LETTERS FROM THE DEAD

Also by Campbell Black

Mr. Apology
Asterisk Destiny
Brainfire

Under the pseudonym of Thomas Altman:

Kiss Daddy Goodbye
Black Christmas
The True Bride
Dark Places

Letters From the Dead

CAMPBELL BLACK

VILLARD BOOKS New York   1985

All rights reserved under International and Pan-American Copyright
Conventions. Published in the United States by Villard Books,
a division of Random House, Inc., New York, and simultaneously
in Canada by Random House of Canada Limited, Toronto.

Library of Congress Cataloging in Publication Data
Black, Campbell.
Letters from the dead.
I. Title.
PR6052.L25L4   1985   823'.914   84-40487
ISBN 0-394-54277-0

Manufactured in the United States of America

9 8 7 6 5 4 3 2

FIRST EDITION

To Rebecca, for her support, help,
insights and patience,
this book is dedicated

Acknowledgment

Thanks are due Peter Gethers,
for his editorial astuteness

*In most ghost stories, possession
is nine-tenths of the law.*

—OLD SCOTTISH PROVERB

LETTERS FROM THE DEAD

Prologue

OTHER TIME FRAMES

[1916]

The sound of a single gunshot echoed throughout the house, as if it had exploded into small fragments of noise capable of traveling from one room to another. Then it died and the girl could hear other noises now, which came to her from a great distance. Outside, in the dark, horses shook their huge bodies and whinnied and hoofs pounded the sand. Glass was shattered and the girl imagined she could see it fall through kerosene light in a million little shards. And beyond, as always, there was the strident call of the ocean, the tide whining and mounting the shore.

Then there were the angry voices of men and the noise of doors opening and closing and harsh footsteps crossing the floors of the rooms below.

The girl listened a moment, her hands gripped round the length of rope. The strength of its fiber surprised her somehow. Its weight was more than she had imagined. She ran her fingers over its rough surface, feeling the intricacy of the way it had been twined. From a simple seed of hemp to a tall plant with small green flowers, it had become transmuted into this flexible object she now held—and she wondered at this for a second, almost as if it were a magical transformation, a form of legerdemain.

But there was no time left in which to stand motionless and gaze at the mysteries contained in a simple length of rope. There was no time left at all, because she could hear another sound now, one that was different from all the others. It was the tap-tapping of a cane on the staircase. *Tap-tap-tap*. The noise filled her with dread. *Tap*. It was coming closer, rising up the stairs.

She fashioned the rope the way she wanted it, her small fingers working quickly. Then, thinking of the gunshot from before, imagining the man slumped dead at the table in the kitchen downstairs, she hesitated. A sense of emptiness, a feeling of sadness, touched her.

She understood what she had to do, but if she didn't do it now there would be no time left to her.

She stepped across the room.

Tap-tap-tap.

The sound was outside on the landing. She heard the raw creak of a floorboard. She imagined she heard the sound of an overcoat brush the wall.

Now.

It had to be done now.

Tiny fibers, detached from the rope, adhered to her hands like soft splinters. She hardly noticed them.

Smiling, the rope hanging from her hand in the fashion of something serpentine, she moved across the bedroom floor. She was conscious, not of endings, not of curtains falling on an empty stage, but of a different beginning, another kind of drama.

Outside, down the darkness, the sea had become wild, the tide churning and the half-moon masked by formless clouds, as if some conspiracy of sea and sky were being played out.

Tap. The creak of a door.

Then nothing save a small dark world filled with silences and eternities.

[1920]

The young man woke abruptly, his body drenched with sweat, bedsheets sticking to his flesh and his hair matted against the pillow. He pushed himself up from the mattress and reached awkwardly for the window, which he struggled to open. He lay back down, gasping, breathing the thick, moist night air. It seemed to clot at the back of his throat, stale and unbreathable and filled with particles of salt. He was thirsty but the water pitcher on the nightstand was empty. For a time, he didn't move. He simply stared at the darkened ceiling.

An image of the girl entered his mind.

He closed his eyes but the image persisted. It was clear and hard and crisp and the passage of four years had done nothing to blur its edges.

He rubbed his eyelids with his knuckles, pressing harder than he should have done. But the image remained, like something branded into the filaments of his brain. He sat upright and gazed at the window. The night was still and heavy and listless, a clammy expanse of dark that suffocated him. He swung his bare legs away from the bed and his feet touched the floor.

He saw a faint night breeze, nothing more than a heavy whisper from the ocean, stir the pale lace curtain that hung at his window. It grazed the sweat on his face and then it was gone and the dark was a vacant hollow again. In his mind he followed the outline of the shore as it twisted away from the village and curved around the headland and meandered past the sea house, whose blind windows he imagined, whose balcony and rooftop and doorways he could clearly see, whose interior rooms stood out with stark clarity inside his head. The presences—he could feel them even now as surely as he might feel warm poultices pressed against his skin.

The presences.

A sound from below the open window drifted up to his room.

It grew slowly until he recognized it as the footsteps and voices of perhaps thirty, forty people. Then there were lights, the pale motions of lanterns illuminating the branches of trees outside his window. A sensation of fear went through him.

Leaning forward, he pressed his hands against the window ledge and, balanced awkwardly, looked down at the cluster of lights. He knew where the procession was going.

And he knew why.

Two days before, a girl had disappeared.

She was the daughter of the Reverend McAllister, a precocious child of about twelve, pretty and carefree and, some said, more than a little headstrong, a little careless. And she had been seen walking out of the village along the sea path that led nowhere else but the beach house.

He stared down into the lights, which had come to a halt beneath his window, inviting him to join the procession. The silence of the group below was sudden and shocking to him and he could see half-lit faces look upward, eyes darkened and little more than unlit pools that suggested the sockets of skeletons.

He would go with them. Reluctantly he would go because he felt a curious sense of responsibility.

He would go out to the sea house even if he had no desire to do so. Even if he never wanted to set his eyes on the place again.

He called to the people below.

It would take him only a few minutes to dress.

Outside, the air was like a damp curtain. When he joined the group he recognized Daniel Braxton and the Reverend McAllister and some of the other faces huddled around the lanterns. The silence was dense, grim, almost as if it existed separately from the procession.

The group did not move for a moment: it seemed to be waiting until it had absorbed him into its midst. And then it stepped forward, the lanterns creating a spectral effect, a nimbus that hovered over the heads and faces of the members, as vague as the aura spiritualists were always claiming to see. The young man felt moist air spread through his thin shirt.

Four years had passed since he had last gone out to the sea house.

Four years, he thought.

And there it was again, bright inside his head, the image of the child as he had found her, and that whole terrible night came back again—

The procession had left the village behind, traveling a narrow dirt road that ran close to the edge of the sands. The feeble light of the lanterns fell only a little way across the beach, and the night was moonless. The young man, his left leg hurting, had the feeling that the world was suddenly empty, that nothing existed save this small group of people and the house to which they walked. He wanted to stop and go back and leave the place alone. He stared out over the darkened beach. Far off, sizzling through the black sheet of sky, there was an abrupt zigzag of lightning that lit the surface of water briefly and then it was gone.

Elyse McAllister.

Would they find the girl out there as they had found the other one four years before?

The young man knew the answer to that without even pondering it, and he experienced a sense of finality. He understood that the members of the group had this same knowledge too; unspoken, even unspeakable, it existed among them with all the sadness of the inevitable.

The sea wind fluttered against the thin flames of the lanterns and shapeless moths swarmed over the lights. Ahead, a mile or so along the strip of the path, the house was visible. The sight of it caused the procession to stop a moment and the young man had the feeling that the group had become suddenly caught up in a vacuum of indecision. He could feel it pull back, pull away, a collective tremor running through it.

There were lights in all the windows.

The yellowy-blue lights of kerosene lamps.

Even though nobody had occupied the place in four years, the house was alive in the darkness.

The young man paused a minute and then he walked forward, conscious of the group shuffling behind him, although with less purpose than before. Four years ago an attempt had been made to torch the building. Men had hurried from room to room carrying blazing straw and gasoline-soaked newspapers.

He had a headache as he remembered it now.

As if the house had been sucked dry of oxygen, as if some odd flaw had occurred in the physical structure of the place, a defiance of logic and common sense and the rules that governed chemical reactions, the fires had all gone out before they had had a chance to damage the property. Whether blown out or doused by some invisible agent, nobody knew. Nobody wanted to find out. And so the house had lain empty and unvisited for four years, a doomed place in the minds of the village people, something dark that sat upon the landscape like a stain.

The young man was not superstitious. He had traveled away from the village, after all, and he had even fought in Europe in the Great War. He had experience of other places. And the simple sight of kerosene flames flooding the windows should not have scared him this way.

Now, as he approached the pathway that led through the grove of trees to the property, he paused. A little more than four years ago he had sold this land to a man who wanted to build a house in an isolated place, a man who didn't want the company of others because he needed solitude . . .

Solitude, the young man thought.

We all know why. We all know why he wanted isolation.

He gazed at the lights burning against the windows.

He had sold the land, and so, in that sense, he had a nebulous responsibility for what happened in this place. He closed his eyes a second and remembered the way the flames had sputtered and died, remembered the scents of burning newspapers and gasoline fumes and scorched straw, remembered how he had climbed the stairway to the upper part of the house.

He was conscious of the group pressing against him and he understood that he was meant to go inside the house alone. The same weary sense of responsibility assailed him. He could have turned around and said that it had nothing to do with him, he had entered into a simple land transaction, that the house and what had taken place inside it was none of his affair—but he did not do any of these things. He accepted the judgment of the group without question.

Still, he didn't move.

The blue-yellow windows of the house seemed to scrutinize him, as if an intelligence lay just beyond the panes of flat glass.

Something that watched.

Yes, he thought. There is something that does nothing but watch.

He moved along the path slowly.

When he reached the porch he stopped again.

From behind he could feel the group urging him to go forward.

The wooden slats of the porch creaked under his feet as he stepped toward the door.

And then he was inside the house, aware of how thick dust lay across all the furniture, conscious of the yellow keys of the piano and sheet music open at a certain page, aware of the flickering brightness of the wall lamps and the faint sound of something moving in an upstairs room. Here and there, relics of four years ago, lay charred sheets of newspaper and stalks of burned straw and spent matches and slivers of broken glass that sparkled in the lamplight. The young man stood in the center of the room, looking in the direction of the kitchen, the door to which stood open. He heard, as though from a muffled distance, the echo of a single gunshot—but that was his imagination, nothing else. A devious trick of his memory.

He did not take his eyes away from the rectangle of light flooding the kitchen doorway.

A shadow passed in front of the light, went away, returned.

The shadow of somebody walking restlessly, relentlessly, back and forth.

The young man stared at it. He moved toward the doorway.

The kitchen was empty.

He had the strange sensation of blood draining out of him, of a fierce chill around his heart.

An empty room. A shadow moving.

This house, he thought, had been designed by an architect from hell.

He rubbed the damp palms of his hands together and went to the bottom of the stairs, gazing upward to the landing, seeing the closed doors of bedrooms that stretched away. Four years ago he had gone up there.

It was not a trip he wanted to take again.

He placed his fingers on the handrail and his foot on the first step.

It seemed to him that he heard—from no distinctive source but rather from the walls of the house itself, from all the rooms and all the lit spaces—a whispered sound which he tried to ignore. He reached the second step, paused, stared up. The lamps were brighter now and the whisper had become louder, more insidious. A voice was forming a name, but he wasn't going to listen to it. It was merely another trick of mind.

Halfway up the stairs he stopped again.

He had fought in a terrible war, he had sustained wounds to his leg, he had lived through the terror of trenches in which he had seen men dying around him, corpses soaked in mud and blood—but the fear that touched him now, as if with a long chill finger, was more than anything he had experienced in Europe. It was amorphous, he could attribute it to no particular sense perception, it even seemed to exist apart from himself—a fear that beat at him with all the regularity of a heart pounding.

He heard a sound in the kitchen and he turned to look down.

The same agitated shadow was going back and forth.

He turned his head again and continued to climb the stairs.

The whispering grew. The sound it made was undeniable.

The name of the girl whom he had found in this house four years before—

But where, for God's sake, was the voice coming from?

He reached the landing and he leaned against the wall. The bedroom doors, each of them closed, suggested mysterious boxes he was meant to open if he wanted to discover the secret of this house.

He opened his mouth and, even though he knew it was useless, called aloud, "Elyse! Elyse!"

There was no answer except for the mounting whisper, nothing save the flickering lights that made soft sighing noises as they danced toward extinction.

"Elyse!"

Nothing.

The flames died, then jumped into life again. He realized that the prospect of darkness in this place was the most terrifying thing he could imagine. Darkness. Blindness. Stumbling into—

Into what?

Along the landing.

A door opened slowly.

Very slowly.

The young man stared at it.

He found himself gazing into a bedroom, seeing the edge of a bed, a dressing table, a rug on the floor, a mirror that caught light and threw it back weakly.

In that room, he thought.

That same room.

And he moved toward the open door slowly, conscious of the whispers filling his head, the flames flickering throughout the house, the presences that seemed now to thrust themselves against him.

He knew what he would find in the room.

But even this knowledge didn't assuage his fear.

He gripped the handle of his cane firmly, as if for courage, and he stepped beyond the door, hearing the sound of laughter that drifted up from a place below.

Those who stood outside the house and gazed toward its illuminated windows saw various shadows pass in front of glass. They heard the wind whip across the sands, and beneath this sound, at some other pitch, there was laughter. Nobody knew whether it was the young man's laugh or that of some other person. Just as nobody could be certain whose shadows they saw moving inside the house. A screen door flapped in the wind, and in that part of a downstairs room which was visible beyond the door sheet music blew upward from a piano and floated across the floor. The kerosene lights died, then flared again, and when they flickered a second time the house became totally dark and the blackened windows suggested eyes suddenly blinded.

Now there was movement on the balcony above. Wooden slats creaked and a figure appeared. As it did so, the assembly below moved backward a little way. The figure approached the edge of the balcony, its shape caught in the pale scattered shafts of lamplight that rose up from the group.

It was the young man who had gone alone into the house only minutes before.

In his arms he cradled something.

Something recognizable.

Something dead.

1

ARRIVAL
June 16

Tommy didn't like the place from the first, didn't like the way the paint peeled from the old wood and how the screens were full of little holes, which meant the house was going to be lousy all the time with sandflies. Plus, he wasn't happy about the way his mother and Rosie were clucking over the joint, like they had just discovered paradise by the sea. And the dump was really isolated, the beach just stretching away for mile after boring mile with no sign of anything he associated with the seaside, no hamburger stands and cotton candy and amusement arcades.

On top of this—and maybe this was the worst thing of all—was the fact he didn't feel too comfortable with Rosie's kid, Lindy, who was thirteen years of age and acted as if girls were the queens of all creation and boys something pretty lowlife.

Tommy struggled out of the beat-up wagon. He shaded his eyes from the sun and looked toward the beach house. It was about a hundred yards from the shoreline and it had really suffered for years, battered by storms, with shingles loose on the roof and slats hanging from the balcony that ran the length of the upper floor. It was a real downer of a color as well, a sort of shit brown. He turned to the wagon and he saw Lindy climb out, pulling herself over a heap of suitcases.

She stood beside Tommy and looked up at him, and he wondered why, if he was the same age as her, she made him feel so goddam inferior. Women, he thought. You could never really tell about them.

He stuck his hands in the pockets of his pants and looked gloomily at the house. The plain fact was, he missed the hell out of his dad and he wasn't exactly receptive to spending the whole summer without him. But then all the other kids whose parents were divorced or separated told him the same thing: Hey, you get used to being split between them because you gotta get used to it and there's no way you can just shuffle back and change the whole deal. It made him feel sad, though, like there was a tiny hole in his heart.

Maybe it wouldn't come to that. Maybe there wouldn't be any divorce. They'd just get back together and everything would be normal and this period of what they called a trial separation would come to an end. He sure hoped so.

Lindy, who had long carrot-colored hair and wore a Judas Priest T-shirt, shuffled her feet in the sandy soil. "Did you see the village back there?" she asked.

Tommy nodded. "The pits," he said.

"Right," Lindy said. "I mean, tell me about a one-horse dump."

Tommy remembered the village about eight miles back down the narrow blacktop, a place called Cochrane Crossing and the nearest place around—but it didn't look like it was going to be a whole lot of laughs going there for a visit. One church and one general store and one tavern. There wasn't even a traffic signal, for Christ's sake. He suddenly thought about his home in Syracuse and he realized he missed the neighborhood already. He missed his buddies, especially Norm, who was his best friend.

"Hey, you guys!" This was Lindy's mother, Rosie, calling. She was standing close to the beach house, her camera slung round her neck and her big black leather camera bag suspended from one shoulder. She was always taking pictures. Every time you turned round, there she was snapping away and looking serious. Tommy's mother, Martha, had some idea of composing a book with Rosie. Martha was going to write the text and Rosie take the pictures. It was going to be about the moods of the seaside, an idea Tommy considered extremely boring. He shaded his eyes now and looked at Rosie, who had the same color hair as Lindy, only she wore it real short, as if she'd been scalped by an angry barber.

"Hey! Why don't you kids start dragging some of the luggage out of the car, huh?"

Lindy sighed and went back to the wagon, but Tommy didn't move for a while because he was watching his mother and thinking how, if he ever got married himself, the woman would have to be as beautiful as Martha. She was small and thin and she had long fair hair that curled around the back of her neck, and she had a kind face with those eyes that always seemed to sparkle. She saw him looking and she smiled, raising an arm to wave. Tommy waved back, then he walked toward the wagon where Lindy was hauling a bag out. The

Judas Priest T-shirt strained as Lindy moved so that you could see her little pointed breasts. Embarrassed, Tommy looked away.

Inside the wagon there was a whole heap of stuff. Suitcases and bags and pieces of moldy food and spoiled fruit from the long trip down here and scattered clothing and Kleenexes. They'd stopped once on the way down, spending the night at a hotel outside Washington, which he'd liked a lot because there was color TV and he got to share a room with his mother, and in the coffeehouse next door there had been a couple of video games. He'd bet anything there weren't any video games in Cochrane Crossing, for Christ's sake. He'd bet there wasn't even TV back there.

He reached inside the wagon and pulled out a suitcase, which he started to drag toward the house. At the back of the house there was a small grove of stunted trees that leaned backward from too much exposure to the wind. They were crooked and spooky and they didn't look like they'd be worth the trouble of climbing. Jesus, what the hell was he going to do here for the next six weeks? Play with Lindy or something. Oh, sure. He imagined she'd be out all day collecting seashells and sorting them into little bundles at night.

Dreary City.

He reached the house and climbed up onto the porch. The two women had already disappeared inside. He set the suitcase down because it was damned heavy and he rubbed his sweaty hands together and looked toward the shoreline. Way out there in the ocean the waves sparkled and rolled. He watched the tide come slithering up on the shore, flecks of foaming water. There was something awesome about the way the whole thing moved.

He shrugged and thought he'd at least get some fishing done this summer and maybe go looking for crabs along the sands. Then, picking up the suitcase, he stepped through the screen door and into the house, where he could hear the sounds of the women laughing at something.

Martha said, "What would you call this kind of furniture, Rosie? What would you say it was? Salvation Army Modern?" And she slumped on the plastic sofa and laughed, looking around the living room at the sticks of bargain-basement furniture and the ugly little pictures on the walls and the threadbare material of the drapes.

Rosie set her camera bag down and put her hands on her wide

hips and whistled. "Thrift-store Contemporary," she said, then she went to the window where she looked out across the beach. "What the hell, it's cheap, and we didn't come here for the luxury. Anyway, we can always make the joint look a bit better."

Martha yawned. The long drive had tired her. She watched her friend stand at the window, seeing the way sunlight made the orange-red hair shine. She wondered sometimes about Rosie's energy, where it came from and the sense of resiliency that accompanied it. You could take Rosie into a flophouse and instead of seeing the cockroaches scurry across the furniture she'd say something positive about the view from the window. It was a matter of seeing possibilities, Martha thought. She stretched her arms and saw Tommy struggle across the floor with a suitcase. The kid paused and looked at her with that small smile that always threatened to break her heart. Sweetness and light. And for a moment she felt a tiny passing sense of sadness because what lay between her and her son was an absence, a concept of a family broken, a missing father.

Charlie.

Why did he have to be such a perfect asshole?

She rose from the sofa, hearing the plastic crackle under her body, and she tried to get the circulation going in her legs. Sometimes, at the age of thirty-five, Martha could feel the body yielding and the bones complaining and the breasts, as if they had lives of their own, sagging audibly in the night.

"This place smells," Tommy said.

Martha moved toward her son and ran a hand through his uncombed hair, and what touched her just then was the extraordinary resemblance the boy had to his father, the same determined mouth and the wide-set eyes and the straight nose. Later, he'd be as handsome as Charlie, but what she hoped was that he wouldn't turn out anything like her husband, with all the fault lines in the personality and the flaws in simple human considerations. Especially she hoped he wouldn't turn out to be, like his father, a liar.

"We'll get the windows open," she said. "Then it won't smell so bad."

She was conscious of Lindy at the other side of the room, Lindy with that strange mixture of arrogance and awkwardness that so many times characterized adolescent girls. She was standing at the foot of the stairs, staring upward, tugging at the waist of her blue jeans.

A foursome, Martha thought. Two women (one divorced, the other separated) and their kids.

A whole lot of spaces in here, things missing, pieces of the psyche broken, memories of pain. Rosie had divorced Herb four years ago and she still spoke about him with extreme bitterness, as if the memory of Herb were a poisoned cell she was destined to carry around forever inside her brain, something locked away in a place beyond the scope of an emotional lobotomy.

Lindy said, "I wonder when somebody last lived here."

And Rosie, drawing a finger through the dust on a windowpane and making a curious curled design, said, "I'd say twenty years ago. Maybe twenty-five. Could be half a century, the way this dust feels."

"Which reminds me," Martha said. "Wasn't there something about the place being cleaned before we moved in? Something about a new paint job?"

"I seem to remember something about that," Rosie said, already spotting something outside that she needed to photograph, already unzipping her camera bag and taking out her Canon, which she handled as if it were a holy relic.

"Let's get that suitcase upstairs, Tommy," Martha said, and she helped him drag the burden upward, listening to the creak of the stairs as they moved, hearing the strange noises of the house all around her—it was as if it had never quite settled into its own foundations and never would, a trespassing thing that would one day be reclaimed by the sea.

On the landing she paused and she put the suitcase down. There were four doors ahead of her along the dim corridor. She pushed the first one open and looked inside: a small bedroom with a window and a door that opened out onto the balcony. The bed was narrow, covered with an old-fashioned patchwork quilt, and there was a dressing table with an oval mirror.

"You like this one, Tommy?" she asked.

The boy nodded casually. "It's fine."

"You sure?"

Tommy shrugged and moved toward the bed, which he tested with the palms of his hands. He appeared satisfied. Then he opened the door to the balcony and suddenly the room, which had been stuffy as the rest of the house, was filled with raw salt smells of the sea.

Martha examined the other rooms.

Each had a door that led to the balcony, each was furnished in exactly the same way as the one Tommy had chosen. Except for the room at the end of the corridor—which was small and had faded wallpaper of an antique floral design—there wasn't much to choose between them. She opened the balcony doors in each of them and let fresh air surge in from the beach and then she stepped out onto the balcony and looked for a time at the sea and the way the damp sands glistened at the shore's edge. It was good after the city to take the biting air into her lungs and let the breeze invigorate her, good to feel it move through her hair and press against the rumpled T-shirt she wore.

She walked the length of the balcony, noticing the grove of twisted trees that grew at the back of the house, seeing a solitary blackheaded gull rise over the arthritic branches and vanish toward the ocean.

A whole summer here, she thought.

A whole summer out of the sweat of the city. A whole summer of not having to listen to any more of Charlie's lies.

She turned her face when she heard the balcony creak behind her. She saw Tommy come toward her, his arms spread on either side as if he were a tightrope walker, his face tense with concentration.

He stopped beside her and she slung an arm around his shoulder.

"So, what do you think, champ? You gonna like it here?"

The kid raised his face and looked at her seriously. "I guess."

"Can't you do any better than that, huh?"

He was silent for a long time, shuffling his feet around, gazing out toward the sea, which seemed suddenly distant and flat, the sun spread across its surface like a flashlight on a sheet of glass.

"Who used to live here?" he asked.

Martha shrugged. "I don't suppose anybody lives here on a regular basis, Tommy. The owner rents it out during the summer. Maybe the fall as well."

"What about winter?"

"I guess it's empty then."

The kid seemed to absorb this fact with great interest, as if he found something unusual in the idea of a house lying empty for months at a time. The truth was, she didn't know whether the place was empty or not—in fact, she knew very little about the property or its owner, having seen it advertised under VACATION RENTALS in a newspaper; then the matter had been conducted by correspondence with a company of lawyers called Bradley Brace and Dunning in Atlanta, who apparently handled everything to do with the place. A contract had been drawn up and a rent check paid and a key had been sent to Rosie by mail, and what Martha had assumed all along was that the house belonged to some absentee landlord who didn't want to be bothered by any details. Indeed, it had been in one of the letters from Bradley Brace and Dunning that the promise had been made to have the house clean and freshly painted—an unkept promise, obviously, but suddenly it didn't seem to matter very much to her.

She hugged Tommy closely against her body.

"We'll have a terrific summer, kid," she said.

He looked up at her and she could see he was forcing an optimism, forcing a bright smile.

"Yeah, we will," he said.

"And you're going to get along well with Lindy, right?"

"Right."

"Right?" she asked again, hearing a tiny doubt in his voice.

"Right."

She held him tighter still as the wind rose up off the face of the sea and the sun, like a candle momentarily doused, slid behind a cloud.

When she'd taken a couple of shots of the shoreline—quick unstudied shots, taken more out of impulse than any real desire to get something good—Rosie stuck her camera back inside the bag and wandered into the kitchen. She knew she'd be doing most of the cooking, since Martha's culinary efforts, if you were charitable about them, left something to be desired.

Taste, mainly.

That and flavor.

One time she'd eaten one of Martha's concoctions, a vegetarian stroganoff, that had left her feeling disabled for several days. It was as if tiny chunks of mushroom and little sticky slivers of onion and dollops of cream had clung to the inside of her head, having traveled an upward route from her mouth. At least Martha didn't pretend to be a decent cook; she was kitchen-clumsy, she didn't know the kind of concentration that cooking needed, she thought everything could be thrown together and done in a hurry.

Rosie stood in the kitchen doorway and ran one hand through her short hair as she stared at the long narrow room in front of her. The refrigerator had been young in the days of Ozzie and Harriet and the sink was discolored porcelain and the kitchen table stood on wobbly legs. She wondered vaguely if you might ascribe the quality of "charm" to the place, but that wasn't going to cut it. She turned "rustic" around in her mind, but that wasn't going to do it either.

Try tacky and inadequate.

She wandered toward the sink, opening closets as she moved, seeing a variety of mismatched ancient saucepans, lids, collections of plates, knives and forks, utensils and an antique juicer that surely belonged in the Oster Hall of Fame. She opened the refrigerator and looked inside at the bare metal shelves. And then she moved to the window, folding her arms beneath her breasts and looking back across the room from another angle.

She had a philosophy, developed across the years of her marriage to Herb, of Making the Best of Things, a rationale that would have to be applied stringently to this kitchen. She raised her face and looked at the ceiling, at the horrible fringed shade surrounding a brown-stained light bulb, and she thought, We're probably lucky that there's any electricity here at all.

"Well?" Martha appeared in the doorway. "*Better Homes and Gardens*, huh?"

Rosie nodded, smiling at her friend. "I've seen worse. When we were first married, we had an apartment in the East Nineties that makes this place a palace." And she remembered that time, bringing back to mind the way Herb would hurry home at night, usually with some small gift clutched in his arms—a plant, flowers, a book, anything that might please her—remembering the heavy sound of his footsteps on the stairs and the lascivious look on his face as he'd enter the apartment, as if he'd been nursing an erection all day long and couldn't wait to drag her to bed.

But that was then and things had the weird habit of changing around you, and love turned, as if it were a passing season of the heart, to something misshapen.

Martha had sat down at the kitchen table and was lighting a cigarette, blowing a thin stream of smoke toward the window. "I checked the bedrooms. Tommy already chose one. You and Lindy can have the pick of the other three. This is a democracy we've got going here."

Rosie turned on one of the water faucets and a rust-colored liquid spluttered out into the sink. "I figure nobody's lived here since last summer. Maybe nobody's ever been here." She turned to look back at her friend. "You think Tommy and Lindy are going to like this place?"

"Sure," Martha said.

"Did you check out that town?"

"Town?"

"I was speaking euphemistically. Cochrane Crossing, whatever it's called . . . Maybe we could leave the kids some night and go take a look at the action."

"I can see it. A few fat good old boys sitting on barstools drinking Schlitz and whittling on sticks while listening to some prehistoric Hank Williams tunes on the jukebox. It sounds like a lot of fun," Martha said.

Rosie looked into the sink. The discolored water was taking a long time to drain away, which meant sluggish plumbing. Then she turned back again to her friend. "Who cares about the town anyhow? Have you had a good long look at the beach? Have you breathed the air around here?"

"First thing I did," Martha said.

Rosie glanced through the kitchen window, watching the tide fall over the shoreline, and what she felt most strongly was the glorious emptiness of everything, the beautiful isolation, the delicate balance between house and ocean, as if a silent partnership had been forged somewhere. And she thought, There are a million photographs to be taken here. You could spend the rest of your life trying to capture the textures of all this. Even if you knew you were doomed to failure.

"It's going to be a good time, Martha," she said.

"I know it is."

"No traffic jams along Erie Boulevard."

"No shopping for A&P specials."

"No kids to hustle off to school."

"No timetables," Martha said.

"I like that bit."

"And no Charlie."

Rosie sat at the table and looked at her friend for a time. There was a slight edge of hurt around Martha's eyes, a vague pain, as if she still hadn't gotten used to the idea of her separation, but Rosie knew that the look would pass. Even if the tiny appearance of pain some-how managed to enhance Martha's rather frail beauty, the look would pass nevertheless.

"Tell you what," Rosie said. "Let's open that bottle of JD we bought and have a couple of shots before we unload the wagon and get this joint into a livable condition. What do you say?"

"I'd drink to that," Martha said.

Rosie grinned and stood up. She moved through the kitchen and out onto the porch, then walked toward the station wagon. She got the Jack Daniel's from the glove compartment, and as she turned to go back toward the house she glanced up at the balcony.

Lindy was standing there, looking down at her.

"What's happening, kid?" she called up.

"Just checking out the scenery," Lindy said.

"It's really something, right?"

Lindy, a hand held as shade against her eyes, said, "Really."

Rosie went back indoors.

She stood on the balcony for a long time after her mother had disappeared inside the house, and what she thought was that the sea was like a kind of music inside her head, not the music you heard at rock concerts or over the classical station her mother always listened to in Syracuse but something else, something she didn't quite know how to define because they weren't notes she'd ever heard before. She walked the length of the balcony and then went inside the room she'd picked out as her own bedroom, the one with the tacky wallpaper, and she stood looking at herself in the dressing-table mirror, pushing her hair back from her face with her fingers, studying her reflection and wondering if she was as pretty as all her friends said she was. Friends, though—they'd tell you almost anything.

She slipped her T-shirt up over her shoulders and looked at her breasts, ran the tips of her fingers round each pale nipple until she could feel goose bumps all over her flesh. Then she let the shirt cover her body again. She could hear the sound of the two women laughing down in the kitchen and there was something pleasant and soothing in the way the sound floated up, filling the house, clinging to the spaces between the rooms.

Pleasant, soothing.

And then the sound suddenly stopped, almost as if Martha and Rosie had reached some serious point in a conversation, something they were mulling over in silence (their marriages, she thought, what else could cause such abrupt quiet?)—and then there was another noise, a vague whisper that didn't come from the breeze blowing in off the sea.

Like a child's whisper. Like a small kid whispering just outside her door.

Tommy.

He was pretty cute with his hair a mass of tight little curls and his long eyelashes, although he was immature and didn't seem capable of stringing too many words together at the same time—but she hoped he wasn't going to be one of those practical joker types. She'd never liked people who sneaked up behind your back and shouted into your ear or had you sit down on whoopee cushions or carried around lifelike rubber centipedes in their pockets.

She stood very still for a second and then, in a quick motion, yanked the door of her room open and looked out along the hallway, expecting to see Tommy close the door of his own room.

But there was nothing and nobody.

Just the gloom of the hallway and the closed doors of bedrooms and a faint light creeping up from the bottom of the stairs.

She stood motionless, as if she were waiting for something.

And then the women were laughing again from below and the mood, whatever it might have been, however you might have described it, was broken.

She went toward the stairs and moved down in the direction of the kitchen, where the wind—blowing in through the windows they had opened earlier—was a little cold.

2

NIGHT
June 16

It was calm and the sea breeze was barely audible as it streamed over the sands and played through the trees at the back of the house. There was a half-moon throwing silver, with the extravagance of a philanthropist, over the surface of the water. Rosie had found a candle in one of the kitchen closets and she'd lit it, placing it on the table in the living room. Martha thought it weirdly hypnotic, the combination of flame and breeze and salt smells, the silences of the house, the idea of the kids already asleep upstairs. It was strange, but she wasn't tired anymore, as if all her exhaustion had been stripped away like layers of old paint. She sat cross-legged on the sofa and gazed at the flame of the candle while Rosie was rummaging through a purse, sifting Kleenexes and tampons and matchbooks. Then there was the soft sound of a cellophane bag being opened and Rosie said, "Found it," and sat down on the floor beside the sofa.

Martha shut her eyes a moment, remembering how she'd first met Rosie in Syracuse and how, initially, she hadn't taken to the woman at all, finding her somewhat overbearing, aggressive, the kind of person who liked to make all the big decisions. It had been at one of those small galleries near the campus where a friend of Charlie's, a photographer called Lyle, was exhibiting some of his material—enormously detailed photographs of strangely juxtaposed objects, a flower lying in a pile of dogshit, a crumpled beer can on a bed of velvet— and Rosie, who appeared annoyed by the entire presentation and seeking some outlet for her irritation, had said to Martha, "This is trash, pretentious trash," and Martha, who didn't like talking to somebody she'd never been introduced to, simply smiled in a pale way and nodded. Then Rosie had grabbed her and, in a series of movements Martha couldn't quite recall now, had marched her into a coffee shop next door and talked at her for the next thirty minutes. The talk had been about the art of photography, about how Rosie had been selling her pictures to magazines for the last three years, about the deterioration of the craft as she perceived it. Martha had not had the heart to say that she knew absolutely nothing about pictures, that cameras were arcane things to her, that she couldn't tell the difference between a holiday snapshot and an Ansel Adams. Rosie's Brooklyn accent, which snapped around vowels and made abrasive sounds out of consonants, had added to Martha's impression of the woman's aggressive nature, especially when she contrasted it with her own softer way of speaking, something she'd learned as a child in Virginia.

They'd met occasionally after that but it hadn't been until the separation from Charlie that she'd really started to develop a relationship with Rosie, actively seeking her out, actively looking for a comrade in the misfortunes of marriage, in which subject Rosie was something of an expert. From this sharing of their mutual marital breakdowns, from their explorations of the ruined geographies of unions, their friendship had flowed, and now Martha perceived Rosie's qualities differently—she wasn't aggressive and overbearing, she was kind and concerned and genuinely passionate about photography.

Martha opened her eyes and, in the flickers of light thrown from the candle, saw that Rosie was laboriously rolling a joint. She put it between her lips and lit it from the candle and inhaled deeply, throwing her head back and passing the joint to Martha, who took it and drew on it tentatively—although she'd been around the substance for years, although it had been an inherent part of the lives of the friends she and Charlie had shared, she hadn't smoked with any regularity until recently. Now she found that it relaxed her before she went to bed (alone, something that was strange to her), and provided that she stopped before a certain point, she didn't reach the silly stage, where everything in the world seemed hilarious.

She passed the joint back to Rosie, who held it in silence for a time. A stem, a seed maybe, crackled and popped inside the roll of paper and there was a quick hiss of smoke.

"I've been thinking we should go into town first thing and get some supplies," Rosie said. For supper they'd eaten fruit and some cheese left over from the trip. A stale meal.

"Supplies" struck Martha as a strange word. It was as if they had become pioneers living at the edge of the world.

"Apart from food, we need Brillo Pads."

Martha felt a gear shift quietly somewhere in her brain. "And Handywipes."

"Let us not forget Handywipes. And Lysol Cleaner."

"Oh, and Windex."

"Windex, for sure. And Fresh Start Detergent."

"Christ, did I leave that out?" Martha asked. "How could I have done that?"

Rosie took a draw on the joint and passed it to Martha. "Ivory Soap, that's a must."

"And Glade Air Freshener."

"Yeah, except I can never decide between lavender and pine."

"And Janitor in a Drum," Martha said, smoking, holding her breath in tight and thinking of a building superintendent incarcerated inside a membranous cylinder.

"Right. And Kleenex in one of the decorator boxes."

"I wish we'd brought our goddam coupons," Martha said.

And then they were both laughing together because this was a game they'd played before, this foraging through the excesses of the consumer world, tossing choices back and forth and arguing the merits of brand over brand—it was as if, having left their domestic status behind, their structured marriages, there was nothing left for them but to satirize the things that had pervaded their previous lives. There was also the fact that one of their mutual friends, Doris Maitland, belonged to a Coupon Clipper's Club and laboriously exchanged coupons with other women and argued the merits or otherwise of various brand names. A domestic counterculture, a barter system run by a network of bored housewives.

"Maybe we can call Doris, maybe she'll send us some," Rosie said and leaned forward, letting her hand rest on Martha's knee.

This was an aspect of her friend that Martha had become accustomed to—she was a toucher, someone who expressed affection physically, without any apparent inhibition. Something Martha had had to learn, even if she wasn't entirely comfortable with it yet.

Rosie took the joint and smoked and a red ash rose up out of her fingers, and then she let the joint die in her hand. "Christ, I still can't believe how peaceful it is here. Can you? I keep waiting to hear an ambulance or a cop car or a fire engine."

Martha, leaning back against the sofa, her muscles relaxed now, nodded her head. It was a different kind of darkness here, a different kind of night from the neon slashes of the city and the all-night doughnut shops and the endless drone of traffic along the freeway. It was almost a perfect dark in this place. And then suddenly she was thinking of the city and of Charlie and wondering—even if she had resolved not to, because there were residues of pain still—which of his literature students he was fucking right now. Which of those flat-bellied, straight-haired, serious girls he was screwing at this very moment. Or maybe it was over and they were sitting up in bed together and smoking and talking about Coleridge and plagiarism, the girl gazing at Charlie with wide-eyed wonder, wanting to pinch herself to see if she wasn't dreaming about having her English professor in bed beside her.

She heard herself say, "Charlie told me he'd had about thirty girls. This was just before we broke up. I didn't know about a single one of them, can you believe that? Holy shit, he must have told some terrific lies in his time. Thirty, he said. Thirty. Like it was this magic number of betrayals. And I didn't know a goddam thing about any of them." A longing filled her; despite herself, there was a yearning right then to think that Charlie was upstairs in bed, waiting for her.

"Charlie's a pig. Herb's a pig as well. Infidelity wasn't his big problem. Indifference was where Herb scored a perfect hundred." Rosie looked at the unlit joint in her hand. "Did I ever tell you I used to try to understand the things that interested Herb? I used to go to the fights with him."

"Fights?" Martha found herself struggling to fix an exact meaning to this word.

"Boxing matches, kid. I used to sit there in these horrible halls and watch two guys pound the shit out of each other. I used to read *Ring* magazine. I learned the difference between a welterweight and a junior welterweight. I knew who all the present champions were. Can you believe that? I knew their names! I mean, you ever hear of Alexis Arguello or Marvin Hagler? Now, that's what I call going out of your way to save a marriage. I did the same thing with football and basketball . . ." Rosie let her hand drop from Martha's knee. "Herb's idea of a big romantic evening was this. We'd put Lindy to bed, right? He'd go out and get a six-pack of one of those imported beers, St. Pauli Girl or Pilsner Urquell, and we'd curl up on the sofa —I'm dressed, remember, in something silk and clinging and he's wearing his robe—and we'd watch a goddam ice-hockey game on TV and somewhere, usually at halftime, there would be a quickie right there on the sofa and then we'd watch the rest of the game. Those were the good nights, Martha. I'm only describing the very best nights, you understand? Herb's idea of foreplay was a grunt in your ear."

Martha watched the point of the candle flicker. She could feel the darkness press in on the house and hear the lazy sound of the faraway tide. Charlie wasn't like Herb at all. Charlie was always romantic and attentive, lingering over lovemaking, stretching it out to that point sometimes where she thought she would explode from the intensity of his foreplay, the way he buried his face between her legs and raised her to a place where whatever inhibitions she might have had were stripped away, where she would think her heart was going to burst open inside her chest. Even now she couldn't imagine him doing the same things with any of his young girls, a naiveté she knew she was going to have to let go. But she'd been naive and trusting and optimistic for most of her life—qualities in her personality she would gladly have changed, if she'd known how to do so.

"I can't compete with the young girls," she said. "How can I hope to compete?"

Rosie was stretching her legs, bending her head forward and trying to reach her toes with her fingertips. "Forget him," she said. "That's my best advice to you. Forget him and go on. Get the divorce. Let the lawyers work it out. Get on with your life. Somewhere down the road, you're going to meet somebody else."

"Somebody else," Martha said and her throat was dry from marijuana. "Have you, Rosie?"

"I've had my moments, dear," Rosie said. "There's a lot of guys out there, and although on my personal register I find a high quota of assholes, now and then you run into somebody nice. The problem with that is you just don't know how they're going to turn out. Herb was nice at the start. Herb was very, very nice."

"Where is he anyhow these days?"

Rosie shrugged and drew her knees up to her chest, hugging them close to her body. "His child support comes with a Santa Monica postmark but I think he moves around a lot. Mainly California."

"Doesn't he want to see Lindy?"

"Who knows? He calls her now and then and he makes promises that I think confuse the kid because he doesn't ever keep them. Daddy's going to take you sailing. Daddy's going to take you camping. Daddy's going to do this, do that. But Daddy doesn't do. Not ever."

A feeling of sadness passed through Martha. Charlie might be an asshole, but he'd never neglect Tommy. She knew that. He'd always want to be a father to his son. There had been a strong bond between them right from the start when—despite the conventions of the time —he'd been present in the delivery room. He'd called it the single most important experience of his entire life. Suddenly the idea of a divorce, something so bleakly final, terrified her. They could patch things back together again, they could mend the punctures in their marriage and start afresh—but then she wondered if Charlie would give up his girls, give up his egotistical infidelities. Those girls seemed to give him something she couldn't—and it wasn't sex, it was the sense of a new conquest. Charlie Triumphant. I love him, she thought. I still love the bastard. She wanted to weep.

Rosie stood up and went inside the kitchen. A light was turned on and Martha could hear her moving around, and then there was the sound of water spluttering from the faucet in the sink. After that there was silence for a while before Martha heard Rosie call her name. She got up from the sofa and went into the kitchen, where Rosie was pouring Jack Daniel's into two frayed Dixie cups.

"A nightcap," Rosie said and shoved one of the cups toward Martha, who took it and sipped, even if she didn't feel like drinking now. They stood at the kitchen table in silence for a time, listening to the noise the sea made as it crawled over the sands and then slithered back, gasping.

"To a peaceful summer," Rosie said.

Martha smiled and raised her cup. "A peaceful summer."

And she stared through the kitchen window at the moon, wondering again about Charlie but she decided she was suddenly too weary to think about him, too weary to want to do anything else but drag herself upstairs to bed and sleep.

A strange bed in a strange house.

She yawned, covering her mouth with her hand.

Fatigue would overcome the strangeness.

Something woke Tommy and he sat upright in bed and it took him a few moments to remember where he was. This wasn't Syracuse, it wasn't his own room in his own house. It was the sea house and the room was unfamiliar—none of his own things, his pictures of Black Sabbath and the huge wall map of The World and the photographs of his father and himself taken that time when they'd gone camping up in the Adirondacks. He reached out for the bedside lamp and switched it on and he watched the shadows of the room dissolve all around him.

He rubbed his eyes and he listened to the house.

He realized he was really listening for a sound of his mother, something reassuring—but that was childish, for Christ's sake, he wasn't a baby anymore, he wasn't going to be afraid of dark places in unfamiliar houses. He looked round the room, the pale walls and the flat surface of the dressing-table mirror and the small fringed rug that lay on the floor beside the bed and—

The closet—

The closet on the other side of the room—

The door was halfway open.

He hadn't really noticed the closet before and if he had he was pretty sure that it had been shut.

He pushed the bedsheet away from his body and stepped onto the floor.

Okay, a door swings halfway open by itself in the middle of the night.

It happens.

It's no big deal.

He rubbed his hands together, which he always did when he was nervous about something, and he moved slowly toward the door, stepping across his unpacked suitcase and the three fishing rods that lay in a heap.

Closets.

Closets don't make you nervous. Holy shit.

He paused at the door and then, reaching out as if he expected something to spring at him from the shadows inside, he caught the edge of the door and yanked it open and sucked in his breath real hard.

And then he heard himself laughing at his own stupid fears.

There was nothing inside the closet except some old books and a bunch of kid's games, a pile of tattered boxes that must have been left here from a previous summer. And the idea that there had been another kid in this room at one time made him feel easy again. He went down on his hands and knees and examined the games. There was Yahtzee and Flinch and Pit and Old Maid and one he'd never heard of before called Ouija. Maybe the kid who'd owned them had just forgotten all about them, maybe his parents had been in a hurry to pack or something like that.

Whatever.

He stood up. He shut the closet door real tight. He was too tired to sift through the stuff right now. Maybe in the morning.

He went back to bed and lay down, drawing the sheet across his body, and he fell soundly asleep with the bedside lamp still lit.

3

DAWN
June 17

It was just after dawn when Lindy woke and, wrapping herself in her bathrobe, stepped out onto the balcony. All night long she'd been having these weird dreams, bizarre turns of the mind in which she'd been drowning, sinking down and down through clear water—and yet she'd always been outside of herself somehow, watching herself drown, so that there was no real sense of panic like you get in bad nightmares but a kind of sadness instead, a resignation to your fate.

So this is how it all ends. Tangled in weeds at the bottom of a clear sea. A waste of a young life.

She walked softly the length of the balcony, careful not to make the boards creak underfoot. The sea was impossibly calm out there, like the tide had just stopped running. The sky was cloudless, quiet, the kind of sky she never saw in Syracuse. She placed her hands on the balcony rail and breathed very deeply, holding the muscles of her diaphragm as tightly as she could because she'd read somewhere that this kind of exercise was good for flattening your stomach.

Those silly dreams, she thought. She had dreamed of her own death before now. She had been present at her own funeral several times, watching her mourners from the coffin, peering at them through half-shut eyes. She had seen them weep over her and shake their heads and hold handkerchiefs to their mouths. Something essentially romantic and tragic in this kind of dream appealed to her, as if she was a heroine trapped inside a gothic novel, somebody who had gone to her death with all her potential unrealized and her wishes unfulfilled. Something romantic and at the same time sexy, in a funny kind of way. Just yielding to death like you were giving yourself to the dark, powerful body of your lover . . .

Relaxing her muscles now, she gazed the length of the beach. She wanted to go down there and walk along the sands and maybe look for starfish or shells or any kind of debris the sea had carelessly tossed up. Pieces of rotted wood, rope, anything the ocean might have claimed only to reject it again. A message in a bottle maybe.

Yeah, a message in a bottle might be neat.

Somebody who'd been on a desert island for years, throwing his last hopes into the ocean and praying the tides would carry his predicament to a sympathetic finder.

What if you opened the bottle and it wasn't from any desert island at all but an obscene message some drunk had just flipped into the sea at Atlantic City? Something like DOES ANYBODY OUT THERE GIVE GOOD HEAD? There would be a telephone number and a name like Al or Danny scribbled across the paper and the bottle would probably have contained something real cheap, like Ripple wine.

She walked the whole length of the balcony until she stood overlooking the grove of trees at the back of the house. If there was anything ugly about this place, she was looking at it right now. The trees just didn't belong here. They were the kind of trees that would grow in the landscape of a bad dream. They twisted at terrible angles, their branches misshapen, their knotted roots visible here and there above the soil.

She clutched the balcony rail again and raised one leg high in the air behind her, a dance-class exercise—

And then, out of nowhere, Tommy was standing at the other end of the balcony, watching her through sleepy eyes. She lowered her leg and felt a little foolish, like she'd been caught on the toilet with her pants at her ankles. How long had he been watching? Had she been talking to herself, saying her thoughts aloud the way she sometimes saw people do when they believed they were alone? She felt a rush of blood to her face and hoped it didn't show.

"Hi," Tommy said.

"Hi."

He shuffled his feet around and glanced in the direction of the beach for a moment. There was a long silence between them and she could feel a pulse beating at the side of her head, something that always happened to her whenever she was embarrassed.

"I found some games last night," he said.

"Yeah?" She tossed her hair away from her face and wondered if the cord of her robe was knotted okay or if there was a gap through which he might be able to see anything. But he wasn't even looking at her and she realized he was as embarrassed as she.

"In the closet in my room," he said.

"What kind of games, Tommy?"

He shrugged. "You know, like card games and stuff?"

"Kid's games?"

"Yeah."

"Wonder where they came from." She was beginning to feel easy again, her nervousness gone; and somehow the perception that Tommy was embarrassed at having sneaked up on her gave her the upper hand now in the situation. She wouldn't show any interest at all in his discovery.

"I was wondering that too," he said.

"Games are pretty dull," she said and she turned away from him, moving along the balcony, hearing him shuffle behind her.

"It depends, I guess," he said.

"When's your birthday?" She spun round and saw that the sudden change of subject had bewildered him slightly.

"My birthday? April twenty-second. Why?"

"That makes you Taurus."

"What does that mean?"

"It's your star sign."

"I don't believe in that kind of stuff."

She ignored him. "It means that you're quiet and practical. It also means that you've got some control over your feelings."

"Oh yeah?" Tommy seemed to turn this over in his head for a time, looking a little pleased. Lindy felt suddenly good, good that she was in control of things again, good that she'd handed him a tiny item of information which, like an unexpected gift, appeared to have given him pleasure.

"What sign are you?" he asked.

"Pisces."

"What's that like?"

"We're the dreamers of dreams," she said, knowing she sounded rather grand and mysterious. "We're the creators."

Tommy leaned against the balcony rail and scratched his head. She looked at the mass of thick curly hair, which she envied. Her own was straight and long and even though it had a pleasing color—according to some people anyhow—she'd never been able to tease it into any kind of shape.

"Creators of what?" he asked.

"Poems. Paintings," and she shrugged, as if she had no further desire to continue the conversation. She would leave him to struggle with what she'd said because she liked the idea of his puzzlement.

"You really believe all that stuff?" he asked.

She didn't answer. In truth, she wasn't sure that she did. She'd read a couple of books on the signs of the zodiac and she always checked her horoscope in *The Syracuse Herald* every day, but she'd never really been convinced. There was, she supposed, some comfort to be had from being able to blame every one of your faults on the stars. She walked a couple of feet, then turned once again to look at the boy. He was reasonably well built, his shoulders broad. Maybe by the time he was sixteen he'd be good-looking and girls would want to go out with him.

He was quiet for a time, then he asked, "Did you bring your radio with you?"

She shook her head. She'd considered bringing the Sanyo transistor but then at the last minute she'd decided against it because it had occurred to her that if you were really going to enjoy the quiet of an isolated shoreline you might just as well not import any alien sounds. Besides, she'd secretly hoped that Tommy would bring his, which was larger and gave out a better sound.

"I forgot mine," he was telling her now. "I left it on the kitchen table." And he snapped his fingers, irritated with himself.

"Then you'll just have to listen to the sea, won't you?" she said and walked away from him again.

"Listen to the sea," he said.

"With both ears wide."

He was smiling at her and there was a quality to the expression— maybe it was a kind of mischievous look, a certain slyness—that she realized she liked.

"You say some pretty weird things, Lindy."

For some reason, this remark flattered her. "Well, if you listen to the sea, you never know what you might hear."

"Yeah? Like what?"

She shut her eyes a moment and felt the growing warmth of the rising sun press lightly against the closed lids. And there was a vague salty breeze beginning to stir across the beach.

"Like what?" Tommy asked again.

Words—

A sentence—

She didn't know where it came from, why it had popped into her head. She didn't know what it meant or even why she chose to say it aloud.

A sentence, a sequence of sounds, utterances.

"The hornpipes of dead sailors."

And, confused by what she'd said, bewildered by the way the sentence had seemingly formed itself of its own accord, she pushed open the door of her bedroom and stepped inside, feeling flushed and disoriented.

4

COCHRANE CROSSING
June 17

There was a sign that said COCHRANE CROSSING POP. 254. It hung from
a pole that had been bent either by a storm or by a drunken driver
unable to fathom the treacherous twists of the blacktop highway. The
sign itself was rusted and almost illegible, as if the inhabitants of the
place were anxious to maintain a certain anonymity. And the village
gave that impression, the small frame houses huddled close together
and the porches masked by shadows, the window of the general store
empty of goods and unadorned by signs, the tavern little more than a
dim cave with no beer signs hanging outside. The whole place might
have been hacked out of the weather-beaten landscape by a race of
people too weary to face any more of the world, a species that had
retreated indoors forever, behind barricades and locks and empty
windows and drab lacy curtains. Rosie had the thought that if Cochrane Crossing were a person it would be wearing dark glasses and
traveling under an assumed name.

She put her foot lightly on the brake as a 30 MPH sign came up in
front of her. "Who was Cochrane and what did he cross?" she asked.

Martha smiled. "He's probably one of those characters lost in
history," she said. "The kind that disappears and just leaves his name
behind like an afterthought."

"I guess," Rosie said, seeing glimpses of the ocean in the narrow
spaces between the houses. "Anyplace else in the world, this would
have been turned into a swinging resort years ago. A boardwalk. A
couple of high-rise hotels. Some nightclubs. I bet there's an entrepre-
neur somewhere just aching to find a joint like this and transform it."

She yawned. She hadn't slept well, waking a couple of times in
the dead of night with a dull headache burning just behind her eyes.
Once when she'd wakened she'd had the odd, dreamy impression that
somebody was walking around the downstairs part of the house—
she'd ignored it and turned over on her side and gone back to sleep
again but she remembered it now, wondering if perhaps Martha or

one of the kids had wandered downstairs for a drink of water. And then she was conscious of how quiet the two kids were in the back seat of the wagon and she glanced at them in the rearview mirror.

"Nothing makes me more suspicious than a couple of very silent teenagers," she said. "I always get the impression that conspiracies are being hatched and devious plots thought up. Am I right?"

She saw Tommy smile in a thin way but Lindy didn't react to her question at all, just continued to stare out of the window as if the village were a leper colony in which she had a morbid interest.

Rosie parked the wagon outside the grocery store and swung round to look at the kids. Lindy—there was something secretive about her own daughter, she thought. Something that was just a little furtive. It was as if she had constructed a portable transparent cage around herself into which she could retreat whenever she felt like it. Adolescence. That was the name of that cage. Adolescence, with its jigsaw emotions. That was where you first started to lose your own kid. It was like making a present of your own flesh and blood to that malignant figure, good old Father Time.

She reached back and stroked Lindy's head. "What's on your mind, babe?"

Lindy shrugged.

It's one of those moody days. One of those days in which the kid just seemed to soak herself in isolation. Rosie often thought that the best way to deal with such times was to leave the child alone until she snapped out of it all by herself, which was precisely what she intended to do right now. She got out of the wagon and stepped up on the sidewalk, where Martha was already waiting in the entranceway to the store.

"They're big on advertising round here," Martha said.

Rosie looked at the sullen window of the store, through which she could see the dull interior of the place and a figure moving around in the gloom. She started to laugh. "I can see Doris Maitland charging in here with a hatful of her coupons only to find that this place won't redeem them."

They went inside. There was an old-time wonderland of smells all at once, of hams, spices, cheeses, pickles, the kind of perfumes that had long ago been expunged from supermarkets by air-conditioning units. There was sawdust on the floor and an antiquated meat-slicing machine and a thin-faced woman standing behind the counter, her eyes the precise color of the ocean that came and went around Cochrane Crossing. She raised her face from a newspaper she'd been reading and smiled at the two women, and there was something so warm and so unexpected in her expression that Rosie suddenly thought, Hey, Cochrane Crossing has a heart after all. So much for your basic first impressions.

The woman leaned forward, gnarled elbows on the counter. "You must be the folks renting the Callahan place."

Rosie moved between stacks of canned goods, items in boxes, noticing the thin layer of dust that covered everything. "The Callahan place?"

"The beach house eight miles down a ways," the woman said.

"Right," Rosie said.

"You like it down there?"

"It's fine, just fine."

The woman picked at something in the corner of her eye. "Must be three, four years, since that place was rented for a summer."

"That long?" Rosie asked, surprised. Three or four years—why would a summer beach house lie vacant that long? Maybe the owner hadn't wanted to rent it. Maybe it was something that simple.

"Must be, I reckon." The woman came around the counter now, wiping her hands against her apron, which was spotless and white. "My name's Darlene. Darlene Richards." And she was smiling again, as if hospitality were as natural to her as breathing the ocean air.

"Rosie Andersen. This is my friend Martha Schuyler."

Martha looked up from a stack of Campbell's soups she'd been examining and smiled at the woman.

"Those your kids out there?" the woman asked.

"One's mine. The other I can't take any responsibility for," Rosie said.

Darlene Richards strolled to the window and looked out at the station wagon, studying the kids a moment. "Bright-looking young-sters," she said. Without turning, without taking her eyes from the children, she asked, "How long you folks staying?"

"Six weeks," Rosie said.

"A lonely place way out there."

"We like it. It's a change from the city."

"I'll say." Still rubbing her hands, Darlene Richards moved back toward the counter. She had thin sticklike legs covered with rather old-fashioned black stockings and she moved in a strange rocking manner, as if there were something wrong with her hip. "Now which city would that be?"

"Syracuse. Upstate New York."

"That's a ways."

Rosie found herself liking this woman and her quaint store, found herself enjoying the smells of the place, what you might call—in the manner of a magazine article—the ambience.

She glanced at Martha and wondered at her friend's silence and her shyness. It was usually like this whenever they found themselves confronted by a third party. Rosie did all the talking, went through all the social maneuvers, and Martha clung to the background like a wallflower.

"Don't know what you'll find to do out here after Syracuse." Darlene Richards pronounced the name *Sire-Accuse*, almost chopping off the last syllable in her mouth. "Some folks go to the bar at night, I guess, and some go to church on Sundays, but mainly there ain't much of anything around Cochrane Crossing. No movie house. No library." The woman shrugged in the manner of somebody who had become accustomed to the backwaters of the world. Rosie watched her and wondered why people chose to live here or if it was the kind of place you were born into and died in, stripped of choice through lethargy or a lack of stimulation or a failure of ambition. She couldn't see herself here all year round—but this was a relative thing: New Yorkers couldn't imagine Syracuse twelve months out of every twelve either.

The little bell above the door rang and she looked round to see Tommy come into the store. She thought how much he resembled his father if you saw him in a certain light. A little double, a replica. She realized she didn't want to think about Charlie right now—she'd never liked the man on those few occasions when she'd met him, finding him somewhat intense and self-centered, wrapped up in his little academic world as if it were the only real one. And she wondered what it was that Martha was still clinging to in the marriage. Did she think clocks could be turned back and deeds erased and the sun would rise again in an unsullied sky? Romantic Martha. She looked back at Darlene Richards.

"You mentioned somebody called Callahan."

"Yeah, right. I did. The Callahans always owned that house out there."

"Do they still live around here?" Rosie asked.

"Only one of them left and that's old Andrew, but he keeps pretty much to himself these days." Darlene Richards propped her elbows up on the counter again. "I got some ham here that would tempt a saint. You interested in ham?" She dragged a huge slab of meat from under the counter and slung it out in front of her.

Rosie looked at the pink meat for a moment, seeing tiny drops of sweatlike moisture glisten on the fatty flesh.

And just for a moment, a terrible moment, she saw something move in the grain of the flesh. Something white, burrowing. A maggot.

There, just beneath the surface of the ham, a tiny worm.

Her stomach turned over and she felt sticky liquid rise inside her throat.

But then the worm was gone and she wasn't sure if she'd seen anything at all, if it was just something she'd imagined in the poor light of the store. She recovered her composure slowly.

"We've got quite a list of things to pick up here. Maybe we'll get around to that ham later." She turned to Martha. "Well, kid, time to stock up," and then she began to move up and down the very narrow aisles, stuffing things into a wire basket.

Martha followed behind her, and Tommy slid off to look at a rack of old comic books he'd discovered tucked away in a corner.

"Is something wrong with Lindy?" Martha asked.

"She's just off on one of her little mental trips. Sometimes she reads something in a newspaper—like maybe how some Buddhist monk has set himself on fire or how kids are starving in Chad—and for a few days she'll haul the burdens of the world round on her shoulders." Rosie picked up a package of Anacin. "These or Bufferin?"

Martha pulled a face. "I'm into Tylenol myself."

"I don't see any here," and Rosie dropped the Anacin into the basket and moved farther down the aisle. She stopped by the toilet tissue. "One-ply or two?"

"I go for the two-ply personally. I like the density."

"Two-ply it is."

They paused together in the far corner of the store in front of a stack of canned meats. Rosie studied the labels for a time, looking at the Spam and the luncheon meats and the whole boned chickens. "Decisions, decisions. Isn't this fun?"

"I'm having a whale of a time, Rosie."

"Me too," and Rosie dropped some Spam into her basket. Martha followed her round the corner of the aisle. Boxes of candies, rows of Baby Ruths and Mounds and Almond Joys, jellybeans glistening like a rainbow of slugs, pink things wrapped in cellophane. A whole sugar nightmare.

"I think we give this section a miss," Rosie said.

"Speak for yourself." Martha tossed three Hershey bars into the basket. "I haven't learned how to handle the munchies like some people I know. I still suffer."

"Which reminds me, we need rolling papers."

Twenty minutes later they were through and back in the street again. They stashed the bags in the back of the wagon, where Lindy was still sitting and watching the street motionlessly. Jesus, Rosie thought, her mood better improve—they were going to be here for six weeks and the last thing she needed was a sullen teenager on her hands for that length of time. But she knew from experience that it was best to let Lindy drift out of it herself. She'd tried the social director approach, the jolly slap-your-knees-and-let's-sing-campfire-songs bit, but nothing like that worked with Lindy. She was like a human submarine waiting for the right kind of weather before emerging.

"You want to look around a bit before we head back?" Martha asked.

"Sure, let's check the scenery," Rosie answered, and as she got inside the car she reached back and ran her hand over Lindy's face. Despite herself, she asked, "You sure there's nothing wrong, babe?"

"I'm fine," Lindy said, and her voice was flat.

"You could've fooled me." Rosie started the car and drove away from the sidewalk. Sometimes, when Lindy assumed a pouting expression, Rosie had flashes of when the kid had been a baby. Back then, the pout had been cute and adorable, and she and Herb had even done things to encourage the look—like playfully removing a favored toy or teasing the baby with some bonbon held just out of reach. That was then, but now was different and the look didn't exactly enthrall Rosie these days.

There were only two streets in Cochrane Crossing, a main street and another that intersected it just beyond the grocery store. Rosie went right, in the direction of the beach, seeing on either side of the car more of the same frame houses, the same porches, the same windows that gave you the feeling there were people watching from behind drawn drapes. The street simply petered out close to the beach, where the pavement was covered with windblown sand and patches of sea grass. She backed the car up and returned the way she had come, crossing the main street and driving away from the shore this time. There was a dilapidated railroad track overgrown with weeds and an abandoned warehouse of some kind just beyond it. A few more houses, and then nothing.

She returned to the main street once more, passing a small church with a bleached-out signboard out front. Pieces of paper were tacked there and they fluttered back and forth in the breeze. Bulletins of some kind. Announcements of forthcoming events. Marriages. Christenings.

Rosie couldn't imagine marriages and births in this place. She couldn't imagine forthcoming events. She couldn't see Pot Luck Suppers and fundraisers or any of the gatherings you might normally associate with a church. There was a certain bleakness to the small white stone building that suggested inactivity, abandonment. But since the big front doors were open a little way and a small kid was peering out, his large eyes impassively watching the station wagon go past, there had to be some kind of activity going on inside.

And then they were going past the bar and the grocery store, and Cochrane Crossing was suddenly behind them, disappearing from the rearview mirror as if it had been the figment of somebody's imagination. Presumably Cochrane's, Rosie thought. Which didn't say a whole lot for the creativity of the guy if that dreary village was all he could dream up.

"The local tour," Martha said. "I guess that's it, folks."

"I guess," Rosie said.

They drove in silence a little way, then Rosie remembered what Darlene Richards had told her about the beach house. "Did you hear her when she said the place hadn't been rented for three or four years?"

"Yeah," Martha answered.

"How do you figure that one?"

Martha shrugged, as if the question didn't interest her. "Maybe it was on the market and they were trying to sell it. Who knows? Maybe they just didn't want renters."

"Why wouldn't they?"

Martha took out a cigarette and lit it; she didn't answer the question. She rolled her window down and let the smoke blow out. In the back seat the breeze flipped the pages of Tommy's comic book, and Lindy sat with her face pressed to the window, her nose flattened against the glass.

Rosie sighed. She had always disliked silences, and the one inside the car right then grated on her a little. What the hell. Some days don't work. Some days people are preoccupied with their own things. Some days they don't really want to communicate. So they have their comic books or their cigarettes or their moods of withdrawal and you couldn't change that.

She gazed at the sea for a time. After lunch, she'd drink some Jack Daniel's and she'd take her camera and go down the beach someplace and lose herself in her own little universe of prisms and lenses and apertures, textures and shadows and compositions. This was only the first day, after all—and the tour of Cochrane Crossing hadn't exactly been uplifting.

5

AFTERNOON
June 17

They had frankfurters and cheese for lunch, a meal that Martha— who had recently come to consider vegetarianism as the road to travel —didn't particularly like. She had sliced off the top of the hot dog and chewed on it before politely getting rid of it into a paper napkin but now, as she walked the edge of the beach, she felt a little queasy.

Maybe it had nothing to do with the food, though.

Maybe it had been the trip to Cochrane Crossing that had bothered her. As soon as she'd stepped inside that grocery store her attention had been drawn to the telephone behind the counter and she'd been filled with an overwhelming urge to call Charlie and hear the sound of his voice. The desire had consumed her with all the persistence of a shrill scream. Go to the phone, dial the number, talk to the man, tell him that you've considered everything and you want the marriage to work no matter what he did in the past. Tell him that in simple words.

Now, removed from the temptation of a telephone, she tried to push the urge from her mind.

She kicked off her sandals and rolled up the cuffs of her blue jeans and waded out into the surf. She wanted to duck under the cold water and immerse herself.

The water curled around her ankles and lapped against her jeans. Bending, cupping her hands, she splashed her face and hair, then straightened up and looked along the length of the beach. She saw the sand dunes stretch away toward the afternoon sun and there, in the far distance, the figure of Rosie, who had wandered off with her camera bag. Rosie's ongoing love affair with the camera made her feel a slight envy because in her own life she'd never had the time or the inclination to take something up, a hobby, say, and turn it into the kind of passion Rosie had for taking pictures. There had always been the chimerical notion of writing something, but her efforts in that field hadn't exactly turned out too well. A couple of monotonous poems, one free-lance article about pollution on Lake Ontario that had been turned down with depressing regularity, and that was about it.

Now Rosie had some strange notion about them doing a book together. Rosie was going to take photographs of the sea and the beach and Martha was going to supply a kind of skeletal text. It had been Rosie's idea and Martha, for her part, wasn't altogether convinced that the concept was any good. What could she write about the sea and the beach that hadn't already been written? And what kind of pictures did Rosie hope to get that hadn't already been taken?

"Yours is a problem of attitude," Rosie had said when the idea first came up. "A problem of confidence and attitude. Your marriage is dying on its feet and you feel pretty goddam worthless right now. But all that can change if you give it a chance. If you start looking on things more positively. So let's give the book a shot, huh?"

Rah-rah-rah.

There was more than a little of the cheerleader about Rosie, as if some aspect of her personality were still dancing up and down on the sidelines of a football field.

What kind of book was it supposed to be in any case?

Rosie had been vague on that point. She sometimes perceived it as a glossy slab of an item you might find lying on a coffee table. At other times it was going to be a little more serious than that, a reflective work concerning nature, sea changes, raw energy. The Critique of Pure Ocean, Martha thought. And I'm not up to it, I'm just not up to it. She bent again and splashed more salt water on her face, then she noticed that Rosie had disappeared somewhere over the sand dunes. She turned toward the house and observed how its shape was different when you saw it from this angle. It was more hunched somehow, like an old man pulling himself in against an expected blow. When approached from the road, however, it had a spindly appearance, as though it had been randomly constructed entirely from driftwood the sea had spat up. She studied it for a moment.

She wondered what the kids were doing in there to pass the time and then she thought, You worry too much about Tommy, too much about whether he's going to be happy this summer or if he's going to get bored and just sit around doing nothing. You baby him and when you do that you don't give him room to develop. He's thirteen and he's not a little kid any longer and he has to find things to do on his own. And then she remembered his interest in arcane rock bands and the sounds that drifted down from his bedroom in the house in Syracuse, she remembered the weird names and appearances of the groups—Culture Club, A Flock of Seagulls, Black Sabbath. The noises they made were alien to her; they might have been created in another galaxy and transported to earth for the single purpose of subverting youth.

You grow old, Martha.

You lose touch.

All mothers felt that way about their teenagers, didn't they?

She knew that Rosie had hard times with Lindy, for example. She saw how Lindy irritated her mother because of the way she yielded to her moods, how she gave in unreservedly to her feelings. Maybe Rosie had just forgotten the way she was at that age.

She waded out a little farther, the water rising to her knees.

Then she turned back toward the house again.

Someone was coming toward her across the beach. It took her a second to recognize Lindy, whose way of walking was always changing, sometimes taking the form of a kind of arrogant strut, sometimes a stoop-shouldered huddle of insecurity. She watched the girl's long reddish hair caught in the breeze. When she reached the edge of the tide, the girl stopped and shielded her eyes against the sunlight.

"Is it cold, Martha?"

"Chilly."

Lindy hesitated a moment and then took off her flannel shirt and stepped out of her cut-off shorts. She was wearing a somewhat modest one-piece bathing suit underneath. She edged toward the water, testing it with her foot, and Martha could see her shiver. Then, abruptly, she plunged into the surf and for a second she was gone from Martha's view. When she emerged, her face and hair were streaming with water and her eyes were shut, droplets glittering on the long lashes. She was going to be a good-looking woman, Martha thought. She had a certain delicacy to her features that was absent in Rosie, a fine bone structure that seemed almost fragile.

She watched the kid shiver.

"I warned you," Martha said.

"Yeah," and Lindy pushed her fingers through her hair, opening her eyes. "I always figured it was best to plunge right in. It gets the worst over with fast."

Martha nodded. "What's Tommy doing, do you know?"

The girl shook her head. "I guess he's in his room. Reading, maybe."

"Tommy? Reading? That's a contradiction in terms."

"Why? Doesn't he like books?"

"Tommy likes pictures and sounds more than he likes books." Martha looked toward the house. For a moment she thought she saw the figure of her son on the balcony, but because of the way the sun was being reflected from the windows she couldn't really be sure. And then the shadow, whatever it was, disappeared from sight, as if devoured by the house.

"I used to bribe him when he was little. I used to give him ten cents for every book he read. I think the last book I saw him open was something called *Truly Tasteless Jokes*."

Lindy said nothing for a time. She had turned her face out toward the sea and there was something in her expression—what? a passing quality of vulnerability? a sudden insecurity?—that touched Martha, and she realized she'd always been fond of this child, seeing aspects of herself in her, seeing tiny shadows of her own history on the girl's face.

"I'm sorry about today, Martha," Lindy said.

"Sorry about what?"

"You know. The way I acted today. It was shitty."

Martha stretched out her hand and touched the girl on the shoulder. "Hey, you can't be up every minute of every day, kid. You can't always be on the ball, you know. I wasn't exactly up to par myself, Lindy, if you noticed."

Lindy smiled, and her smile was a generous thing, like a gift you never expected, something dazzling. "I think that place gives me the creeps, Martha. I think that's what it really was. That village."

The creeps, Martha thought. Had she felt something of that herself? There had been a vague depression, certainly, but she hadn't been sure of its roots.

"I guess there's something about it I don't like," Lindy said. "I don't know what, though. It's just kinda empty."

"I know what you mean," Martha said. Kinda empty.

"And then there's my mother. I mean . . ." Lindy ducked her head under the water again and Martha could see tendrils of red hair float outward from her skull like a gorgeous seaweed. She rose up, dripping, massaging her face with her hands.

"What about your mother?"

"She always expects me to smile, you know? I hate to disappoint her. I can't always go around smiling when I don't feel it inside. I don't want to go through that kinda fake behavior just to please her."

Martha hesitated. A delicate balance of things here. The girl needed somebody sympathetic to talk to, somebody who would listen and, in return, offer sympathy—you just had to be careful what you said and whether it would be the right kind of thing and hope you didn't come off sounding like an adult, an authority figure. The level you needed was equality. "You ever talk to your mother about this, Lindy?"

Wrong. Wrong thing, bimbo. Lindy's expression changed and she looked away and Martha was embarrassed by the inadequacy of her response to the kid. She could hear the sound of a door closing on some distant room. I could have said something else. I could have said, Hey, any time you want to talk with me, feel free, let's you and me be close friends, confide in me, trust me, I know what's going on, let's leave your mother out of this, let's keep this one to ourselves. Instead, she had stepped aside. She had stepped aside and tossed the ball back into the wrong court. Fragile glass, china, everything stacked precariously on a shelf and ready to topple at any moment— dear Christ, the emotions of adolescence.

Martha let her arms dangle at her side, her muscles limp and slack.

Lindy said, "You know my mother," and then she was gone across the water like a fleet mermaid, spray rising behind her as she swam, her arms digging the surface of the sea and her head lowered.

Martha moved out of the water and back onto the beach, where she sat down and lit a cigarette. The smoke was rough at the back of her throat and she wished she could quit the habit altogether, especially here where the air seemed so goddam pure and her lungs felt grateful for it. She watched the girl swim, her thin body rising and falling with the tide. Then she stubbed her cigarette and stood up, picking holes in the soft sand with her bare toes.

Lindy was coming out of the water now, walking to where Martha stood. She sat down on the sand, Martha's shadow falling around her, and she looked out toward the sea in silence for a while.

Her face was pale, as if the tide had sucked all color out of the skin.

Then she said, "I guess you're right. I guess I should talk to my mother about it."

Martha sat down beside the girl. "You don't have to."

Lindy glanced at her. "No, but I should."

Martha reached out and held the kid's hand in her own and she wondered how anyone managed to survive the furnace of this age, the white heat and the changing temperatures, how they managed to get out of it all alive. "Lindy, listen, anytime you want to talk, you know you can come to me. It's hard sometimes between a mother and her kid, don't ask me why, and it helps if you've got a friend you can speak to." Martha was silent a moment, then she added, "I don't mean this to sound corny, Lindy. I really don't."

"I know." Lindy was drawing a shape in the sand with a stick of driftwood. "Sometimes I don't understand the things I do. Then sometimes I understand them perfectly."

It gets better, Martha wanted to say.

But she wasn't sure of the truth in that. If you came in on it from a certain perspective, it only got worse. Doubts deepened and anxieties rose like hot mercury in a glass tube. But you couldn't say that to a thirteen-year-old kid, could you?

Lindy threw the stick aside and turned to Martha. "Can I ask you something?"

"Sure."

"Why are you separated from Tommy's father?"

Separated, Martha thought. Was there any one good answer to the kid's question? Any one that would satisfy, reduce everything to a simple explanation?

"He had too many girlfriends, and because of that he told too many lies." A basic statement, emotional facts stripped to the cold bone.

Lindy nodded. "He screwed around on you."

"In a nutshell." Martha looked away, staring along the beach and seeing Rosie come into sight in the distance.

Then Lindy stood up and knocked sand from her legs. "How did you find out about it?"

A flash of pain. Martha shut her eyes. The noise of the sea crowded her brain, the tide beating against skull bone. She felt her breath caught tight in her throat. "Well," she said. "It was an accident, really . . . I just happened to see him with a girl when he had told me that he was attending a faculty meeting." She concentrated. Reduced to a single sentence like that, it was all so damned simple. The words didn't convey the strident sense of terror she'd experienced when she'd seen Charlie come out of a house with his arm around a yellow-haired girl who had her own hand slung casually, intimately, at his hip. A simple suburban house in a street lined with oak trees and white spring sunshine threading through the tangle of branches. And yet it was the most terrifying street she'd ever seen in her life.

Lovers—

Charlie and the girl with the yellow hair.

Lovers, easy in the spring sunlight.

Lindy nodded her head and was silent a moment, as if she were trying to reconstruct Martha's betrayal.

Her next question came out of nowhere, emerging from some odd train of thought that Martha couldn't quite follow. A bizarre inquiry, nothing you could link to what had gone before. A young kid's grasshopper mind.

"Do you know what a hornpipe is?" Lindy asked.

"A hornpipe?"

"Yeah."

Martha brushed a fly away from her face. "I think it's some kind of wind instrument."

"Like a whistle or something?"

"Like a flute, I guess. Also, it's the name of a dance. A kind of folk dance, I seem to remember." Martha smiled. "I wasn't expecting that question, Lindy. You got any more like that?"

"Nope," the girl said. She reached down, touched Martha's shoulder in a shy gesture of friendship, then she was skipping away across the sands in the direction of the house.

A hornpipe, Martha thought.

And she smiled to herself.

Tommy finished reading the comic book he'd picked up at the grocery store in Cochrane Crossing and lay for a while on his bed, gazing at the ceiling, watching how the sun crept across it and how the shadows in the room kept changing. He went out onto the balcony once and saw his mother talk with Lindy down on the beach, and what he remembered was the way he'd seen the girl that morning when she didn't know he was there. He hoped she didn't think it was something he did on a regular basis, this spying on people, but it had happened pretty much by accident. Maybe he could have coughed or something to announce himself—but he'd been fascinated by the way she was standing on one leg, like a stork, the way she was balancing herself as if she were poised on a tightrope and afraid of the fall.

But all that star stuff, for Chrissakes!

What was he supposed to make out of all that?

And her airs, the way she seemed to talk to him down the length of her nose, which made him feel real small, even though he was about two inches taller than she was.

Girls.

He sat up on the edge of the bed, remembering Josie Lindstrom, who was in his math class, recalling how he sat directly behind her and gazed at this intriguing little hollow at the back of her neck and the way her curls fell all around it—sometimes it was a great effort not to give in to the temptation to put out his hand and just feel the hollow with his fingertips. Sometimes he really had to hold himself in check if he wanted to resist the urge, and his body would feel strangely tense all over. Like that time, about a year ago, when he'd kissed Frances Muldaur behind the gymnasium (Norm had bet him he wouldn't do it). He remembered the way his body had tensed then and the strange sensation of her soft lips against his and the surprising moment when the tip of her tongue had touched his teeth very lightly before she'd pulled away and pretended to be indignant.

He gazed round the bedroom. He wondered what his mother and Lindy were talking about. Then he stared at the door of the closet. This was the damnedest thing because he'd closed it last night and at some point—it had to be when he was on the balcony—the thing had swung open again.

He rose and moved toward it.

The hinges, he guessed. That and the oldness of the latch.

It wouldn't stay shut. That was all.

He pulled the door toward him and, as he did so, realized he was alone in the house—and suddenly he was aware of an excruciating silence. A silence that reached everywhere. It even sounded like somebody had switched off the sea for a moment.

Or else—

The sounds from outside weren't getting through to the house.

Something was preventing them.

One day here, Tommy, and it's like you're stir-crazy, imagining weird stuff, making things up. What it is, you miss your radio. You miss the constant background noise. You miss your music, your tapes, the way you're always playing them back home. That's what it is.

But he'd never known such an intensity of quietness, such an absence of sound, like the world had turned upside down and every single noise had drained out of it and now there was nothing left to hear except the pounding of his own blood inside his head, a fast pulse, a quick beat. This silence was a pressure you imagined you might measure if somebody had invented the right instrument for the job. Something heavy in the air, heavy and cloying and draining, something so heavy that you thought it might pin you to the floor and hold you there by force. He thought, I'm going deaf, that's what it is, suddenly I'm going deaf, I didn't get any warning about it, I never had any symptoms, my hearing is just shot—and he felt a panic, as if he'd been shut off forever from a part of the world he had treasured. He put his hands to his ears and looked inside the shadowy closet, feeling dizzy and disoriented, listening to the race of his own blood. He looked at the boxes and books, his hands still cupped over his ears, and he had the unsettling feeling that the closet was deeper than he'd imagined before, that it extended beyond the wall and connected with other closets in the house in a series of tunnels, coldly silent tunnels with damp walls.

Bzzzzz. Bzzzzz.

He dropped his hands from his ears when he heard the faint sound of a fly winging around his face. Then other sounds came back slowly, the quiet beat of the surf, the cry somewhere of a gull, the breeze making the balcony creak—and it was like one of those moments of joyful discovery when the crippled guy dips his feet in the waters of Lourdes and says, I can walk, I can walk! He went to the balcony door and opened it and breathed the air in as deeply as he could inside his lungs, trying to relax now, trying to overcome that panic he'd felt before.

The depths of that silence, Christ. What did it mean? Did he need a checkup or something? Was it waxy buildup inside the ears?

He pulled the door shut. He went to the mirror and studied his own reflection. I look okay, he thought. I don't look any different from before—but what did I expect to find staring back at me any-how? Some thin tubercular guy with red-rimmed eyes and pale lips? He laughed at his own face and then, in the center of the room, he did a couple of jumping jacks and he could feel his blood flow warmly through his veins. You're okay, he thought. There's nothing wrong with you.

Nothing at all. You're not deaf and you won't need one of those little gadgets that sit in your ear and amplify the world for you.

Then he went back toward the closet again.

He sat down cross-legged on the floor and began to haul the stuff out. The books, the boxes of games. They had an odd mildewed smell that reminded him of the stink in old Mr. Warford's basement that time last year when he'd had to go down there to get back a baseball that had slipped through an open window. He shoved the games aside and flicked through the books. Real young stuff. Pages filled with big printing and colored pictures. Fairy tales. Old stories of knights in armor and magicians and castles. He closed the books, leaving them scattered across the floor of his room the way he did with his stuff back home, which was when his mother would get on his case about tidiness.

And then he sifted through the boxes of games, wondering how long they'd been there in the closet and trying to imagine whom they might have belonged to. He opened the only one that was unfamiliar to him, the Ouija game (how the hell were you meant to pronounce that word anyhow), and he saw a lettered board and a small triangular thing, whose purpose he couldn't immediately understand. He read the rules inside the lid of the box, but it didn't seem like much of a game to him—people sitting round and asking questions and waiting for the small triangle to move. There wasn't even any way of scoring points, so far as he could see.

So how would you know the name of the winner?

It looked like a totally pointless game. Which was the kind he didn't like at all because he enjoyed the spirit of competition, the idea of doing battle with the other guy and trying your damnedest to win. He tugged on his earlobes, as if to reassure himself of his hearing power, and then he reached inside the box and removed the small triangle, holding it in the palm of his hand.

After a moment, he dropped it back inside the box and replaced the lid.

.   .   .

Rosie usually liked to photograph people. There was something about the diversity of human appearances that intrigued her. The nose, for instance. Everybody's nose was constructed for the same purpose essentially—that of breathing—and yet you encountered a perplexing variety of structures. The squat, the flattened, the long, the pinched, the widespread. She enjoyed eyes, hair, the turn of mouths, the way in which all these elements came together, as if by an act of impossible human architecture, in that thing called the face.

But this was different now. Here she was in the center of a landscape devoid of human presence, conscious of her own solitude, which, in a way, made her slightly nervous. When it came to taking pictures of people, there was a kind of bonding, a relationship you entered into between yourself and your subject—like a contract of sorts that allowed you to steal another person's image and capture it on celluloid—but this kind of relationship, which she'd always found comforting, wasn't possible in the middle of rolling, empty sand dunes. And when she sat down among a thicket of sea grass and opened her camera bag, she didn't take the Canon out immediately. Instead, she removed the fifth of Jack Daniel's she'd begun at lunch and took a quick swallow from it. She put the top on the bottle and stuck it away again, realizing that the landscape must have unnerved her more than she'd imagined—otherwise, why would she be looking for this fake courage?

She slung the Canon over her shoulder and walked a little way.

When she turned to look back, she couldn't see the house any longer. The sea might have swallowed it. She went down on one knee, and raising the camera to her eye, adjusting the lens, she rattled off a couple of quick shots. To get the feel of the thing, she thought. Just to start things rolling. And then she pointed the Canon toward the water and took a few more pictures, after which she continued to walk. She paused only to drink from the Jack Daniel's bottle again, shoved it back in the camera bag and realized she'd never before had an alcoholic drink of any kind while she was out with her camera. It was something she'd formed a taboo about, as if any edge of insobriety would diminish her perceptions, erode her sense of professionalism. So why the hell now?

Because, babe, there aren't any people around.

And this is a big landscape, a big canvas.

And you are all alone in it.

She clambered over the dunes, feeling soft sand slide and slither under her sandals. She sat down on the top of a mound and gazed seaward. She had sold about a hundred photographs in the last twelve months to places as diverse as *Camera* and *Lady's Circle* and *Parade* —the income from which, along with Herb's child support, made her life tolerable if not entirely free from financial worries—and she intended to go on building up as much of a reputation as she could as a reliable and talented free-lancer. But her own attitude today was a puzzle to her. The bottle of booze and the sense of tension and the acute awareness of being alone, none of these things were conducive to what she wanted to do out here.

Goddammit. You need to get up off your butt and get on with it.

So she slithered down the dunes toward the shoreline, where she turned around and pointed her camera back the way she had come, trying to get the texture of the tracks she'd left in the sands. She was more careful this time, taking her time with her shots, her framing, trying to get her body to relax, her muscles to loosen. She took three or four pictures of the dunes and then started to walk back along the beach. She turned her camera out toward the ocean when she paused again, and she saw the sun flare off the incoming tide, flare and die and flare again, as if a series of tiny explosives were being set off across the water.

Christ, though, she didn't feel good about it. She didn't feel she'd accomplished anything. She just knew that nothing she shot today was going to turn out right. It was the same feeling she'd had when she'd first started out taking photographs with a camera Herb had given her on their third wedding anniversary. Maybe he had imagined she'd be content taking snapshots, vacation pictures, anniversary shots, that kind of thing. But Rosie had thrown herself into the art of photography, devouring books and subscribing to magazines and spending long hours in cold places to get the shot she desired. There was a certain lust in photography, an irrational desire to seek out and capture The Shot, The Biggie, the one that nobody had ever caught before . . . The Myth of the Perfect Picture. The one that would forge your reputation for you forever. One day, she thought.

Perhaps . . .

Even as she saw the beach house come in sight again, she couldn't rid herself of the disappointment she felt. And then she reminded herself that this was her first day out with the camera, that this whole landscape would take longer to understand, that she couldn't expect to enter this sea-world cold and hope to catch it on a roll of celluloid just like that. Tomorrow—as all her tomorrows were intended to be —would be better. She put the Canon back inside the camera bag and zipped it shut.

She looked at the house and saw Martha come across the sands toward her. She raised one arm and waved and thought how delicately Martha moved, as if she were afraid of placing her entire weight on the ground. Maybe it was a certain grace, maybe it had nothing to do with any fear or shyness. Alongside Martha she sometimes felt clumsy and large-boned and awkward. Unrefined.

Martha had her hands in the pockets of her jeans. "Take any good pictures lately?"

Rosie made a slight grunting noise. "It was one of those days. You know the kind."

"I think I do."

"Shit, even the camera didn't feel right in my hands, Martha." Which was perfectly true. It had felt hard and alien to her, as if it were no longer the tool of her trade but something hostile and unyielding, whose functions she couldn't quite work out.

Martha clapped her on the shoulder and smiled. "Tomorrow," she said.

"That's what I've been telling myself."

"You're good at what you do, Rosie. Keep that in mind. If there's one thing you know anything about, it's how to take pictures."

"Do I get the impression you're trying to cheer me up?"

"Would I do something like that?"

"It's usually the other way round."

Rosie stopped and looked at her friend, and suddenly her disappointment withered away. When she wanted to, Martha had the quality of turning on lamps in black rooms. Rosie slung an arm around the other woman's shoulder and laughed. There was no point in being troubled by the failure of a single afternoon's shooting, was there?

Martha looked in the direction of the house. "You know what I think? I think we're all still a little tired after the trip."

"I think you're absolutely right," Rosie said. And she was already thinking about tomorrow, about the pictures she'd take, the shots she'd get, was already anticipating a triumph over this whole place, a conquest in celluloid.

Lindy paused in the grove of trees, reaching up to touch a twisted branch. There was a sound coming from somewhere, a strange creaking that might have been the throaty call of an exotic seabird. She listened a moment: was it the branch of one of the trees? But then it stopped, and in the silence she experienced a strange nervousness. She turned to look at the house and she saw Tommy come down the pathway toward the station wagon. He opened the front door and sat behind the wheel, unaware of Lindy observing him. He adjusted the rearview mirror, then gripped the wheel in his hands, and a look of dark concentration came over his face.

He imagines he's driving, Lindy thought.

Then she remembered how he had pestered the two women to be allowed to drive the last stretch from Cochrane Crossing to the beach house and how Martha had refused. Her refusal had seemed less to do with Tommy's driving skills than with the fact that the boy had learned to handle a car under the tutelage of his father. Family jealousies. Little currents that twisted this way and that in the blood.

Lindy studied Tommy a while longer, then she walked down through the grove. She stopped, stood with her back to a trunk, and she was nervous again. An unidentifiable apprehension, like a thin vapor forming in her mind.

The sea.

I am thinking about the sea.

But nothing had happened, had it?

Nothing had really happened when she'd been in the ocean a short time ago, had it?

She had ducked beneath the surface and then—

Then what?

Something damp, something coated with slime, had slid against her inner thigh.

No.

It had caressed her. That was the word. Caressed her flesh. Made her shiver.

When she'd opened her eyes and looked down, she had expected to see a clump of seaweed or some kind of aquatic vegetation floating against her leg, but there hadn't been anything. No tendrils of weed. No sign of life.

Just the gray water pressing upon her body.

Just that.

A caress. A lingering touch that had seemed deliberate to her.

She smiled at herself. It hadn't been anything but a current of water, a freak of the undertow, an eddy of tide.

6

THE SECOND NIGHT
June 17

By the time they had finished supper it was almost dark. Rosie had prepared a pasta with mushrooms and butter and a simple green salad, which they ate at the kitchen table. Martha got up, gathering the dishes. "Great food, Rosie," she said.

Rosie was pouring two glasses of Jack Daniel's at the table; the kids had gone upstairs. Martha could hear them clumping around overhead.

"No telephone. No radio. No TV. Terrific. This is the life we were all made for," Rosie said. "Who needs the bullshit of freeways and supermarkets?"

Martha heaped the dishes in the sink and sat down at the table. "And no dishwasher."

"What do you call these?" Rosie held two hands in the air, smiling. She pushed a shot of Jack Daniel's across the table and Martha picked it up. Booze and dope, Martha thought. I am going to the dogs.

She sipped the alcohol and looked in the direction of the kitchen window. Outside, only faint slivers of daylight remained, striping the sky with pale streaks of pink. She yawned and stretched her arms.

"I'll get around to the dishes later," she said. And she felt as if she were shirking some vital chore, reneging on her part of a bargain, that while Rosie would do the cooking she would do all the cleaning.

Rosie lit a cigarette. "I'd like to take a walk along the beach. You feel up to that?"

"Sure."

"Something about the seaside and the moon," and Rosie sighed in a mocking way. "It's romantic."

Romantic. What a strangely hollow sound there was to the word. Martha picked up her drink again. From the upstairs part of the house she could hear Tommy laughing and she felt suddenly good—it had to mean he was getting along with Lindy, which was something that had troubled her when they'd first planned this trip. The kids didn't know each other particularly well, they went to different schools and they had different groups of friends, and Tommy hadn't wanted to come down here anyhow. But Charlie, who had some kind of fellowship to write one of his papers—the subject, she recalled, had to do with Coleridge, like everything in Charlie's life had to do with Coleridge—was too busy to look after Tommy. He would, however, find time for one of his girls, she supposed. He would always find time for that. Expecially on those nights when the paper was bogged down and the ghost of old S. T. Coleridge wasn't particularly inspiring and his sex drive was overwhelming his academic ambitions—which, given the intensity of those ambitions, the relentless quest for the holy grail of tenure, the furious need to publish, was really saying something about his lust.

"It's an unbelievably lonesome stretch of beach," Rosie said. "I think maybe that's why I didn't get much done today. I'm not used to places like this. I can hear my own heartbeat, which isn't something that happens to me often. You don't walk around the streets of Syracuse listening to your own heart, do you?"

"Not often," Martha said. She finished her drink and could already feel the hotness spread through her body. There was the sound of more laughter from upstairs, both Tommy's and Lindy's this time. "Those two seem to be enjoying something."

Rosie nodded and stuck her index finger into her drink, pushing ice cubes around. "I wonder if she's ever had sex."

"Who?"

"Lindy. I sometimes wonder if she's ever been laid."

"She's only thirteen—Christ."

"Where have you been hiding yourself these last few years, kid? Did you miss the new liberation of children or something? They start out at ten these days."

Martha stared at her friend for a moment; the idea of Lindy and sex seemed totally incongruous to her—just as it did when she thought about Tommy with some girl. They were both too young, too immature, too uncertain, maybe finally too self-conscious for sex. Or am I just being naive as usual? She felt she would have known, in some mysterious maternal way, if Tommy had ever had a girl. As for Lindy, she was pretty sure the kid was still a virgin, but then on the other hand it wasn't as if she walked around with a sign hanging at her neck. VIRGIN HERE. PLEASE KNOCK BEFORE ENTERING.

"I don't think she has," Rosie said, filling up both empty glasses. "But you never know these days." She stood up and looked out of the window, her elbows propped up on the ledge. "I know one thing for sure, though. She wouldn't tell me about it if she had."

A tiny note of isolation in Rosie's voice; it was as if having gone through one divorce from her husband on the grounds of incompatability, she was now being forced through another, this time from her own daughter on the grounds of puberty. Martha got up, setting her glass down. She was already beginning to feel a certain buzzing inside her head.

"You want to take that walk now?" she asked.

"Sure."

They went out of the house and moved slowly across the beach to the edge of the ocean. The moon was up, a silvery disc muffled by clouds. The sea, like some great slavering beast, licked the sands and then fell back only to come again, as though its appetite were unsated. Martha put her hands in the pockets of her jeans. There was a touch of cold in the night air and she shivered a little.

They walked in silence some way, then Martha paused and looked back at the house. With the windows lit and a feeble electric glow emerging from it, it gave the impression of a half-sighted old man, his eyes yellow, peering toward the ocean.

"How old do you think the house is, Rosie?"

"Hard to tell. Fifty, sixty years. Considering the way it's had the shit kicked out of it by the sea, though, it could be younger than that." Rosie lit a cigarette and flipped the dead match toward the tide. Then she kneeled at the edge of the tide, dipping one hand in the cold water. She raised her face and looked at Martha. "Do you ever wear your wedding ring these days?"

"My wedding ring?"

"Yeah. I noticed you don't wear it anymore."

"I stuck it in a drawer as soon as Charlie moved out." Martha felt water lap round her bare feet and she took a few steps back from the tide. She no longer thought about the ring; it seemed to belong to somebody else anyhow, a fresh-faced bride in an old photograph, surrounded by confetti and good-hearted relatives and all the snow-white paraphernalia of a church wedding. "What made you ask that question?"

Rosie stood up and shrugged. "Idle curiosity. I still wear mine sometimes, but only when it's practical. At PTA meetings. Or when I find myself in a singles bar and I don't want anybody to get the impression I'm up for auction in the meat market. I always keep it at the bottom of my purse the way some guys keep condoms in their wallets. I use it as a kind of prophylactic."

Martha smiled. The ring as a protective sheath. It was something she hadn't considered. But there were any number of things she hadn't had time to consider; the separation had left her vaguely numb and a little empty inside and she sometimes had the feeling that everything was temporary somehow, everything hanging in some purgatory of the transient, that her solitary condition was something that would change eventually, even if she wasn't sure how.

They walked a little farther along the sands, then Martha turned to look back at the house, which was partly obscured now by the dunes. She had the odd impression that the sand was crawling up the beach to bury the place, devour it stick by stick, plank by plank. Sea and sand, an awesome combination, a terrible power. Even as a child in Virginia she'd always been overwhelmed by the ocean when she'd gone there with her parents. She remembered all at once the feel of her own thin tears and the sobbing noises she'd made when her father had first dipped her feet in the sea. It didn't matter that he was clutching her securely. She still had the feeling that she was going to be sucked back by the tide and dragged underneath and deposited on some distant beach. Dead, prunelike, beyond recognition.

"Did you hear something?" Rosie asked suddenly. She had paused at the edge of the tide, her head inclined slightly in an attitude of listening.

"Only the sea."

Rosie held up one hand. "No, something else. Listen."

"What am I listening for?"

"Sshh. Just listen."

Martha heard the tide, the soft sound of water over sand, but nothing else. She looked at her friend. "What did you hear?"

"I'm not sure." Rosie looked puzzled. She shrugged. "I thought I heard a voice, I guess."

"A voice?"

"Yeah, a man's voice."

Martha stared the length of the dark beach. She couldn't see any signs of life, but then it was difficult to see much of anything in this kind of darkness. A man's voice, she thought. There's nobody out here except me and Rosie, nobody at all.

"What kind of voice was it?" Martha asked.

"I don't know. A voice is a voice," and there was a slight note of irritation in the way Rosie spoke, as if she found Martha's question silly and unanswerable.

"What was it saying?" Martha was conscious of the fact that she was whispering now.

"I didn't catch any words," Rosie answered.

Martha listened again. The trouble was, you could imagine things in a place like this, you could take the sounds of the sea and translate them into human voices, you could hear sentences in the movement of the surf if you wanted to.

"Maybe it's some guy with a girl," she said. "Maybe it's something like that."

"Yeah." Rosie hesitated a moment. "Let's walk back."

"Sure. If you want to."

"I think I want to."

"You sound spooked, Rosie."

"Do I?"

"Yeah."

"I guess I didn't expect to hear somebody out here."

"You imagined it."

"Probably."

They turned and moved back in the direction of the house, the lights of which seemed suddenly welcoming to Martha, like candles left in windows by anxious friends anticipating your return.

Tommy said, "Just listen to this. 'Explore the mysteries of mental telepathy and the subconscious with this time-tested favorite.' " And then he laughed, raising his face from the lid of the box and looking at Lindy. "The Mystifying Oracle," he went on. He laughed again, and this time Lindy thought she detected a strain in the sound, like he was nervous about something or there was an undercurrent of slight anxiety. She held the small plastic triangular piece in the palm of her hand—it was called the message indicator, according to the Ouija instructions—and she wondered if the thing really worked or if what actually happened was that you made it move across the lettered board without being aware of what you were doing. She was sitting on the edge of the bed in Tommy's room because he'd asked her to come in to look at the games he'd found and she'd agreed halfheartedly. The room was the pits, she thought. Clothes spilling out of a suitcase, books all over the floor, boxes of games.

She placed the message indicator on top of the board of letters and stood up, smoothing her blue jeans with the palms of her hands.

"You leaving?" he asked.

"I guess." She balanced on one leg, reaching down to scratch the other. There really wasn't anything to stay for. She wasn't up to playing one of the games or just hanging out shooting the bull with Tommy.

"I figured maybe . . ." He licked his lips.

"Maybe what?"

"Well, maybe we might try this Ouija thing."

He pronounced the word *ooo-ee-jah* and she laughed, holding one hand up to her mouth. "It's pronounced *weejah*, Tommy."

"Yeah?"

"French."

Tommy reached for the message indicator and studied it, and then he held it up to his eye and stared at her through the transparent plastic disc at the center of the thing. "You want to try it out? Just for laughs, I mean?"

"I don't know," she said. "I don't like the idea of messing around with the thing. I've heard some pretty heavy-duty stuff about Ouija boards."

Tommy stifled a yawn. "Like what?"

"I can't remember exactly," she said. And she couldn't, but she knew that somewhere along the way she'd heard spooky things about these boards, weird messages being spelled out and people being freaked by what they received. That sometimes these messages were malicious and misleading.

Tommy gazed at the board. Then he made a funnel of his hands and spoke into it in a voice that was meant to sound hollow and scary. "Are you there? Are you out there? Spirits? Do you hear me?"

Lindy laughed, even if she didn't really mean to. "Hey, I'm trying to be serious, Tommy. You don't want to mess around with those boards."

"Come on. Why don't we try it?"

She shook her head. There was a distant sound of alarm inside her, a bell going off in a faraway room. And she remembered how that odd word "hornpipe" had popped into her mind out of nowhere and she thought how strange it was when you didn't have any control over the things you thought up or the words that came out of your mouth. You were like a puppet or something—except you didn't know who was running the show.

She looked at Tommy. "I don't think I really want to. Maybe some other time."

"Aw, come on."

"No."

"A couple of minutes?"

"No."

"And if nothing happens we'll give it up."

She was still shaking her head. "Look, I don't want to."

"Okay, okay, okay." He appeared slightly offended and shoved the board aside, and the message indicator slipped from the bed to the floor. Lindy bent down, picked it up, set it back on the board again. Although she didn't want to play Ouija with him, at the same time she wasn't anxious to offend him or hurt his feelings—he might be immature, but she had caught an edge of sensitivity around him, a quality that was almost delicate. Besides, she was still feeling a little guilty about the way she'd treated him on the balcony, exercising her superiority over him like that and probably making him feel bad about himself. Shit, she thought. This is a no-win situation. She watched him get up from the bed and squat on the floor among the books, which he sifted through in an idle, bored fashion.

You've got a whole summer ahead. You've got to get along and try to be cooperative, Lindy. You've got to get down to Tommy's level now and then. A whole summer—and suddenly that prospect filled her with a sense of determination to make things work out, at least as far as she was capable of doing. Six weeks. Six weeks of sea and this beach house.

"I wonder who owned all this stuff," Tommy said.

She gazed at the books. The pages were yellowy. She could smell dampness rise from the paper even from where she was standing. "I guess there was a kid here once." Go right ahead, she thought, state the obvious if you must, just because you feel you want to make conversation for the sake of Tommy's feelings.

Tommy looked up at her, as if he were going to say "That's a bright insight," but he didn't say anything. He just looked at her from under his long, curling eyelashes.

"Is there a name on the books?" she asked.

"Uh-huh. I already looked. Nothing." He tossed the book aside and stifled another yawn.

Lindy stared at the half-open closet door for a moment. It isn't going to hurt, is it? It isn't exactly going to ruin the rest of your life and your prospects of marriage, kids and a brilliant career if you spend five minutes with him playing that goddam game, is it? She picked up the board, sat down on the bed, placed the board on her lap.

"All right," she said. "Five minutes."

Tommy smiled and sat down beside her. They touched knees together—she felt embarrassed a second, as if this contact had somehow exposed her—and they placed the board between them.

"A question. We need to ask a question," she said.

"You do it," Tommy said. "Ladies first."

"You're such a gentleman." She closed her eyes and tried to come up with a question but her mind was appallingly blank just then and she couldn't think of a thing. Of course, there were questions she might have asked if she'd been on her own—would Todd Smith in her homeroom ever smile at her or would she get a scholarship to an Ivy League school—but these felt too private to ask in front of Tommy.

"You try, Tommy."

"Me?"

"Yeah, you go ahead."

"I don't know . . ."

"There must be something you want to ask."

"I guess so." He screwed up his face in concentration. "Okay. I'll do it." He stared at the board and placed his fingertip on the indicator and Lindy did the same thing. Then he asked, "Is there anybody out there?"

"God, Tommy, what kind of question is that?"

"It's a question."

"But it's so vague, I mean."

"I don't think it is."

"Okay. It's your question." And she looked down at her finger on the edge of the plastic triangle, noticing how it differed from Tommy's. Hers was long and thin, his wide with a ragged nail, as if he spent a lot of time chewing on it. Is there anybody out there, she thought. That wasn't the kind of question she would have asked.

A minute went past. The plastic triangle didn't move.

Tommy sighed. He was already becoming impatient so maybe he'd just want to quit quickly, which suited her fine.

"Boy," he said. "This is exciting. I haven't had this much fun since the football coach made me run twenty-five laps."

"Be patient," she said.

He sighed, looked around the room, started to tap his foot on the floor.

Another minute.

"You want to quit now?" she asked.

"Pretty soon."

Good, she thought.

And they waited.

Tommy said, "Maybe nobody heard my question. Maybe I should ask it again," and there was a grin on his face now, a silly expression, as if by demonstrating the uselessness of this game, he'd scored some kind of point over her and ridiculed her earlier fear of even trying. He tipped his face back and stared up at the ceiling and, like a wolf baying at the moon, shouted his question aloud. "Is there anybody out there!"

Which was when the triangle moved.

Just like that.

Sliding, slipping, seeming to try to run out from under their fingertips, it shot rapidly across the smooth surface of the board, and she felt something move inside herself, a clammy sensation, as if a hot hand had clutched her heart and was holding it tightly—

It went to the letter Y.

"Holy shit," Tommy said.

The letter E next.

Lindy shut her eyes a moment. She didn't like this, she didn't like it the way she hated riding a roller coaster, the feeling in your stomach and that awful sense of the world turning upside down.

S.

Tommy took his hand away from the board.

"Yes," he said. "It said yes."

She opened her eyes and was about to say something when she realized he was already asking a second question. "Who are you?"

It came back quickly and Lindy could feel a mild vibration go through the tip of her finger.

M E.

"What kind of bullshit answer is that?" Tommy asked. "Don't you have a name?"

The plastic piece didn't move for a long time, and then when it did, it did so as fast as they could follow it, swinging from one letter to the next in a pattern that was both erratic and orderly, logical and illogical, as if whatever force were moving the object had become impatient with this limited means of communication.

WHICH NAME—

No more, Lindy thought. Let's stop this now. I don't like this feeling.

DO YOU WANT?

She pulled her hand away and let it drop at her side; it was still tingling and she thought she was going to throw up because she could feel waves go through her stomach. She stood up and looked at Tommy.

WHICH NAME DO YOU WANT?

"I don't think I want to do this anymore, Tommy. Okay? I think I've had enough right now. I hope you don't mind." She realized she was talking fast and breathing hard, as if she'd just come from a long, hard run.

"You're gonna quit? Just when it's getting started?"

"I think so, I really think so."

"Come on, this is just starting to get good."

"No."

He looked at her with disappointment. "I was really enjoying it. It was pretty weird." He glanced back down at the board and the message indicator, picking the plastic object up in his hand, turning it over, examining it to see if maybe there wasn't some hidden mechanism. "I mean, I don't know how it works or anything, but it's weird."

A faint suspicion formed in her mind all at once. Maybe he'd been playing a game with her, pushing the object around the board, goofing off on her because he'd seen how reluctant she had been to play in the first place. Maybe that was what the whole thing came down to. "Tommy," she said. "Were you making that thing move? Tell me the honest truth."

He looked at her and he seemed amused by her question. "I thought at first maybe you were the one doing it. It wasn't me."

"You swear?"

"I swear."

"I don't know if you're being serious or not, Tommy."

"I'm serious, honest."

She walked toward the closet. The acrid aroma of dampness was very strong suddenly, rising from the enclosed space of the small closet and the pages of the books.

"Real weird," Tommy said again. "The whole thing's weird. I don't just mean the way that gadget moves across the board but the answers we got. Which name do you want—what do you suppose that means?"

"I don't know," she said. "I don't think I want to discuss it." She felt a stiffness inside, a hardening, as if all her nerve endings had frozen solid. "I think I'll go to my own room."

Tommy shrugged. He had picked up the board now and was scrutinizing it like a mechanic peering into the guts of a car. Only there was nothing to look at, just a plain smooth board with a bunch of letters on it, nothing else. Letters and numbers and the word G O O D - B Y E. She didn't want to look at it, she didn't even want to be in the same room as the thing. And she had the strangest feeling that she was about to cry, about to break down in front of the boy and just cry her heart out, even if she wasn't sure why. Tension and nerves and that queasy thing in her stomach. You're upset, that's all, you're upset because you didn't want to play the game in the first place and you didn't like it when you did. Which name do you want? She clasped her forehead with the palm of her hand. She was burning up. And she thought, Great, I come on vacation, I get a fever, which I need like I need a dentist's drill inside a cavity.

She moved from the closet and went toward the door, pulling it open. She looked down the darkened hallway at the stairs.

"Later," Tommy said, holding the board against his chest like a shield.

"Sure." She drew the door shut and moved toward her own room. Inside, she lay down on the bed and shut her eyes. There was a bad taste in her mouth and a dryness at the back of her throat. A virus, she thought. Maybe that's what I've got. She turned over on her side and gazed at the black window, and for a moment she wished she was back in the city, back where you could hear night noises and the dark wasn't saturated with such silences. Which name do you want?

What was that supposed to mean?

If Tommy hadn't been pushing the indicator around on purpose, and she hadn't been conscious of doing so herself, then what was it that had made it move? She found herself imagining another world, one that was composed of disembodied voices and shadows, a world filled with the sounds of the dead, a world that surrounded this one and sometimes overflowed into it so that the two became confused— it was an unlit place, a place where the sound of a footstep on a stairway didn't mean you could see anybody climbing or where the motion of an object didn't mean that there was somebody actually touching the thing. It was a big formless universe, she imagined, its restless inhabitants always reaching out, with desperate, invisible hands, to touch the surface of the world of the living.

Words out of nowhere.

Whispers in dark hallways.

Something shoving a plastic object across a plastic board.

Two worlds in contact.

Two different worlds.

Where did one end and the other begin?

Or were they in a state of some constant overlap?

She opened her eyes. She heard the porch creak beneath her window and the sound of the two women coming back from their stroll along the beach.

Rosie opened the door of her daughter's room and stuck her head round. "What's happening?" she asked. "Did I miss anything interesting?"

Lindy shook her head and smoothed her long hair away from her face. "I just didn't feel very good. Like I'm getting a cold."

Rosie sat on the edge of the bed and held the kid's hand a moment. Then she touched her brow, which was slightly warm. "I'll get you some aspirin," she said.

"It's okay. I'm beginning to feel better."

"You sure?"

Lindy nodded. "Yeah, I felt feverish, but it's passing."

Rosie studied the child a moment. Why did she always have the feeling that she was making conciliatory gestures toward her own kid, as if the relationship were nothing more than a series of quick skirmishes and fragile truces?

"I was thinking that maybe you'd like to come out with me tomorrow when I take the camera," she said. "I could use some company, babe. You feel up to that?"

"Sure. Why not?"

Rosie stroked her daughter's hair for a time, marveling at its soft strength and the way it shone beneath the bedside lamp. "It's a lonely life out there on the beach."

Lindy raised herself up, leaning on an elbow. She was obviously distracted, her attention someplace else, the way it frequently was these days. Rosie wondered when she'd first started to lose the girl, when it was that the kid had begun, in almost imperceptible ways, to slip out of her life. At ten? Eleven? Somewhere in there, sometime during those years; that was when she'd begun to retreat behind closed bedroom doors and held long whispered conversations on the telephone. You're a mystery, kid. A sweet mystery.

"I tried the Ouija board with Tommy," she said.

"I didn't know he had one of those things."

"He found it in his closet."

"So what happened?"

"Nothing much," Lindy said. And then fell silent.

A door opens, a promise is made, a door closes. Rosie looked at her daughter a while longer, then she kissed her on the side of the face and stood up.

"Well . . . I guess I'll call it a day," she said. "Good night, kid."

"Good night, Mom."

"Sleep tight."

She left the room, shutting the door quietly behind her. She went inside her own bedroom and looked at herself in the mirror. She ran her hands through her short hair, pouted her lips, moved toward the bed. She undressed and dropped her clothes carelessly on the floor and put on a long flannel shirt that had once belonged to Herb.

She reached for the bedside lamp, turned it off and lay listening to the lulling sound of the tide. And she remembered the voice she thought she'd heard on the beach, a man's voice mumbling someplace nearby, uttering words she hadn't been able to understand. The sea, she thought, just the sea playing tricks on her ears.

Simple tricks.

Even the fact that she imagined she'd recognized the sound of her own name in the muttered words was just another deceit of the mischievous tide.

Even that.

7

THE CHILD
June 18

Tommy woke, knowing that the weather had changed. The air was heavy and clammy and his body stuck to the bedsheets. He thrust them aside and looked toward the balcony door. The sky was gray and there were enormous black clouds scudding along, driven by the wind. He could hear the change in the sound of the sea, too, the tide no longer monotonous and lulling but angry. He got out of bed and went onto the balcony and looked in the direction of the ocean. The color of the water was different as well, gray and miserable, and the waves were swollen, rolling up on the beach in a crazy, ragged way. He thought of a mad dog foaming at the mouth, and then, shivering in the wind, he turned and stepped back inside his room.

The goddam closet door was open again.

He went toward it and kicked it shut with his foot. This was turning into a kind of competition between himself and the door, a game he was determined to win. He heard it close with a satisfying sound, then checked the handle to make sure it was going to stay shut. He sat on the edge of his bed, scratched his head, yawned and wondered if anybody was up yet and if there was a chance of some breakfast downstairs. He couldn't smell anything cooking, though, so maybe Rosie hadn't wakened. He was filled with a sudden longing to catch the scent of bacon frying.

After he'd put on a pair of blue jeans and a sweater, he stepped out into the hallway and looked in the direction of the stairs. All he could hear was the noise the wind made as it blew around the house, making things creak. He wondered if this place was safe, if it was sturdy enough to stand up to a storm, then he figured it had to be since it looked like it had been around a long while.

He rubbed his hands together and went down the stairs. *Creak creak creak*. The kitchen was empty. What was more bleak at breakfast time when you were hungry than the sight of an empty kitchen? And breakfast was his favorite meal of the whole day, the only one he really loved. Not those skimpy cereal things, little bits of sugar and corn afloat in a bowl of milk, but the Real Thing, bacon and eggs and hash browns and pancakes and orange juice. He looked inside the refrigerator, which was when he felt a slight edge of panic—where was the goddam bacon, for Chrissakes? He rummaged through the shelves, looking for the familiar package, finding nothing. Stacks of cheese and eggs and milk and a couple of tomatoes but no bacon.

This is the end of the world, he thought.

A breakfast without bacon. It was like taking a shower with your clothes on.

He moved to the table and sat down, drumming his fingers on the surface. And then he remembered that his mother had recently been babbling about vegetarianism, which, coupled with the fact that Rosie had a thing about organic foods, didn't look too promising so far as the old bacon went. He stood up, walked to the sink, poured himself a glass of water. Then he wondered if he should just go ahead and scramble a few eggs and make some toast, but when he turned to look for the bread he saw it was that brown Roman Meal junk, which he hated. There was no good white bread anywhere.

This sucks, he thought.

He drained the water and put the glass down in the sink. Then he heard the first sound of rain slapping against the kitchen window, shaking the glass. And for a moment the whole house seemed to tremble, like it was about to float up in the air and plunge out toward the sea, dragged up by its roots and just flung across the sky like a crazy Frisbee. He stared out of the window. This was going to be one terrific day. He stuck his hands in his pockets and shuffled his feet around and wished he was back home because at least he had friends there and he could hang out with them.

He turned when he heard a noise from upstairs. *Creak creak creak* again. Then Rosie came into the kitchen, her eyes a little puffy and her hair untidy. She was wearing baggy khaki pants she might have stolen from the corpse of a dead soldier six inches taller than her— but Tommy understood that some women found military clothing quite fashionable these days, for reasons he couldn't begin to fathom. He'd seen Rosie one time in a camouflage jacket. She had looked as if she was concealing hand grenades in her pockets.

"Tommy," she said. And as she passed him she reached out and rubbed his shoulder in a friendly way. "You're up early."

"I guess. What time is it?"

"Seven-thirty. What happened? Couldn't sleep or what?"

Tommy shrugged. He liked Rosie, except she had this habit of always touching him, rubbing his hair or his shoulder or the back of his hand. "The wind woke me," he said.

Rosie stood at the window a moment. "I like this weather."

"I don't," Tommy said.

"Tommy, Tommy," she said and then, to his embarrassment, she gave him a quick hug. He caught some kind of scent, a sweet sickly smell of perfume. She stepped away, opening the refrigerator. He felt suddenly brighter at the prospect of breakfast. "The thing is, when you're going to live by the sea you have to get used to all its moods. You have to learn to live with the elements, Tommy. You'll see, you'll start to like it here when you think with that kind of attitude."

The elements, he thought. He wasn't really sure what she was talking about. He watched her take out eggs, which she started to break one by one in a mixing bowl. Scrambled? Omelette? French toast? He liked the suspense of anticipation. Then she was whipping the eggs into a froth with a whisk.

"I hear that you're trying to converse with the spirits," she said, glancing at him and smiling.

"The Ouija board thing?"

"Lindy says you found one in your room."

"Yeah." And he recalled the weird way Lindy had behaved last night, almost as if she were scared of something, then accusing him of pushing the indicator around. Which he hadn't been doing at all. He'd figured maybe that she'd been the one doing it, and if not, then the whole thing was too strange to think about.

"Did you try it out?"

"Some," he said.

"Why is it that when I try to have a conversation with either you or Lindy I feel like a dentist?" She tried to imitate him, moving her head from side to side with each word she said, her voice deep. "Some. Yeah. Sure. I mean, Tommy, don't you sometimes feel this great need to use words of two or three syllables?"

Tommy watched little bubbles form on the surface of the eggs as Rosie moved her wrist back and forward. Then he sat down once more at the table. Sometimes you wanted to talk and sometimes you didn't, and there were times when you didn't want to talk with any adult anyhow.

"So what happened with the Ouija?" she asked.

"Nothing much."

"Nothing much," she said. "I rest my case. How do you want your eggs?"

"Scrambled's fine."

Rosie rolled up the sleeves of the sweater she was wearing, then she hauled a big black skillet out of a closet and dumped it on the stove with a clang. She melted some butter and poured the egg mixture into it, after which she tossed in some seasonings Tommy wasn't altogether sure about—thyme, basil. He was strictly a salt and pepper man. But when you're this hungry you don't stop to ask questions, you just eat. He heard his stomach moan deep inside. Suddenly the kitchen was filled with a delicious smell.

"Got any plans for the day, Tommy?"

"I'm not sure. What about you?"

She looked at him thoughtfully a moment. "I've got to try to take some pictures, I guess."

"In this weather?"

"I wouldn't be the first person to photograph a rainy beach. Anyway, there's something different about seaside rain. It's not like the city kind. Maybe I'll get lucky today, maybe I'll get something dramatic."

She put a plate down in front of him and he attacked the eggs with a ferocity that seemed to amuse Rosie, who grinned at him, shaking her head.

"You ever hear of the verb 'to chew'?" she asked.

Crazy time to ask a question when your mouth's full and you can't answer because then you get a lecture about not talking with food in your mouth. He nodded his head and went back to the eggs.

"You eat like there's a house on fire, Tommy."

"Good eggs," he mumbled.

"Gracious of you to say so," and she turned away from him, stepping back toward the stove. He finished eating and carried his plate to the sink. He felt some need to please Rosie, as if to thank her for the breakfast, so he figured he could do it best by being tidy—which wasn't often the case at home. He folded his arms against his chest and watched her whisk some more eggs in the mixing bowl.

"You like it here, Tommy?"

"It's okay, I guess."

"It'll grow on you. You'll see. Later, you'll look back on this vacation and you'll think it was a great time."

He turned this over in his mind, doubting it.

She was touching him again, this time smoothing a curl of hair away from his forehead. "You've got great hair, anybody tell you that?"

"Yeah."

"I bet," she said. "I bet all the girls tell you, huh?"

He shuffled his sneakers on the floor. People were admiring his curls all the time. Sometimes he wanted to take a pair of scissors and lop the whole lot off, which would give his mother a stroke.

He watched Rosie a while longer, then he went over to the window and looked out. You could hardly see the ocean now for the rain, which was streaming across the window in great quick drops. He pressed his nose against the glass. The wind came up and rattled the pane and he heard the house whine all around him.

He blew on the glass, steaming it up, then he drew a pattern in the condensation with his fingertip. A gallows with a hanged man. He stared at it, erased it, pressed his face back against the glass and looked out.

Something moved out there.

Something moved behind the thick curtain of rain, a flash of yellow, bright yellow, then it was gone.

Yellow, he thought.

What's yellow and walks across a beach when it's raining?

It sounded like one of those sick joke questions.

A banana *sand-witch!*

He looked at Rosie and was about to mention what he'd seen but then he realized he wasn't absolutely sure how to describe it other than to mention the color, which didn't amount to anything very much, did it? Maybe he was just seeing things. Maybe that's all it was.

Somebody, he thought. There had been somebody out there.

Somebody small dressed in something bright yellow.

Walking along the beach through the rain.

Big deal. It was probably somebody from Cocksucker Crossing.

He stared out a few minutes more but decided that the person—if there had been a person—must have gone farther down the beach. Then he left the kitchen and climbed upstairs to his room, thinking you'd need to be some sort of loony to wander around in this weather.

He stepped inside his bedroom and had the strangest feeling, the

kind of feeling you get when you enter a room just after somebody
has left it and you can still catch an edge of their presence, the way
you might hear a tune in the distance. He moved toward the bed,
then glanced at the other side of the room.

Where the goddam closet door was open.

Martha said, "Sometimes, Tommy, I get the impression you intend
to remodel this room. I imagine you sitting in here with hammers and
nails and all kinds of floor plans, working out the changes you're going
to make. I mean, how am I supposed to explain all the noise you
make otherwise?" She was standing in the doorway of her son's room
because what had wakened her was the banging sounds that had
come from there. It wasn't bad enough that she'd got up with a
piercing headache, she'd had to listen to Tommy taking his room
apart. She looked at the debris on the floor, shirts, shorts, socks,
shoes, boxes, books, fishing rods, and she wondered how—unless he
had a very peculiar, presumably arcane method of arranging things
—he ever managed to find something he was looking for. She was
about to tell him to get the room in some kind of presentable shape
but the pain in her head was bad and she didn't have any energy and
besides she didn't want to start her day off by moaning at her son.
Some mornings, if you woke moaning, the remainder of the day was
a downhill slide into depression, when every little thing snagged your
nerves.

"It's that door," Tommy said. "I was trying to get it shut. It keeps
opening all the time."

Martha looked toward the closet, the shadowy space beyond the
half-open door. "And you thought you'd kick it into submission, did
you?"

"I banged it a few times, Mom, it was no big deal," the boy said.

"And it still doesn't stay closed?" she asked.

"That's right."

"Maybe you'll have to learn to live with the absolutely shattering
fact that there's something wrong with the door, Tommy, which
shouldn't be too difficult." She put one hand to the side of her head
and tried to rub the spot where the pain was the strongest. She hated
herself for her sarcasm with the boy. It was cheap and pointless and
what made it worse was the slight whine in her voice. Don't nag, she
told herself.

"It gets on my nerves," Tommy said.

She sat alongside him, laying a hand on the back of his wrist. "I've got a terrible headache. I didn't sleep too well. I didn't mean to jump on your case this early in the day, Tommy. I'm sorry."

"Yeah. Me too. I didn't know I was making so much noise." Tommy shrugged and looked in the direction of the closet. She followed the line of his eyes, then studied his expression and realized that this business with the door was really bothering him more than she would have thought. He was not an overly imaginative child, and there wasn't much of the dreamer in him—but she recalled how, when he'd been very small, a certain closet at the top of the stairs had always troubled him. He'd always had difficulty going past it, especially at night, and even after she'd demonstrated how the closet contained nothing more sinister than linen and towels he'd been afraid just the same, as if he imagined a family of demons waiting for him behind the closed door. Waiting, ready to spring out at him. But he'd grown out of that quickly. She wondered what was involved here —some decrepit memory emerging? A flashback to a time she was sure he could barely recall?

She watched him rise from the bed and go toward the closet, where he kneeled and examined the latch and the handle. He was chewing on his lower lip and frowning; he had always been a determined child, sometimes to the point of stubbornness, and she could see how he had made up his mind not to be defeated by a simple door that wouldn't stay shut. But why did it matter so much to him, she wondered. Why couldn't he just ignore it?

She stood up and looked at the closet. The hinges were very old and the latch had a shiny, worn-down look. And then she looked inside the closet itself, seeing how the space rose up into the gathering of shadows beyond the shelves, as if perhaps at the very top there was an entrance to an attic. There was a smell of dampness, but what else could you expect to find in a beach house? She took a step back, colliding with the boxes and books Tommy had discovered.

"I can't figure this thing," the boy said. "I mean, it really should stay shut," and he prodded the latch with the tip of his finger before he stood up. He looked at her, his face tense, the muscles in his jaw tight.

"You're making a mountain out of a molehill, Tommy. It's not so important, is it?"

"I guess," he said.

"You can learn to live with it, right? If you'll pardon the expression, Tommy, you won't let a goddam door unhinge you, will you?"

She was hoping he might groan at the feebleness of her pun, but he didn't.

He nodded his head. She watched his face, realizing that it was something she should have found as familiar as her own, but it kept changing—just when she really thought she knew it, when she really felt she understood every expression, every little gesture, she found something new written there. Like right now: she'd never seen quite this look of tension. She put out one hand and massaged his shoulder very gently. His muscles were tight, locked in place. She wished there were something she could suggest, some kind of outing or activity, but he had outgrown the promises of Disneyland or the State Fair, things that might have pacified him or interested him in the past, and besides, what could she possibly suggest for him to do around here on a day as savage as this one was turning out to be?

She kissed his forehead, thinking that pretty soon she'd have to stand on tiptoe to reach his brow because he was already a half inch taller than her and growing at a surprising rate.

She went to the door, glancing once again at the boxes of games and the pile of picture books on the floor. Then she said, "I better go in search of an aspirin, Tommy," and she blew him a kiss across the room before she pulled the door quietly shut.

She stepped into the hallway, moved toward the top of the stairs, then paused. She listened to the roar of the rain on the roof and the noise of the wind crying around the house as if it were a great bird in terrible pain—and then there was the sound of a door banging from below with the pulselike regularity of a hammer rising and falling steadily on the head of a nail. She went down the stairs. Across the living room she saw that the front door was wide open and the screen door beyond slapping back and forth against the outside wall. The sea wind, as though it were an aggressive trespasser, was blowing through the house, causing the pictures on the walls to tremble and the curtains to shake and the threadbare oval rugs to flap against the floorboards. The whole house might have been seized in the wicked grip of a giant's hand, raised up and shaken and about to be crushed.

She hurried across the living room and drew the screen door shut by reaching out through the rain to grasp the slippery handle. Then she closed the wooden door and listened to the click of the latch.

She sat down on the sofa and shut her eyes because her headache was getting worse now. She clasped her hands together and thought, This house has a problem with doors.

Doors that blow open, that won't stay closed.

A problem with doors. A problem with security.

The need to feel safe, protected, sheltered.

She shivered, went to the window.

Outside, she saw Rosie make her way through the driving rain in the direction of the sands, and for a moment, without quite knowing why, she wanted to throw the window open and call out to her to come back inside.

But then Rosie had gone, swallowed by the weather.

Something dramatic, Rosie thought when she'd stepped out onto the porch. The wind that blew rainsqualls against her face had the ferocity of an animal, and for a moment she couldn't catch her breath. Something dramatic indeed—it wasn't a day for taking pictures at all. The wind was too strong and the rain too dense to make anything possible, and besides, her Canon hadn't been built for this kind of weather. You needed a good underwater job for this kind of day, something watertight. She walked to the steps and moved toward the sands. The wind flapped at her sou'wester and tugged her waterproof hat. A blind, wet day. Unless it cleared up, the camera was going to remain safely inside its bag.

She struggled across the damp sands. There was something gorgeous and unanalyzable in this kind of weather. Something that seemed to release you, offer a transitory kind of freedom. It was as if forms and shapes and anything recognizable had been wilted and changed by the violence of the sea rain, and the basic geography of the landscape altered so drastically that you were plunged into a world both maddening and invigorating. The skin tingled and the blood rushed and you had this feeling of astonishing aliveness, a sense of self you rarely experienced.

She turned her face away from the sea, because rain was driving under her hat and into her eyes, and she looked back at the house. It was strange—the house was no longer there, obscured completely by the falling rain and blurry drifts of spray that the wind blew up off the tide. It might never have been constructed. It might have belonged inside some odd fantasy she'd built for herself, a dream populated by people—Lindy, Martha, Tommy—who had never existed. Then she faced the ocean again and began to move, bending into the wind, feeling her lungs work furiously behind her ribs as she struggled for air. It makes sense to go back indoors, she thought, and get the hell out of this storm because you're not going to get any pictures today. But you had to persist if you were going to be professional, you had to plug and just keep plugging away for as long as it took. And she raised her face upward, wondering if there might be a break in the cloud cover, maybe the promise of better weather to come, but the dark shifting mass overhead was ominous and complete, while the wind was growing stronger by the second, making her coat rise up against her body and threatening to dash her hat out to sea.

There were no boundaries, she realized, between earth and sea and sky, everything had overlapped, spilled into one another. It would be easy to get lost out here where you didn't have a sense of direction any longer and there were no recognizable landmarks to guide you. She pulled her hat down on her head and turned her back to the wind, clutching her camera bag tightly against her side.

She walked back the way she had come, studying her own footprints as she moved, following the trail she'd already left. She'd been crazy to come out here anyhow, imagining there might be some small hope of taking pictures. Dream on.

There it was through the rain, through a space in the thickness of the rain, the beach house, looking impossibly fragile and frail, like a folly somebody had constructed against all sound advice.

But there was something about the way it looked now, drenched and sunken and miserable, something about the mad weave of rain around it, that appealed to her. I want a picture of this, she thought. I need to try and get one picture of this forlorn house from precisely this angle in exactly this kind of weather, and she undid the snap of her camera bag and reached inside for the Canon, wondering how she could contrive to keep rain from blowing directly into the lens. She shielded the camera as best she could, took her picture quickly, then let the camera fall back inside the bag.

She looked back at the house again.

There was a small child standing on the porch.

A kid of about eight or nine wearing a yellow rainslicker and a pointed yellow hat, just standing there and watching her through the blur of rain.

A girl, a pretty little girl.

Rosie moved forward and the wind abruptly changed direction, swinging at her from the house and the road beyond, forcing her to pause a moment. A kid, she thought. What would a kid be doing out here on a day like this?

A neighbor, maybe.

She hadn't seen any other houses nearby but that didn't mean there weren't any. There might be dwellings elsewhere along the shore in places she hadn't explored.

But why did she have the feeling that this wasn't the case, that the child wasn't somebody who lived in this vicinity at all?

Somebody lost. A little person lost in this terrible weather.

She called out, "Hey! Hey, little girl!"

Then she struggled forward, the wind and rain filling her nostrils and blinding her eyes and choking the breath from her body, and when she reached the house she clambered gratefully onto the porch and called out again, "Hey, kid!"

She moved round the side of the porch.

"Little girl? Where are you?"

Behind her, the boards of the porch creaked and she swung round, but she didn't see anything—and even though she walked the length of the porch again and tried to peer through the ragged drift of rain, even though she shouted at the top of her voice a few more times, she saw nothing and her cries went unanswered, unless you counted the mocking responses of the storm.

There was just the howling wind and the whipped-up sea and the steady *beat beat beat* of rain against the roof and windows.

But no kid. No little girl. Had she gone indoors for shelter?

She pushed the door open, stepping inside the house, half expecting to see the kid in the living room or the kitchen, but there were only Lindy and Martha drinking coffee at the kitchen table. She stared at them, conscious of the way water dripped from her clothing onto the floor.

"Did either of you see a little girl come in here?" she asked. And as she looked at their blank responses, at Lindy's sleepy face and Martha's vague frown, she realized she wanted them to tell her, Sure, she came in here, we saw her, everything's okay, don't worry about a thing, Rosie. She wanted the stamp of authenticity on what she'd seen outside. A nice black stamp, a mark of verification.

"What little girl?" Martha asked, gazing across the rim of her coffee cup.

"I just saw her on the porch, a kid in a bright yellow rainslicker with a matching hat." She heard her sentence fall into a vacuum, heard her words being sucked into a silence that was almost conspiratorial. "If she didn't come in here, then I don't know where she could have vanished to."

Martha was shaking her head. "You sure?"

"It's hard to mistake a bright yellow slicker—Christ." Control your voice, Rosie, do not sound so irritated.

"What would a kid be doing out here in this shitty weather?" Lindy asked and sipped her coffee.

"I don't know, I honestly don't know."

Martha stood up and went to the stove and produced a cup of coffee, which she set on the table for Rosie. "Get out of your wet clothes and drink this. You don't want to catch a cold."

Rosie sat down slowly and ran a fingertip round the warm cup. "Look, I know what I saw, Martha."

"Maybe she went the other way."

"What other way?"

"Away from the house, I mean. Maybe she walked back to the road. Maybe she came from a car parked on the road," and Martha shrugged, as if there might be a simple, reasonable explanation for the abrupt appearance and disappearance of a small child in the middle of a storm.

A car parked in the road, Rosie thought.

Why not? It made as much sense as anything else. She stared at rainwater slithering from her sleeve and forming a puddle round the base of the cup. I am not given to seeing things. I am not the kind of person who sees tiny phantoms, whether they are dressed in yellow raincoats or in full Halloween regalia. I do not see things any more than I hear voices.

Hear voices, she thought. She shut her eyes very tightly. Somebody is driving along the road, a girl and her father, the father has to pull over for some reason, maybe he has to pee—whatever—and the little girl takes the chance to slip out and check the storm over, then she hurries back again. Now there was one plausible scenario. One highly practical way of explaining a faint mystery. You could easily imagine an anxious father searching for his daughter in the wild rain, couldn't you?

Yes. You could.

She drank some of the coffee and licked her lips. "You're probably right, Martha. Yeah, you're probably right."

It was better than broaching the impossible; it was better than admitting that perhaps—just perhaps—your perceptions had been vandalized by a rainstorm and that you were simply seeing things.

You are not the kind of person who sees things, Rosie.

You have always prided yourself on a certain levelheaded quality.

"It just blew my mind for a moment," she heard herself saying.

"The last thing you imagine is seeing a small child alone out here on a day like this."

"Well," Martha said. "I just hope she made it back to the car okay."

The car. Already that had become the version, the gospel they accepted. Rosie looked at the rainy window, seized by the feeling—which she could not quite articulate—that the child was still out there somewhere, her yellow coat shining at the center of the storm, like a brittle fall leaf clutched at the heart of a hurricane.

8

COCHRANE CROSSING BREAKDOWN
June 18

The storm did not die until late afternoon, and even when it had drawn back, even when the rain had stopped and the sea ceased raging along the shoreline, the sky was still heavy and bloated, dark clouds hanging across the watery sun. Lindy stood on the porch and watched her mother take pictures along the edge of the sea; Rosie had been pretty antsy all afternoon, like somebody who'd been cooped up too long, and as soon as it had quit raining, she'd seized the camera and hurried outside, almost as if she were afraid the entire landscape might disappear forever before she could get it pinned down on film. Like there's a holocaust just round the corner, Lindy thought—and she wondered about this mad passion of Rosie's, which she'd started to develop just after the departure of Herb. She was pretty damn good, you had to admit, and even when her pictures were being rejected at first, there were always real encouraging notes from editors. After she'd started to make a few sales, the refusals had been less frequent—although they still happened now and then.

Lindy leaned against the porch wall, her arms folded under her breasts. From upstairs, through the open door of Tommy's room, she could hear the kid singing. His voice was high-pitched and a little unsteady, and he was massacring the tune he was trying, which she recognized as Ozzy Osbourne's "Diary of a Madman." The air was stuffy after the storm, clammy and damp and unpleasant to breathe. She had a sudden yearning for her air-conditioned bedroom in Syracuse. She went to the other end of the porch, away from Tommy's singing, and then Martha came out of the house, although she moved so quietly you could hardly hear her.

"Did Tommy drive you outdoors as well?" Martha asked.

Lindy smiled. Sometimes, in those moments when she yielded to unforgivable thoughts, when she just gave in to voicing her most private feelings to herself—good and bad—she found herself half wishing that she had Martha, instead of Rosie, as a mother. They were more attuned to each other, she thought, more alike. And Martha always tried to treat her as an equal at least. It was the kind of thought that filled her with sadness because she knew that Rosie really loved her and that she tried very hard, even if her efforts were often clumsy and transparent. Maybe it would get better somewhere down the road and they would grow closer together.

"I think my son has the scary ambition to become a rock and roll star. He sees himself up there on a stage, surrounded by all this glitter and girls throwing love letters at him. I don't have the heart to tell him that he doesn't have the voice for it. Maybe I'm wrong." Martha took a pack of Camel Lights from her shirt pocket and lit one. "Maybe his is the kind of voice the public is just craving."

Lindy thought she was a very good-looking woman. She had an oval face with strong cheekbones and the kind of eyes that seemed always to see straight through you. She had a good figure, too, and when she moved it was always with a certain elegance, as if she'd been taught to dance some years ago and had never lost the knack of easy motion. I want to be a little like Martha when I'm her age, she thought. And she was overwhelmed by a sudden warm feeling toward her, wanting to reach out and hold her but unable to overcome the vague inhibition she felt. It was always like this when she really wanted to touch somebody; she didn't have her mother's ease—quite the opposite, she shied away from contact. She remembered the first Junior High dance, when she'd danced a couple of times with Jay Brewster and how, somewhere along the way, had found herself wondering what it might be like to kiss him—but when he'd asked her to walk outside with him she'd refused, scared all at once of the prospect of the boy's mouth pressed against her own and the idea of his hand slipping inside her dress. No, not scared really, that wasn't quite the word: she'd been thrilled in an odd way, attracted by the notion and at the same time fearful of stepping over some nebulous boundary she'd drawn in her own mind. Besides, she'd had the intuition that Jay Brewster wasn't right, that he wasn't going to be The One, he wasn't going to be First.

Martha was blowing a stream of smoke in the direction of the sea. "I admire your mother's energy," she said. "I wish I could get into something the way she does . . ."

Lindy glanced at her mother snapping away at the edge of the tide. She seemed to have the camera pointed upward, trying to catch the dark clouds and the weak sunlight that filtered through here and there.

"Yeah, she's got energy all right," Lindy said. "She dragged all her developing stuff down here. She said she wasn't sure she could get good service where we were going."

"She was probably right," Martha said. "If you gave your roll of film to the grocery store, they'd sent it to the nearest town by carrier pigeon."

"Or Pony Express."

Martha flipped her cigarette away and it sizzled somewhere on the sands beneath the house. Lindy watched it die and then she saw her mother come back up the beach toward the house.

When Rosie stepped onto the porch, she put her camera bag down.

"You look happy," Martha said.

"I think I might have got something this time," Rosie answered, and she looked pleased, her smile lopsided, the smile she always reserved for her greatest moments of pleasure. "That's a wonderful sky out there. Terrific cloud formations."

Lindy gazed toward the sea. Terrific cloud formations, she wondered. She attempted to see them through her mother's eyes and failed. What she perceived up there was menacing, another storm in the making, as if the dark clouds were black castles about to topple and, stone by stone by stone, crumble over, crack in pieces, split by swords of lightning.

"At least it was better than yesterday," Rosie said. "I feel pretty damn good but I'll reserve judgment until I see how they turn out." She breathed deeply a couple of times, like a long-distance runner after a hard race, and then she clapped the back of Martha's hand. "I feel like a small celebration. What do you think?"

"What have you got in mind?"

"Well . . ." Rosie paused, reaching down for her camera bag and hoisting it up on her shoulder. "Maybe we could hit the local tavern. The kids are too old to need a baby-sitter. We could have a few drinks, relax, check the local talent." Rosie winked and, reaching lasciviously with her elbow, nudged Martha.

"What local talent?" Martha asked.

"Hey, you think it's all hicks with sand in their ears around here?"

"That's exactly what I think."

"I have a suspicion you're right." Rosie moved along the porch to the door. "But I could go for a couple of drinks. Lindy, you wouldn't mind staying home with Tommy for a few hours, would you?"

Lindy wondered about this for a second. She wouldn't have any objections unless Tommy dragged out that Ouija board again and insisted she play it with him. "It's okay with me. If it's okay with Tommy."

Martha said, "He won't mind."

Rosie dragged the camera bag indoors and after a few moments Martha followed her into the house. Lindy could hear their voices floating out through the screen door. Rosie was laughing at something. Sometimes, when the two women were together, they could be like a couple of kids getting ready for a party. Bright-eyed, eager, as if they had just been released from detention room. Their voices rose and fell excitedly, Rosie's sharp-edged Brooklyn tones, which were hurried and breathless, and Martha's more measured way of speaking, a softer sound that often suggested the cadences of poetry.

Lindy turned her hands over and looked into the palms, searching —as she sometimes did—for a sign of a future in the lines that criss-crossed the skin. What she wanted was a contented life, one unblemished by sorrow or divorce, a life of creativity and construction. Sometimes she could imagine a man in her future, a husband, a bunch of little kids. At other times there was a filmy shadow that formed across this picture and she would find herself longing for something quite different—an artistic existence, living in a loft in Greenwich Village or studying in Venice or just drifting round the capitals of Europe.

She dropped her hands and decided it was idiotic to expect to see the future in some random markings on your flesh, for God's sake.

Who needed to know the future anyhow?

It would take the unexpected out of life.

She shrugged and stuck her hands in her pockets and went inside the house. The trapped air left in the storm's wake was moist and insufferable indoors.

She stepped into the bathroom, where there was a dilapidated cubicle that passed as a shower, and she undressed, dropping her sticky clothes on the floor. She turned the faucets and adjusted the hesitant flow of water until it was lukewarm, then she plunged her head under the stream.

Greenwich Village. Venice. A series of exotic lovers.

Shower dreams.

She kept her eyes shut tight as the water snaked from her forehead and cascaded between her breasts and dripped down into the tense curls of her pubic hair. She leaned back against the tiled wall and spread her legs a little way and she thought how, with only the slightest skip of the imagination, the drumming of water could become the sly rubbing of fingertips against her.

The feeling gave her pleasure and she heard herself, in a voice that wasn't quite her own, moaning quietly.

And then suddenly, as if something had happened in the depths of the house to obstruct the plumbing, the stream of water stopped dead. Lindy opened her eyes and stared upward into the silent shower nozzle.

A freak. A flaw in the pipes. A blockage.

But why, when the water had ceased like this, did she continue to feel the strangely pleasant stroking between her legs? Was it some kind of sense echo? Something like an afterimage? She clasped her hands together and, feeling dizzy, a little dislocated, pressed them against her pubic hair as if she were caught naked in a public place and wanted to hide herself.

It's your imagination, Lindy.

It's only your imagination. A weird flight of fancy.

But there it was, the undeniable feeling of pressure, of something trying to force her hands apart, something trying to lay her bare again.

She stepped quickly out of the shower and wrapped herself in a towel. She gazed at the discolored tiles, rust stains and chipped porcelain and loose grout. It was just an old shower stall, that was all. It was nothing more, nothing less. Everything else was a product of your mind. Abruptly, with a loud sputtering noise, the water was storming through the tiny holes in the nozzle again.

And what she felt was that she had been quietly violated, almost as if somebody had whispered an obscenity at the heart of a very pleasant dream.

"I think it freaked me out to see that young kid today," Rosie said as they were driving away from the beach house. "It was the last thing I expected. It upset me somehow. You know what I mean?"

Martha looked at her friend. It was always strange to see Rosie with makeup on her face. Lipstick, eye shadow, a light dusting of something called Creamy Powder Blush, which darkened her complexion. Strange, too, to see her in a skirt and blouse, because she always wore jeans or those military pants she favored. She might have been dressed up for a big night on the town instead of a quick trip to a backwater tavern. Martha wondered what Rosie expected to find in Cochrane Crossing. A man? The chance of some brief summery fling without any troublesome complications?

She turned her face and looked out of the window. Darkness had fallen now and the clouds had drifted away, leaving the night starry and vast. There was a forlorn pocked moon low in the sky.

"You think the kids are going to be okay?" she asked.

"They'll be fine," Rosie said. "I guess I just wanted to get out for a while. You didn't mind, did you? I'm not dragging you along against your will, am I?"

Martha shook her head. She found she always went with Rosie's flow, bending to suit her friend's plans and schemes. Once, reluctantly, she had even agreed to a double date, a dinner with two men she'd never met before. They had gone to a restaurant on the outskirts of Syracuse where Martha's date had turned out to be a real-estate salesman in a two-piece bronze-colored polyester suit, a guy with chubby hands and, she suspected, a wife tucked away somewhere in the background. She'd been uncomfortable all through the talkative meal, listening to Rosie's excited laughter and resenting herself for having consented to the invitation. Invitation wasn't exactly the word; command might be closer. She'd resolved then never to give in again to Rosie's wishes, but here she was once more, going out because it was something Rosie wanted to do.

She recalled how the salesman, Hal, had tried to kiss her in the parking lot later. She remembered his boozy breath and his paws pressed against her body and the way she'd stepped aside, laughing, trying to make a joke out of the whole thing. It was a situation that need never have arisen if only she'd listened to her own instincts and turned the date down. Now she stared at the unstriped blacktop glistening in the full beams of the car and she wished she'd stayed home with the kids.

It all boils down to the fact that you've never really liked to say no to anybody, always imagining that you might hurt vulnerable feelings. She took a Camel Light from the pocket of her shirt and she lit it, gazing at her friend in the darkness of the car.

The weathered sign that read COCHRANE CROSSING came up in the headlights. Ahead, Martha could see the lit windows of houses. Despite the scattering of lights, she had an impression of bleakness. What do they do in this place? How do they whittle the nights away? The darkened grocery store came into view, then the tavern across the street. There were a couple of cars and pickup trucks parked outside the place, but the bar itself seemed unlit and quite abandoned. Rosie turned the engine of the wagon off but didn't get out at once.

"Now there's a joint that's really jumping," Rosie said, squinting through the windshield at the doorway of the bar. She pushed her door open and stepped out, smoothing her skirt with her hand, then checking the buttons on her blouse.

Martha joined her on the sidewalk. She was conscious, from the corner of her eye, of a shadowy movement inside the grocery store. She turned and stared across the street: was Darlene doing some nighttime inventory or something? Now she had another impression —that of several people inside the grocery, faces clustered together and staring out across the narrow street.

Then the shadows were gone and she was following Rosie through the door and into the tavern, a long narrow room, badly lit, murky as a clouded puddle, a pale red neon beer sign hanging behind the bar and several men sitting up on stools with the kind of stoic appearance of habitual beer drinkers. They sat perched as if they were waiting for something to happen, something that would alter forever the shapes of their lives. There was a big old-fashioned jukebox glowing in the far corner, like something that had traveled to earth from a galaxy too distant to measure. Take me to your leader, Martha thought. She followed Rosie to a stool at the bar and climbed up, fully aware that the men were staring at them with a mixture of curiosity and vague resentment, as if this were a private club for males only. The bartender shuffled toward them, an old guy with a glass eye and the kind of greasy hairstyle that had gone out of fashion in the nineteen-thirties. Martha was reminded of a lapsed member of a barbershop quartet, somebody who'd forgotten to pay his dues.

"Ladies?" the man asked and his glass eye glinted in the pale light.

Rosie ordered a double scotch on the rocks, Martha a single. When the bartender returned with the drinks he set them down on the counter and surveyed both women, as if he were auditing their appearance for some inscrutable accounting of his own. Martha felt that the fly of her jeans was undone or that the buttons of her shirt were open and a nipple peering through.

"You'd be the ladies renting the Callahan place, I guess," he said eventually.

"That's right," Rosie answered.

"How do you like it out there?"

"It's fine."

"Walter's my name." And he held out a thin hand to be shaken.

"I'm Rosie. And this is Martha." Martha took the hand. It was unexpectedly firm, the skin cool.

A couple of men along the bar had shifted around, staring quite openly now. Martha glanced at them—but it was hard to see their faces in the poor light. Then she was conscious of somebody sliding down from a stool and moving slowly toward them. A big man, broad-shouldered, dressed in a plaid flannel jacket and blue jeans. He was about forty, his fair hair sparse across his skull. He stuck himself between the stools, spreading his large hands on the bar.

He had a deep voice that seemed to vibrate inside his chest. "Which one's Martha? And which one's Rosie?"

More introductions. Martha felt her hand being seized and held a moment longer than she thought necessary. "My name's Marshall Braxton. Folks around here usually call me Brax," and he threw his head back and laughed, as if he found something wildly comic in his own name. Martha couldn't figure what.

"I own this bar. I'm also the Mayor, the Fire Chief and the Chief of Police. If there's a vacant office anywhere in Cochrane Crossing I'm the man they always ask to fill it. I'm what you'd call the big fish in the small pond," and he was laughing again. It was an infectious sound and Martha could feel herself smiling. "Allow me to buy you gracious ladies a drink."

Walter, seemingly anticipating this, was already approaching them with two more scotches, which he set down on the counter.

Braxton studied Rosie a moment. Then he said, "What brings you ladies way out here anyway? That's a real lonely spot."

"A vacation," Rosie said. She was smiling at the big man, and Martha recognized that particular expression—Christ, she was already half flirting with this stranger the way Martha had seen her do several times back home with other strangers.

"Wouldn't be my idea of a vacation," he said. "I'd go stir-crazy out there, I figure. How do you pass the time?"

"I take photographs," Rosie said.

"Photographs." Brax turned this word around in his mouth as though the camera had only been invented last week. "And the little lady here, what does she do?" He turned to Martha.

Martha shrugged. "I don't do much of anything, I guess."

"She's a writer," Rosie said—somewhat charitably. "We're going to be working on a book together."

The book. Why did that idea seem to have faded into a mist? Martha had hoped that Rosie might have forgotten it, but Rosie never let any project slip once it had crossed her mind and she'd found it viable.

"A book writer and a photographer," Brax said. "We've never had them out at the Callahan house before, if my memory serves me."

"What kind of people have rented the place in the past?" Martha asked.

"Oh," Brax said. Then vaguely, "Most kinds."

"It's been vacant for the last few years, I heard."

Brax raised one of his huge hands and stroked his chin. "Yeah. Old man Callahan just didn't want to rent, I guess. He's a contrary son of a bitch, if you'll pardon my French, ladies."

"So why is he renting it this year?" Rosie asked, letting the tips of her fingers rest on the man's sleeve.

"Needs the money," Brax said, shrugging. "You never know with old Andrew, though."

In the corner the jukebox was whirring into action. After a moment the room was filled with the sound of Willie Nelson. Martha glanced the length of the bar. After the initial flurry of curiosity, the men had gone back to whatever they'd been doing before—which had apparently been some form of silent communion, their hands round their beer glasses and their faces looking downward. Night after night, she thought. They must meet each other every goddam night of their lives. What was there left to talk about? Old skeletons of conversations, things they'd said before and forgotten they'd ever said them, exchanges of useless information, repetitions. The intellectual life.

"What happens around here?" Rosie was asking.

"Well, the high point of the social calendar would be the Christmas dance at the church over there. Yeah, I reckon that would be it," Brax answered and laughed again, like the notion of a social calendar was ridiculous.

Christmas seemed distant and impossible to Martha somehow. She lit a cigarette and Walter immediately pushed an ashtray toward her.

"There's no real social life round here, Rosie."

"So what do you do all the time?"

"Collect food stamps and sign up for welfare." Brax directed this remark beyond the women to the guys along the bar, and they all laughed. "Seriously, we get the occasional passing tourist, who's usually lost his way. Sometimes we get parties of hotshots who need to go fishing and we take them out on boats. Mostly, though, this is what you'd call a depressed community. There aren't any jobs unless you happen to deliver the mail."

"Why do you stay?" Rosie asked.

An expression that might have been one of suppressed pain went across the big man's face. It was extraordinary how the whole face altered when he wasn't smiling or laughing. Martha could see, behind the bonhomie, some other person, as if Marshall Braxton were troubled by something that his laughter couldn't solve. "Where else would I go?"

The music stopped now. There was a deep silence in the room, which lasted only a few seconds. And then the jukebox stirred into action again and Martha heard the whining voice of a female singing something about satin sheets and tears. It was so goddam maudlin. She finished her first scotch, then reached out for the one Brax had bought her. She sipped it, only barely listening to the ongoing conversation between Rosie and the big man. She caught the words "Syracuse" and "kids" and "divorced" and she guessed Rosie was into the standard version of her autobiography, the one she always dragged out when she was talking to a total stranger. Martha got down from her stool and looked at Walter. "Where's the toilet?" she asked.

"Little girls' room's right out back," and he pointed to the rear of the bar with a skinny finger.

Little girls' room, she thought. Why did some people always use that bizarre expression? She walked past the jukebox, glanced at the selection available—Tammy Wynette and Ferlin Husky and Conway Twitty (which she considered a totally suitable name for a caged bird rather than an adult male)—then found herself moving down a narrow corridor until she came to a door marked LADIES. She went inside —into complete darkness. The door swung shut behind her and for a moment she panicked, fumbling against the wall for a light switch.

Which she couldn't find.

Maybe there isn't a light in here, she thought. Maybe they don't bother to replace burned-out bulbs because women don't come in this bar very often.

But then she found the switch and flicked it and saw that she was in a very small room with a sink and a john and a towel dispenser, from which a length of soiled cotton hung down. She drew the bolt across the door.

She looked at her reflection in the mirror, pushed her hair away from her face and then swung round abruptly to face the locked door —she had the odd feeling that somebody was standing just on the other side of that door. She stared at the handle, expecting it to turn at any moment. But nothing happened.

It had to be one of the guys from the bar.

If there was anybody there at all, if this wasn't some figment of her imagination, then it had to be one of the drinkers who'd followed her out into the hallway.

But why?

Some kind of joke?

And then she heard the sound.

A fingernail being drawn across the wood.

Slowly, deliberately, scratching back and forth.

"Who's there?" she asked. "Is somebody there?"

Why did her voice sound so stupidly cheerful?

There wasn't any answer. Just the sound of slow scratching, on and on.

"Who is that?" The question seemed utterly inadequate to her. She should have just seized the door and whipped it open and confronted the nuisance, but somehow she couldn't bring herself to do that.

The scraping noise stopped a moment. And then there was the slow rise and fall of knuckles on the wood.

Rap rap rap.

"Who the hell is it?" Martha said again.

Silence. Even the soft noise of knuckles, of bone on wood, had ceased. Martha glanced at her own reflection in the mirror. Her face was pale and she looked drawn, pinched, her skin stretched tightly over cheekbones.

She shivered.

The little room was suddenly very cold, icy, a shaft of winter thrusting under the door, strong enough to stir the light hairs on her legs and blow her skirt upward a little way. She stepped back from the door, conscious of goose bumps all over her body. She thought: Somebody left the door open farther along the hallway.

The nuisance, the pest, whoever he is, has gone away and left a door open and the cold night wind came sneaking beneath the door, that was it.

Cold night wind, Martha?

Here in humid Cochrane Crossing?

There was no such thing as a cold night wind unless the weather had turned with abrupt violence outside. Unless a ferocious storm had suddenly blown in from the Atlantic, spitting an icy wind through the village.

Unless unless—

She ran a hand across her forehead and turned back to the mirror.

She closed her eyes quickly.

Consider, she thought. Keep calm and consider this: a mirror is a mirror is a mirror, it catches light and it throws back reflections and that's all a mirror does . . .

So why the hell was the glass blank when you looked at it just then?

Why was there no image of yourself, just this empty space, reflections of the tiny room, the walls, but no images of Martha?

Why?

Confused, she opened her eyes.

Slowly she looked at the mirror.

Her own face stared back at her. White as cotton, eyes dark and highlighted by anxiety—her own face nevertheless.

She clutched the edge of the washbasin. She felt weak, as if within her veins her blood had simply stopped flowing and her hammering heart was just pumping at empty arteries. A well gone dry. Okay, she thought. The deal is that I suffered some kind of sensory hallucination. That's what happened. Either that, or I am coming down with some major virus. Meningitis, say.

She shook her head and splashed cold water over her face.

I'm healthy, she told herself.

Physically fine.

Say stress. The stress of the legal separation, stress at having to deal with those most smarmy of creatures, lawyers, the stress of Charlie's confessions about his philanderings. Stress covered a lot of mileage and, besides, it was a convenient label when you got right down to it. Good old stress.

She drew back the bolt on the door and made her way along the corridor to the bar, going to her stool and glancing at the group of men, who were still sitting around as sullen as they had been before. Years of living with the vicissitudes of the sea appeared to have bleached all possibility of expression out of them.

Rosie was still into her conversation with Brax. Martha reached for her drink, sipped it, smoked a cigarette. Now and again she would look along the bar, but nobody was paying any attention to her. The jukebox was still playing a dreary tune.

More drinks were being fetched by Walter and she felt her head spin slightly. Three was somewhere close to her limit. After that, it was the twilight zone. Uncharted territory.

Rosie leaned toward her. "How are you doing there?"

"Fine."

"I like this place. It's got a certain ambience."

Martha stared into her drink and remembered what had happened to her in the ladies' room and she decided that the tavern had all the ambience of an old-fashioned ice house. She raised her head and looked along the length of the bar again. Was one of these guys a practical joker? Was one of them responsible for the noises at the door? Maybe—but how could any one of them be responsible for the absence of her reflection in a mirror? Jesus, that would have to be a hell of a trick. And the wind blowing beneath the door: how could any one of those guys have done that?

She had a sudden sensation of vulnerability as she looked at the hooded faces, and she thought, These guys know that two women and two kids are living in an isolated beach house alone—what if they got drunk one night and decided on some serious fun? What if they piled into a pickup and rattled along the blacktop to the house, popping beer cans and muttering about what they were going to do with those two city women? She picked up her third scotch and looked down into the drink and a wave of nausea went through her; she

didn't have anything like Rosie's capacity for liquor. Besides, it pro-
duced morbid thoughts in her brain, such as the possibility of a mul-
tiple rape perpetrated by a gang of Good Old Boys.

She sipped her drink, forcing the alcohol into herself. There was
a stage of inebriation she reached where she always felt immensely
nostalgic, given to moisture in her eyes and thoughts of her childhood
in Virginia, but these fond recollections were a danger signal because
she always threw up immediately after the outburst of sentimentality.

She was thinking about Virginia now, her parents, the house she'd
grown up in, the horse she'd ridden when she was about nine, a
Shetland pony called Cinders. These images were alarm bells going
off inside her head so she shoved them aside and put the scotch down
too and she realized that Brax was leaning toward her, asking a question. She made him repeat it.

"What do I write? That's what you want to know?" And to her
horror her words were slurred. "I'm writing a novel," she said. She
looked at the expression of surprise cross Rosie's face. "I'm writing an
epic novel about . . ." She hesitated, seeking some inspiration to in-
fuse into the lie. "Appalachian life at the turn of the century."

"That right?" The big man seemed impressed.

Rosie leaned forward from her stool. "It's going to be a big best-
seller. It has a cast of thousands and a movie company has already
expressed interest in it, which means, Brax"—and here she patted the
back of his hand—"that you're talking to somebody who is going to
be a rich woman one day soon."

"Yeah?" Brax smiled at Martha.

Don't do this to me, Rosie, Martha thought. Don't embroider the
simple lie, I have no inventions left. She looked across the bar. Walter
was standing at the far end, his glass eye askew. The scene had the
quality of a still life.

"Warner Brothers, wasn't it?" Rosie said.

"MGM."

"I always get them confused."

"Me too," Martha said, remembering that Rosie always thought it
funny to embellish stories for total strangers in bars. You can tell a
stranger anything, she had once said. You can make up your life to
suit your mood. An epic novel, Warner Brothers and MGM, fabulous
riches, fame—Martha could feel herself cringe; she'd never been
good at even the most innocent kind of lie.

She wanted to go outside, let the fresh air bring her back to life,
but she didn't move. She was aware of Rosie and the big man moving

away from her, and she realized after a moment that they were going to dance to the jukebox. She couldn't believe Rosie at times. She couldn't believe her social drive, the way she collected people wherever she went. She twisted her neck and watched them shuffle across the floor to some God-awful country tune. What was Rosie playing at? Had she drunk enough to be attracted by this man? But then the music had stopped and she was coming back to her stool and the big man had vanished somewhere.

"Need another drink?" Rosie asked.

Martha shook her head. "Warner Brothers, for Christ's sake."

"Well, I wasn't sure if it was MGM or somebody else. You know I never keep these things straight in my head." And she laughed, leaning toward Martha and kissing her cheek.

"Where's your boyfriend?" Martha asked. It came out as one word. Wheresyourboyfriend.

"He had to split. Maybe there's a house on fire someplace or a criminal lurking out there who needs to be arrested."

"You always go for the big shots, don't you?"

"You know me, kid," and Rosie did a little dance, a sort of soft-shoe shuffle round her stool. "Anyhow, you ready to leave?"

"I'm ready."

Unsteadily, Martha climbed down from her stool. They went outside together and stood on the sidewalk and listened to the sound of the surf come up through the empty streets of Cochrane Crossing. There wasn't a trace of coldness in the night air: rather, the atmosphere was heavy with warm moisture, the clammy aftermath of the storm.

They moved toward the wagon and Rosie said, "Nice place. We'll come back again."

Martha opened the passenger door and fell into the seat, losing her balance badly. Rosie got behind the wheel, laughing.

"You're a lightweight, Martha."

Rosie started the car and they drove past the village sign. The dark blacktop glistened in the full beam of the headlights, then Cochrane Crossing was gone. Sleepy, her eyelids leaden, Martha looked at the unstriped road stretch ahead. Locked rooms, she thought. Knuckles on a wooden surface and cold blasts of air climbing your legs and blank mirrors—it was Séance Time, communications with the Spirit World, elliptical messages from Beyond.

She sniffed the air. There was a faint scent of burning rubber inside the car. "What is it?"

"I don't know. I'll tell you one thing, we're losing power."

The car was slowing, stuttering as it began to lose speed.

"Ah, shit," Rosie said. "Shit shit shit."

Four miles from the beach house, on a stretch of lifelessly dark road, the wagon—without any of its idiot lights coming on—quit on them, died on a downhill slope and rolled to a halt.

The smell of burning rubber was stronger now.

Rosie got out of the car and Martha could hear her clatter around under the hood. It was the only sound out here on this lonely road except for the relentless cry of the tide along the black shoreline.

9

OUIJA
June 18

"I told you I don't want to play again."

"Why not?"

"I don't feel up to it."

"Sure you do."

"No."

"Come on."

"En oh."

"A couple of minutes, that's all."

Tommy tipped his chair back against the kitchen wall. Why was she making such a big deal out of something that was only a goddam game in any case? He looked at her as she stood beside the refrigerator, an apple in her hand, and he wondered why girls had to be such a big mystery, why they were always hiding themselves behind arguments that seemed to him perfectly irrational. Sometimes it was like they occupied another world altogether, where everything didn't always add up.

He looked at the Ouija board on the kitchen table.

"Lindy . . ."

Her face was stuck inside the open refrigerator now and he couldn't see her expression.

"Lin . . . dee . . ."

"Tommy, will you quit it?" She slammed the door and turned to stare at him, little blood-red dots high on her cheeks. He watched her and he thought, It's not like I'm asking her to play doctor or anything. It's only a board game.

"You allergic to games, Lindy? They bring you out in a rash or what?"

"I don't enjoy games. I think they're a waste of time."

Now she was taking her high and mighty approach. He fiddled with the plastic indicator in his hands and then he set it down, shoving it slowly back and forward across the board. "I can't play it by myself."

"Tough. Then you won't be playing at all, will you?"

"You scared?"

"No."

"Yeah, you gotta be scared."

She sat down at the other end of the table from him, her teeth crunching into the big red apple. And she fixed him with a look he found uncomfortable—it was like she was saying, Don't bother me, small boy, I have better things to do with my time. He turned the indicator upside down. It looked like a large dead insect flat on its back. He whistled monotonously for a few seconds, then, with his fingertips to his mouth, pulled at his lower lip and let it flap back in place.

"You look stupid doing that."

"Yeah?" He did it again. Pull and flap. Pull and flap.

Lindy turned her face to the side. "He'll get tired of doing that soon, poor thing," she said, as if there were a third person in the kitchen. "He always does. Then we just tuck him back in his straitjacket and he calms down. He just can't help himself. Sad," and she was shaking her head.

"Ha-ha," Tommy said. He put the indicator down in the dead center of the board. For a time he sat in silence, just listening to the house. Rosie and his mother had gone about thirty minutes ago and the rest of the house was empty—so why did he imagine just then that he'd heard the stairs creak? He kept listening but the sound didn't happen again. A house like this has to make all kinds of little noises, he thought. Slates, boards knocked loose by the wind—a house like this has to be able to create all its own sound effects.

Lindy was nibbling on the core of her apple and gazing out of the kitchen window where, beyond the undrawn drapes, the black sky pressed against the glass. Tommy thought of the stretch of empty beach outside. "Hey, you want to take a walk with me?"

She shook her head. In the palm of her hand she was holding a bunch of apple seeds. "I don't feel like it."

He sighed. You try to be nice. You suggest a game. No, thank you. You suggest a stroll. No, thank you. What did you have to do? What gestures did you have to make so that somebody would recognize the fact you were just trying to be kind? He had run into the wall of mystery again and he couldn't see beyond it. He got up from the table and walked to the window. He looked out. Somewhere out there the sea was rolling up on the beach but it was invisible in the darkness. It might not have existed at all except as a series of tidal sounds.

He went back to the table and sat down facing the girl. She flipped the apple core into a trash bag and then propped her elbows up on the table. Tommy watched her and realized quite suddenly that she wasn't bad-looking at all, if you liked her color of hair, if that kind of red appealed to you. He sneaked a glance at the small breasts beneath the plaid shirt she was wearing and she caught him, her face flushing —he felt like a criminal apprehended in the act of snatching an old woman's purse. He looked away. Jeez, it had only been one quick look, that was all. It wasn't as if he'd tried to *touch* her tits, so why did he feel so bad about it now? Because she was looking at him as if he were one of those dirty old guys who stand in bushes with their peckers out and a pocketful of candy for unsuspecting kids.

Then he was conscious all at once of the fact that he was alone in a house with a girl, and the idea disturbed him in ways he couldn't quite figure out because it wasn't as if he hadn't been alone with a girl before, but he felt hot, sweat rising from the very fine hair under his arms, trickling across his chest. He scratched the backs of his arms.

"If you don't want to take a walk and you don't want to play this game with me, what *do* you want to do?"

Lindy shrugged. She removed a stick of chewing gum from the pocket of her pants and slid it into her mouth, and her jaws moved for a while. Tommy studied her a moment, seizing an opportunity when she wasn't looking straight at him, and wondered about her curious mixture of moods, how it was that she could be real friendly sometimes and then put on this cool act at others. Like she was doing now, chewing her gum and just staring into space almost like he didn't exist or wasn't worth any of her attention.

She turned her face toward him. "Okay, okay, okay. I'll tell you what. I'll play for ten minutes on one condition, if it's so important to you."

Tommy shrugged. "It's not all that important," he said, trying to meet cool with cool.

"Hah! You've been bugging me about it all night!"

"I wasn't bugging you."

"Sure you were." She chewed her gum for a second, then took the small pink pellet out of her mouth and tossed it into the trash.

"What condition?" he asked.

"You've got to promise never to ask me again, okay? You've got to promise you won't bug me anymore . . ."

He stared at her. He felt like he was in the presence of a baby-sitter who was being paid by the hour to look after him. He felt patronized and silly. A deal, he thought. Where did she get off?

"Well, it's up to you, Tommy."

He hesitated. Maybe she was really trying to be kind, even if her kindness had a condition to it.

"Well? I think it's a pretty fair offer, Tommy."

"Except you don't really want to do it, do you?" he asked.

"I'm waiting for your answer," she said.

"Yeah, okay." He felt he had lost something here, something he just couldn't quite define, but it was connected to his pride. It was as if he had come through long and complex negotiations for a contract and had yielded at the last moment to the other person's terms. He sighed and pulled his chair around the table toward her.

"One other thing," Lindy said. "I don't want to do it on our laps like we did before. Let's just leave the board on the table."

Tommy shrugged. His earlier interest in trying the game was beginning to wane; Lindy had eroded his enthusiasm with her orders, her conditions, her attitude.

"You ready?" he asked.

"Ready." She put her finger on the indicator.

Tommy did the same. "Your turn to ask a question, Lindy."

She shut her eyes the way a kid did before blowing out the candles on her birthday cake, trying to dream up some terrific wish.

"I want to know . . ." Lindy paused. Her tongue ran across her lips. "I want to know your name."

"That's what I asked before," Tommy said.

"It's my choice, okay?"

They sat in silence for a time, looking at their fingertips on the plastic surface, and Tommy felt slightly ridiculous—he'd made all this fuss about playing and now the heart had gone out him. How was it going to look if he just stood up and said, Sorry, I don't want to play, Lindy? She'd probably throw something at him.

"Tell us your name," Lindy said, and although she tried to make her tone light, Tommy could detect something else underneath, an edge of some sort, a tension. She doesn't want to do this. She's only doing it because I wouldn't quit bugging her. And now I'm the one who can't be bothered. Why was life so goddam contrary? Why were moods like balloons that were easily punctured?

"Your name," Lindy said again.

The plastic moved very slowly, as if it were magnetized to the board. Tommy's eyes followed it across the letters.

Y.

Then O.

And it stopped for a time.

He felt sweaty again, little drops forming on his forehead and scalp. It had to be the humidity in this dump.

It moved once more. It slid toward the letter U.

Y O U.

Tommy opened his mouth and whispered the word to Lindy, who whispered back, "I can spell, Tommy."

It stopped moving again, this time for a minute or so, and Tommy could feel a certain weight in his eyelids; he wanted to yawn.

Then C.

Y O U C, Tommy thought. What kind of name was that supposed to be?

The letter U.

Y O U C U.

The indicator seemed to vibrate against the tip of his finger, then it slipped rapidly toward the next two letters before it became completely still.

N T

Lindy took her hand away from the object and stared at Tommy. "You did that, didn't you? You can't deny that you did that yourself. I could even feel you giving the thing a push."

"Hey, I swear I didn't," and he wanted to laugh because the message was the last thing he'd ever have expected. If he believed there was some kind of spirit edging the indicator around the place, then it had to be one with a sense of humor. "Lindy, I promise you, it wasn't me."

"Then why are you smirking like that?"

"I am not."

"You are."

Tommy looked down at the board. "It didn't answer your question, did it?"

"I don't give a damn. The whole thing's foolish as hell."

"Ask the question again," he urged her. "Go on."

"What for? You'll only play another of your idiotic tricks."

"I am not playing tricks, Lindy." He paused a moment. "Okay, I'll ask. What's your name?" And he looked at Lindy, realizing for the first time that she had striking green eyes. If you saw them in a certain light they were gray, but right then they had become a delicate shade of green.

This time there was no movement from the indicator, and Tommy had the feeling that the board was completely dead beneath his hands, that it was no more than reinforced cardboard covered with a coating of some kind of plastic—but that's what it had been all along anyhow, he thought. It had never been anything else. It didn't have mystical properties, no matter how the plastic doodad behaved under your hand. There was probably some really simple explanation, like the heat from your skin making the thing move, something rational like that.

The wind was coming back. It could be heard shivering against the sides of the house. Tommy looked up at the window and saw the screen tremble. He hoped it wasn't going to storm again. He didn't like the idea of his mother being out in bad weath—

It moved. Suddenly it moved.

It slipped quickly beneath their hands and Tommy could feel a terrible burning sensation course the length of his finger like a lick of flame, and he wanted to drag his finger away but he couldn't do it, somehow he couldn't do it, as if his whole hand were paralyzed, and when he raised his face to look at Lindy he realized she was going through the same thing exactly. Her mouth hung open and there was a frightened look in her eyes and he could see the thin veins in the back of her hand stand up, as if the blood that traveled through her body had swollen like a rainy river. The letters were being covered in a fury, faster than he could even remember them, the triangle of plastic rushing across the board like something squirming, trying to get free. And the message made no goddam sense at all, just this curious jumble of letters that went on and on in a meaningless sequence of the alphabet—I A M X Z Z R X O B B B S B B W W C O M M E—like wires had been crossed someplace and all kinds of fuses blown and terminals shorted out. He listened to the odd gasping sound that Lindy made and he understood he wanted this to stop, he didn't need to go on with this because it was scary and incomprehensible, but he still couldn't get his finger away from the board, still felt as though he was being sucked down into the letters as if his hand were being drawn into quicksand and his whole body would follow after that, and down he would go, down and down and down, into a murky place from which there was no return.

"Tommy," she said. "Tommy, Tommy, make it stop, please make it stop," and there were tears in her eyes now, spilling over the lids and running across her cheeks. "Please, Tommy!"

He opened his mouth to say something but his tongue felt heavy, bloated, as if somebody had laid a piece of lead inside his mouth. And his throat was dry, constricted. I can't make it stop, what can I do to make it stop?

I X X X Y Y M Y B G L O O Y K Y I R W T N G F O R Y OU.

Then, gradually, it was beginning to slow down and suddenly the air in the kitchen was no longer heavy, like somebody had switched a fan on someplace, dispelling the humidity.

Slower and slower.

Crossing the board with a kind of serenity.

Forming the name—

R O S C O E

The burning sensation left his finger and he could see Lindy, her face no longer pale, her expression no longer panicked, sit back in her chair as if she was exhausted. After a moment she dragged herself up and moved across the kitchen to the door. Tommy dropped his hands at his sides and listened to her climb the stairs. He looked at the board and then he followed the girl, calling her name.

The door of her bedroom was open, a faint light spilling out into the hallway. He looked inside, saw her sitting on the edge of the bed with her hands clasped together, a Kleenex pressed between her fingers. She raised her face. Her eyes were red from crying. What was he going to say? That he was sorry he'd ever suggested the idea of playing? He stuck his hands in his pockets and stepped into the room.

"What happened? What the hell happened down there?" he said.

She didn't say anything for a very long time. She just kept staring at him. Then, "Burn it, Tommy. Burn that thing. I want you to burn it."

He nodded. Then he went to the bed and sat down beside her, overcome by an urge to hold her hands and in some way comfort her —but he felt awkward, clumsy, afraid that if he took her hand he'd manage to hurt it somehow.

"Will you do that?" she asked. "Please?"

"Sure," he said. "Sure I will."

This seemed to cheer her and she tried to smile. "I don't know, I just don't know what happened in the kitchen, I just know I didn't like it and I don't want it to happen again, that's all."

"It was spooky . . ." He looked round her room, which was neat and tidy, little jars of things on the dresser, a comb stuck into the bristles of a brush, a box of Kleenex. A girl's bedroom, he thought, and he felt like he'd penetrated some dark, fundamental secret of existence. "I couldn't take my finger away, Lindy. Like something was holding it there. That doesn't make any sense, I guess."

She nodded. "I know what you mean."

"And those strange letters," he said. "I wonder what that was all about."

"I'd like to forget, Tommy."

"Yeah . . . and then the name Roscoe. Where did that one come from?"

She reached for the Kleenex and snapped a tissue out of the pop-up box. She touched it to her face. "I don't know where it came from and I don't care. I just want you to swear that you'll burn the thing."

"Cross my heart." He understood he felt weak now, like he was living at some distance from himself, hearing the pulses in his own body beat like clocks that ticked away in a distant cellar. Roscoe, he thought. Why Roscoe? It wasn't the name of anyone he knew.

He got up from the bed and shuffled his feet round in the bedside rug. All at once he felt very close to the girl, as if they had shared something intimate between them, something that would bond them together. They had a fear in common and to Tommy that seemed more of a link than love would have been. He scratched his curls and moved toward the door.

"Lindy, look, I'm real sorry I talked you into that thing, I mean . . ."

"You didn't talk me into it. I did it all by myself."

"Well . . ."

"You've got nothing to be sorry about, Tommy."

"I don't know," and he stepped out into the hallway, afraid of the shadows of the house, afraid of the prospect of his room and that goddam closet—afraid to go down into the kitchen and look at the board or even touch it, as if there were some presence lingering down there. What am I thinking, he wondered. What am I afraid of, Christ? You've grown out of boogeymen and monsters in attics and shapeless forms in basements. You left those things behind with Dr. Seuss.

Didn't you?

He went to the edge of the stairs and looked down at the light falling through the open kitchen door and he had the impression that somebody was inside the room, somebody who was just pacing very slowly back and forth. And maybe he imagined he saw a shadow passing in front of the light, that he heard the very soft sound of footsteps, before he started to go down the stairs.

10

NIGHT WALK
June 18

"Cars, fucking cars," Rosie said. "They're a testimonial to the failure of the American imagination, Martha. I fell for the advertising, you see. I fell for some bullshit patriotism spewed out of Detroit, and at the last minute I decided I wasn't going to buy a Subaru so I got this damned Dodge wagon. Holy shit." And she raised her fists in the air as if she were railing—not at Chrysler or General Motors or any other faceless corporation in Detroit but at God himself and his unwilling-ness to intervene at times of such crises as flat tires, busted water pumps and hoses with holes in them, those times when you really needed The Big Guy, when you were stranded on some bleak freeway on a rainy night and there was no help in sight.

The two women had decided to walk back to the beach house rather than go on into Cochrane Crossing, where, at this time of night, Rosie felt there wouldn't be any assistance available to them; presumably tomorrow they could make the walk into town when it was light. Now they had left the road and the broken-down car and were walking across the sands, feeling the wind that had just come up with renewed vitality thrusting itself out of the sea almost playfully. Rosie could feel a coldness press against her legs and she wished she'd worn jeans instead of this thin skirt. Why she'd decided to dress up for a visit to the tavern in the village she wasn't really sure. Besides, she thought she was allergic to the powder she'd rubbed over her face because her skin was starting to sting a little.

"I wonder how much farther it is," she said.

Martha, who had been silent for the last five minutes, said, "I figure at this clip we've covered a mile max."

"Christ," Rosie said. "A mile, that's all?"

"The sand doesn't make for fast travel."

Rosie looked in the direction of the ocean. "We should have kept to the road. Why didn't we? Don't answer that. We're trudging along this beach because it was my idea. Why don't you sometimes hold up your hand like a traffic cop, Martha, and tell me my ideas suck?"

"They seem all right at the time, I guess."

Rosie reached out and slung an arm around Martha's shoulder. "I bully you, don't I?"

"I don't think so."

"Yeah, I do, I know I do. Next time I try to steamroll you, say something. Stamp your feet. Shout. Call me a bitch. Anything. Okay?"

"The car was going to break down anyhow. It could have happened in daylight."

Rosie rubbed her friend's shoulder. "You're too nice for me, Martha. You know that? I mean, how did somebody like you and me become such good friends in any case? An attraction of opposites?"

"Something like that."

Rosie shivered as the wind drifted in from the black sea again. There was no longer a moon, and clouds had obliterated the stars. All you could see of the ocean were tiny white flecks sliding like powder over the fringe of the beach.

"I don't think I've ever been on such a goddam lonely road in my life," she said. They had kept to the blacktop for perhaps half a mile and nothing had passed in either direction. Rosie continued to anticipate a pickup truck coming along and some kindly backwater type— all bone and Adam's apple—stopping to fix the Dodge. But zip. There hadn't been a thing. A world devoid of autos. Which wasn't bad in theory but at times like this left much to be desired. You could go with exhaust pollution for the convenience of easy transportation. What if the storm blew back in right now, for example? They'd be stranded here like two beached fish. She dropped her hand from Martha's shoulder.

"Why did I have to suggest that drink? It's not like we don't have liquor back at the house, is it?"

"It doesn't matter now," Martha said, her tone conciliatory.

Rosie stopped and looked along the beach. She couldn't see anything. There was no sign of the house yet. No tiny flickering light. Everything seemed cold and empty to her. They walked a little way in silence.

Then Rosie said, "This reminds me of summer camp when all us girls used to walk a mile every night because the counselors—who I suspect were in league with the devil—thought it was damn fine for our growing bodies. Out in those woods, you couldn't see your hand in front of your face. We used to sing songs. I remember that. I remember 'It's a Long Way to Tipperary.' I think I even know the words . . . you feel like singing, kid?"

Martha smiled. "I'm tone-deaf. Got one of those tin ears. I never could carry a tune."

Rosie cleared her throat and sang the first two lines of the song.

> *"It's a long way to Tipperary*
> *It's a long way to go,"*

and then, because her voice sounded feeble as the wind whipped through it, she stopped. "Why am I singing, Martha?"

"To keep our spirits up."

"Why? Are we downhearted?"

"I don't think so."

"Good. I hate downhearted. I think downhearted stinks. My favorite word is 'buoyant.' I used to like 'gay' before it became limited." She realized she was talking just a little too quickly, rattling on as if she were afraid of silences. Afraid of what she might hear if she stopped talking. What exactly? The wind slurring across the waves? "How far do you think now?"

"Mile and a half. About two and a half to go. Maybe we can walk a little faster," Martha suggested.

"We can try."

They quickened their strides as much as they could but the sand, wet still from the rains, was too mudlike for them to make fast progress. And then there were dunes rising up all around them; a scrambling process was involved in clambering over them, an undignified posture that reminded Rosie of how crabs scuttled.

"We could take this opportunity to discuss our book," she said.

"Book?"

"How quickly they forget. The book. The *book* we planned."

Martha hesitated a moment. "I don't think I've got the confidence to try it, Rosie. Every time I think about it, I get butterflies in my stomach."

"Nonsense."

"No, I do, really. I think about how good your photographs are and then I think about my prose and I can't make a reasonable equation out of the two. You need a pro, Rosie."

"I need you," Rosie said. "I won't take no for an answer. And if I sound like a bully again, it's only because I honestly think we can do this thing together. Truly I do."

"I know, I know."

"Try something tomorrow. Try and get something down on paper tomorrow."

"If the mood strikes—"

"Mood mood. Mood's got nothing to do with it. A professional doesn't sit round on his ass waiting for a good mood."

Martha tried to light a cigarette, shielding her match from the wind by cupping a hand, but it didn't work and she gave up after the third match. By the brief flicker of flame, Rosie could see her friend's face and she was reminded of something as delicate as china.

They walked a little way in silence. Rosie thought about the pictures she'd taken that afternoon, immediately after the storm had passed. There had been a thin, watery sun and streamers of pale light coming through the cloud banks, the kind of sky that cried out for a sound track of religious organ music. She'd gone through a whole roll of film, convinced that with each click of the shutter she was getting closer to something terrific. The sky, the dunes, the ocean, the storm's wake. She was bound to get at least a couple of great shots.

Thinking about the photographs now, she felt uplifted, and whatever depression she'd experienced about the broken-down car just evaporated. A car was just a car, but the prospect of a great photograph was like a taste of nectar in her mouth. Tomorrow she might set up her equipment in the bedroom and develop the film.

She glanced at Martha, who'd been very quiet, pondering something.

"What's on your mind, Martha?"

"The kids," Martha answered.

"What about them?"

Martha turned her face toward Rosie. "I don't know. I guess I was just wondering if they're okay."

"Sure they are."

Martha shrugged. "I just had a weird feeling, that's all."

"What kind of feeling?"

"I don't know how to describe it."

"A mother's intuition?" Rosie asked.

"Something like that, I guess."

"Can you be more precise?" Martha often took refuge behind vague statements, Rosie thought. It was as if she thought of words as butterflies too beautiful to pin down.

"I don't think so."

"Well, was it a bad feeling or what?"

"I'm not sure."

"Martha."

"Really, I'm not sure."

Rosie placed the palms of both hands flat against Martha's shoulders. She's so frail, she thought. So skinny and small. How could she possibly stand up to the world? "Listen, I'm a great believer in a mother's intuitions, so maybe you can spell this out for me a little better. Did you feel something bad?"

"Maybe . . ." Martha was struggling for language like a diver, his oxygen tank draining, fighting for breath on the ocean floor. "I had the feeling there was something wrong, only I don't know what exactly. I can't define it, goddam."

"They're okay, Martha. Lindy and Tommy are okay. What could happen to them away out here in any case?" Martha was trembling a little. "Look, they're thirteen now, they know how to take care of themselves. And nobody comes out this way, obviously. They're fine. I'm certain of it. Relax." And she started to stroke Martha's arms but the trembling didn't stop.

"I'm okay. Really. I'm fine." Martha laughed, as if her own indefinable fear was very foolish.

"We can try to walk a little quicker," Rosie suggested. "Get back faster if we can."

"Sure."

They scrambled over the dunes, feeling the sand clutch at their feet. The faster they tried to move the more the sand seemed to impede them. When they were over the next clump of dunes and the sea grass had thinned out, they were both breathless. The house was still nowhere in sight.

"I don't have the lungs for this kind of slog," Rosie said. She could feel the heaving of her heart, her lungs opening and closing like clamshells in a frenzy.

"Me neither." Martha was bending from the waist, her hands on her knees. "Too many cigarettes . . ."

They continued to walk, more slowly this time. Rosie could feel the rebellion of muscles in her legs, the mutiny of sinew in her calves. Then there were more dunes to cross, which they did laboriously, their feet clogged by clinging damp sand.

There it was. The beach house, Windows lit both upstairs and down. Rosie stopped a moment, trying to get her strength back. "Home," she said.

Martha was looking toward the house, hands on her hips, her breath coming very quickly. Exertion or nerves, Rosie wondered. They moved across the last stretch of sand, the dunes behind them now. And then they were only about fifty yards from the house.

There was somebody on the porch, somebody silhouetted against the light from the kitchen window.

Somebody who stood very still and stared in their direction.

Rosie felt a tiny scream in her heart.

Because it wasn't Lindy and it wasn't Tommy and it wasn't any little girl in a yellow slicker. This was a man, tall, his shoulders broad, his hands placed against the porch rail. A man, she thought. And then she was running toward the house, running as hard as she could, conscious of Martha trying to catch up with her.

A man, why would a man be out here like this—

Why—

She could see the man's shadow shift very slightly, his head moving almost as if he were laughing at her strenuous efforts to get to the house.

"Rosie," Martha was saying. "Rosie, Rosie, what is it?"

Rosie stumbled up onto the porch and looked in the direction of the kitchen window.

She saw nobody.

She shook her head back and forth and felt something claw inside her chest, a large hook scraping the bones of her rib cage and she thought—

You see a little girl in a yellow raincoat and then a man standing out here on the porch and they vanish, both of them just disappear into thin air, so maybe, just maybe, Rosie, you're imagining things, seeing things that aren't there, dreaming up phantoms.

She sat down on the porch with the light from the kitchen window falling across her face and she shut her eyes. She was conscious of Martha standing over her.

"Rosie? What is it? Why did you start to run like that?"

Rosie shook her head. She opened her eyes and looked up at the other woman. Don't tell me you didn't see the man, she thought. Don't tell me anything like that, Martha. Because I don't want to hear it.

"I know I said I was worried, Rosie, but I've never seen you run like that. It was like you were being pursued by something."

Rosie rose very slowly to her feet. Her legs were shaking. (You saw a man standing right where you're standing now. Unmistakable. Undeniable. A fact made of iron. You saw a man.) She looked at Martha. And when she spoke her voice trembled. "I thought I saw . . . I thought I saw a man. I guess . . ." You guess what, Rosie? You guess you were confused by shadows? Worried by Martha's instinct to the point where you created your own specter right here on this goddam porch?

"A man?" Martha said. "I didn't see anybody."

"You didn't?" A sinking inside, a sensation of something slipping down through her body, like a vital fluid draining out of her.

Martha shook her head, and her face looked serious in the light from the window.

Rosie rubbed her lips with a fingertip.

She felt Martha's hand cover her own. "Let's go inside and check the kids."

(I know what I saw, I know what I saw, Rosie thought.)

They went indoors, inside the silent house.

They found the kids in their bedrooms, Lindy fast asleep and Tommy sitting on the edge of his bed with the Ouija board on his lap.

11

BAD DREAM
June 19

Martha said, "How upset did she get, Tommy?"

"Crying and stuff." The kid looked at her apologetically.

"Because of this board?"

"Right."

"But it's only a game. It's not as if there's anything serious about it. It's only the subconscious that makes it work."

"The subconscious?"

"It's like when you do something you don't realize you're doing, Tommy. But if it affects Lindy like that, I don't think you should play it anymore, do you?"

"I guess not." Tommy looked down at the board. "She asked me if I'd burn it."

"Well, you don't need to go that far. But maybe you should put it away. Stick it back in the closet there," and she looked toward the half-open door. The shadows within. "While you're at it, you might think about tidying up your room, kid."

"Yeah."

"Promise?"

"Promise."

Martha got up from the edge of the bed, looking at the board in Tommy's lap. She remembered sitting once, in the very early days of her marriage, with a Ouija board stuck between herself and Charlie, a night when they'd been drinking wine and laughing a lot, and Charlie had dragged the board out and talked about invoking the spirits. Then he'd proceeded to push the little plastic doodad around deliberately, spelling out the words I L O V E Y O U, M A R T H A. But that had been her only experience with the thing and she'd always associated it with a happy time in her life, a time of love and great expectations, when everything in the future looked glossy and secure. Back then, she thought, when dinosaurs were young.

Charlie. She could feel her hands tense, the skin stretch across knuckles. Why did he have to go and louse things up the way he had done? She gazed at her son and she was conscious of the fact that she loved Charlie still, that perhaps it wasn't too late to mend all the broken corners of their love and put it back together again. Forgiveness, that was the rub. How could she sleep with Charlie and lie in his arms and be possessed by recurring images of her husband in bed with his various girls? She wasn't sure she had the strength for that. She knew only that she wanted Charlie by her side right now, and the realization of this created a terrible sense of his absence. Was she going to go through the rest of her life with the feeling that there was something always missing? A phantom limb, a phantom husband?

She laid her hand on the board and saw a downcast expression on Tommy's face. Obviously, the experience had troubled him as much as it had Lindy. But young minds were gullible. Young minds were prey to casual phantoms—hadn't she herself believed as gospel those ridiculous photographs of Conan Doyle's purporting to depict fairies when she'd been twelve? She smiled at the idea now and moved toward the door.

Ouija boards and Rosie imagining a man on the porch and strange happenings in the lavatory of a tavern—maybe there was a kind of sea madness, a form of temporary insanity that attacked you through the salty air and leaped up at you from the droplets of spray.

"Your room, champ. Don't forget." And she blew him a kiss, stepping out into the hallway and shutting the door behind her. She paused outside Rosie's door and tapped lightly on the wood, and when she heard Rosie's voice she went inside.

There was a bunch of mysterious photographic equipment stashed in one corner and clothes draped carelessly over the back of a bedside chair. The room was almost as cluttered as Tommy's. Rosie was lying back across the bed, dressed in a dark blue robe which lay open, revealing an area of breast. She made no effort to cover herself as Martha came into the room.

"You okay?" Martha asked.

"Fine," Rosie said.

There was a pause. A man on the porch, Martha thought. She looked away from Rosie's pale brown nipple and gazed at the heap of equipment. "You setting up shop?"

"Tomorrow, maybe," Rosie said. She yawned and turned over on her side, propping herself up on one elbow. Both breasts were clearly visible to Martha for a moment, then Rosie pulled her robe back in place. "I'm over my little horror show. My own private demon." And she smiled. "You know, I really did think I saw somebody out there. What do you imagine's happening to me, Martha?"

"It was an anxiety attack." She couldn't think what else to say.

"A good old anxiety attack. Right." Rosie swung her legs off the edge of the bed now. She had long slender legs that Martha sometimes envied in a mild way. "I don't know. I was just all of a sudden filled with this great panic and I guess that helped to blow things out of proportion . . . At least the kids are okay."

"Yeah. So much for my intuition," Martha said, feeling slightly foolish now when she remembered the wave of dread that had coursed through her on the beach. It had undeniably happened, though, and she had given in to it for a moment, allowed it to sweep right through her, letting it carry her away. Dread—what was worse than some completely nameless dread that came at you like a quick stroke of lightning? Cretin, she thought. Yielding like that. And starting up a chain reaction that affected Rosie.

"We mothers worry," Rosie said. "It's probably the thing we do best."

They laughed together, as if they were trying to shake some dark spell loose and turn the mood of the night around. Martha sat down in the bedside chair, pushing aside Rosie's dress and blouse and underwear.

"The car," Rosie said, as if she'd just remembered something. "Shit, we're going to have to walk to the village tomorrow."

"If you want to develop your pictures, I wouldn't mind taking the kids and walking in with them."

"You sure?"

"Sure I am."

"I'd appreciate that." A brief expression of doubt crossed Rosie's face, then it was gone. "I could use the peace, I guess."

"You got it." Martha stood up, tired now. She stifled a yawn, then she looked at Rosie. "I talked with Tommy about the Ouija thing, by the way. I told him he shouldn't mess with it anymore."

"It's a good idea," Rosie said. "If Lindy was as upset as he said she was, then I don't think they should screw around with it."

Martha yawned again and walked toward the door.

"Martha?"

"Yeah?"

Rosie ran a hand through her short hair. "Listen, I'm sorry about tonight . . ."

"You can't help cars breaking down."

"No, I don't mean that. The other thing."

Martha looked at her friend for a while and then she smiled. She stepped out of the room and thought, You can't help the overheated imagination either.

But it wasn't like Rosie. That was what troubled her a little.

It wasn't like Rosie at all.

Someone is moving along the porch.

Someone is moving slowly.

Boards whine.

And then silence.

And then the noise of fingernails scratching at glass.

And then a handle turning, turning.

And then and then.

The door opens and the room is suddenly filled with cold air. The coldness of a granite crypt. The chill that sinks through your bones. Freezes your brain so you cannot move an inch. Your muscles are stiff and your nerves numbed and you cannot do anything but lie there and wait.

Wait as the door opens.

Then the whole house shifts, tilts, creaks on its rotted-out foundations and you think of a world turning upside down, even as the

door

opens

smells of the deep night sea floating through spaces

and you cannot move

somebody steps into the room, only it's another room in some way, it's changed and the changes make the walls slope differently and all the alterations are like little bells tinkling in the sea wind

a door opens, closes quietly again

there's freedom now, an easy freedom, a sense of liberation that allows all your muscles to move and you hear yourself moaning, waiting as the door whines shut and

you hear somebody come across the floor

and you're waiting, you're waiting for

him

(who? waiting for whom?)

Come, come to me, come to me.

Please come to me now.

Let it be now
please
And you raise your arms and hold the body that lowers itself close
to you
(who is he? who is he? you don't know him but it doesn't matter,
does it?)
come come come come come
come
and something touches you very lightly between the legs, the tip of
a finger, something cold touches
and then it all changes, it shifts to some other level and you are
clutching empty air and shivering as the chill passes and you hear the
door swing shut and the sound of somebody moving back down the
balcony
silence
the stark, brutal penetrations of silence
stark, beautiful
quick as any thing of wonder
You open your eyes.
And all the sounds die down the balcony, even the rattle of the
sea wind.

"Baby baby baby, what's the matter? What is it? What happened?"
"A nightmare."
"What kind of nightmare, Lindy?"
"I don't remember. Funny, the only thing I seem to remember
. . . somebody scratching at the balcony door, that's all, I guess . . ."
"You're okay now. You're okay. Everything's okay. Trust me. You
don't have to worry about a thing. You don't have to scream any-
more."
"I'm okay now. Really. I'm fine."
"Are you sure?"
"Sure. Really."
"Nightmares are terrible because you don't have any control."
"Yeah . . ."
"I used to keep having this one when I was a kid, only it doesn't
sound like a nightmare when I talk about it. I'd fall sound asleep and
I'd be in this forest and birds were whistling. Which sounds absolutely
fine, but they wouldn't stop, they just wouldn't stop, and the noise

would fill my head until I thought I was going to explode and even when I woke up I could still hear those goddam birds, Lindy. For hours, sometimes. And instead of sounding cheerful the way birds are supposed to, I don't think I've ever heard a more menacing sound in my whole life. You know that? Nightmares can be *stu-peed*."

"I wish I could remember the whole thing."

"Why, for Christ's sake?"

"I don't know."

"Nightmares are things you forget, babe."

"Yeah. I guess so."

"Things you forget real fast."

"Yeah."

"Things you just let go of. Okay?"

"Okay."

"Now give me a kiss. Thank you. I love you, Lindy."

"I love you too, Mom."

"It doesn't always seem that way, does it?"

"Well . . ."

"I didn't like my mother when I was thirteen either. But when I was seventeen I figured she was one of the most beautiful people in the world . . . that's the way it went for me. You think that's gonna happen to us, babe?"

"I hope so."

"No more bad dreams, all right?"

"No more."

A pause, a sigh.

"It's almost daylight, babe. I better get some sleep. Maybe you want me to sleep here beside you?"

"No, I'm fine. I'll be okay."

12

THE SEA DOLL
June 19

The sea was unfettered, the waves high, the wind rising sharply from the water. There was a bright sun burning across the sand dunes. Martha thought that it wasn't a day for nightmares, it was a day in which you were glad to be alive—and she remembered how she'd been awakened in the night by the sound of Lindy crying aloud from her bedroom. A nightmare, a kid's nightmare, like some dark animal come to feed on the child's brain. She put her arm around Lindy's shoulder as they crossed the dunes. Tommy was walking some distance ahead, pausing every now and then to examine something. A crab, maybe. Or a starfish. She glanced at Lindy, whose face was shining from the sea wind.

"You feeling better now?" Martha asked.

Lindy nodded, smiled at Martha. "I don't even remember the dream," she said. She kicked her feet in the sand and glanced out toward the sea. "It was like there was somebody in my room . . ."

Somebody in my room, Martha thought. And what had Rosie said at breakfast about the nightmare? Fingernails scratching against glass? Something like that. Martha stared a moment into the yellow sun. There were connections here that she didn't like to think about, a linkage that distressed her. A scratching on doors. Fingernails drawn back and forth. Claws. She felt the wind surge under the toilet door again and she repressed a shiver, but the surface of her skin was chilly.

"How far is it to the car?" Lindy asked.

"Three miles, maybe four."

Lindy shrugged. "It's a nice day for a walk."

Tommy was turning round, coming toward them, holding something in his hand. Something concealed in his closed fist. Martha thought, Don't let it be something gross, like the carcass of a dead gull. Something gross and worm-riddled. Tommy had the odd habit of fetching dead things inside the house back home. Once, about three or four years ago, he had brought home a desiccated frog; another time it had been a small bird whose rotted bones swarmed with maggots. He must have outgrown such morbid curiosity by this time: *please*. He was grinning as he approached them and Martha could feel herself flinch.

"Tommy, whatever it is, I don't want to see it," she said.

"It's nothing."

"Hey, I know that look on your face, kid," Martha said. "What is it this time? What have you got hidden in your hand? A mangled octopus? A squashed fish?" And she looked away, watching sunlight glint on water.

"I swear, it's nothing," Tommy said, and he opened the palm of his hand very slowly.

Martha glanced quickly, aware of an object in her son's hand, aware at the same time of Lindy moving closer to Tommy to examine whatever it was he held.

Sea-drenched, misshapen, its brown hair streaked, its glass eyes dulled and bleached—a child's toy, a doll in a lacy dress whose colors had been ruined by the sea. A simple tiny doll, delicately molded from porcelain. Lindy put out her hand to touch it.

"See," Tommy said. "I told you it was nothing."

"It gives me the creeps," Lindy said.

"Why? It's only a kid's toy."

"I don't know," and Lindy shrugged. "It's probably been in the sea for ages by the look of it."

Martha gazed a moment at the blank features of the thing and she tried to imagine it rising and falling in the motions of the ocean, floating upward, downward, twisting and turning in the tide like some strange dead fish. Specks of sand crusted the hair and eyes. A little girl's lost toy, a sad misplaced thing. It looked old, almost antique, and she wondered how long it had been tossed around in the sea. A sea mystery: the child who had owned it was probably a middle-aged woman by this time.

"It was just lying over there in the sand," Tommy said, as if he were seeking an excuse for having picked the thing up in the first place.

"What are you going to do with it, kid? Take it home as a souvenir of your summer vacation?" Martha asked.

"Yeah. Right. I can show it to my buddies," Tommy said and looked suddenly sullen.

Martha reached out and took the doll from the boy and held it between the palms of her hands. The porcelain surface was cold against her skin, colder than she had somehow expected. She gazed at it for a time. And what she wondered was why it seemed so oddly sinister to her, almost as if—and this thought spooked her—it had been left out on the sands for some reason. Tommy was meant to find it, stumble across it, fetch it.

Goddam, that was such an idiot idea, she had to dismiss it from her mind entirely. The sea claimed all kinds of things, driftwood and beach balls and rubber rafts and oars, it claimed the bones of dead men and the ships they'd sailed in—why wouldn't it also seize away the small doll of a child, for heaven's sake?

A kid lets the tide suck it away.

Simple.

Very simple.

Maybe there's a few tears and a sense of loss and then forgetfulness as the years go past.

The random sea, she thought.

It takes away, then it gives back, and it works to no schedule, it operates to no known clocks. Tidal movements. Shifts of silt. The silent stirring of sand.

Now she held the doll rather awkwardly, as if she wasn't sure what she was supposed to do with it: Give it back to the ocean? Rescue it from the sands and the tides?

"It's ugly," Lindy said. "I mean, it's really ugly, Martha."

"I guess," but Martha wasn't sure if she agreed. There was a quality of sadness, a forlorn feeling, to the thing.

"Throw it away," Lindy said.

A note of adamance in the girl's voice. A command. Throw it away, Martha, get rid of it, there's something wrong with the thing, it belongs to somebody else and we have no right to touch it.

"Back into the sea?" Martha asked.

"Sure," Lindy said. "Why not? That's where it came from."

Why was she so reluctant to discard the damn thing, Martha wondered. She held it a moment longer, glanced at Tommy—who had lost all interest in the proceedings—and then she walked to the water's edge, laying the doll face upward in the tide. It turned over, its lace dress billowing as it caught water; it turned over and over, the eyes opening and closing weirdly as the tide tugged at it and sucked it backward and then it was as substantial as a jellyfish, barely visible beneath the strength of the running sea, drifting as carelessly as any piece of flotsam. Martha watched it go until she couldn't see it any longer.

Lindy said, "It's logical," and there was something final in her voice. Ashes to ashes. Water to water. Everything goes back to the sea eventually. Even old dolls. Martha ran a hand softly through the girl's hair and then they walked along the beach, Tommy still moving a little way ahead, kicking sand up as if the act of finding the doll had pissed him off thoroughly. Martha watched her son a moment, the stooped shoulders and the sea breeze scurrying through his curls and—for no good reason she could think of—she was consumed with an extraordinary sense of love for the boy. A raw connection of emotion coming out of nowhere, flaring up out of nothing, just the sight of the child shuffling through the sand.

The intensity of a mother's love.

The terrifying vulnerability of caring without question, without doubt.

"How much farther?" Lindy asked.

"Three miles, I guess," Martha said. Three miles of soft sands and a stinging breeze and a sun that seemed cold at the very core of its heart—as if it had lost interest in warming the recesses and shaded places of the planet.

The doll, Lindy thought.

A doll that lies in the sand like a dead person.

An abortion.

A fetus.

Only porcelain and fake hair and unreal eyes and nothing else.

Nothing else, not really.

Not really anything, not anything at all.

And yet—

Yet

How did you know, how did you know the name of the goddam doll, how did you know that once upon a time some child had called that doll Sarah? How the hell did you just get that feeling out of nowhere, where did that come from?

Information just doesn't fall out of the sky like a shower of meteorites, but you knew that once a child cradled that doll and called it Sarah.

Sarah Sarah Sarah.

Now how did you know something like that?

Creep City. The doll talked to you, right?

The doll just came right out and said:

Hi, Lindy, I'm Sarah.

That was bullshit. That was just plain old bullshit of the kind your imagination is always spewing up inside your head, all the vomit of the crazy things you can't stop thinking about, dreams and nightmares and somebody scratching on glass and a finger touching you in the private place between your legs and the weird sense you felt of wanting to be filled, filled and possessed and loved—

It fades.

It just fades.

A nightmare and a doll called Sarah.

She stopped and took off her sandals and shook sand out of them and then she stared across the dunes at Tommy and watched the way he moved, watched the slenderness of his hips and the motion of his body and the way the wind teased his thick hair, and what she suddenly wondered was whether Tommy had been the intruder in her dream.

But that wasn't true at all.

She just knew the man's name.

Spelled the way it had been spelled on the board.

The stupid board.

R O S C O E   R O S C O E, whoever Roscoe was, whoever he might have been once.

(Once, past tense, why did she think of it like that? Why did she give it any kind of credence at all? A stupid board game with Tommy just screwing round, goofing off on her, why should she believe there had ever been any human being called Roscoe—when it hadn't been anything except a part of Tommy's retarded game, nothing more than that, so why why why did she think it had been Roscoe who had come to her in the black heart of her dream and opened the balcony door and touched the wet center of her body with the tip of his finger, why would she think that when it wasn't anything more than a game Tommy had played on her—but she knew, she knew, *she knew* there was a Roscoe, there had been a Roscoe once, maybe last week, last year, maybe a century ago, but she knew there had been a man called Roscoe and she knew it was this man who had come to fill her nightmare, who had opened the door of her room and touched her, God, *yes, yes,* had touched her and made her feel something she'd never

felt before, yes, yes, Roscoe, not Tommy's game, not anything like
that, no no no. . . .)

She pushed her fingers through her hair and she could feel the
sea breeze slip through the thin material of her T-shirt and the way
the nipples of her small breasts hardened as the breeze, with a cold
touch, thrust against them.

And she turned her face to look out toward the horizon, where
the chill sun glinted and no ships sailed and the world was empty, as
if it had never been created at all. She crossed her arms beneath her
breasts and for the first time in her life she thought, I want someone
to stroke my breasts.

To suck them.

I want Roscoe.

13

DEVELOPMENTS
June 19

There was a magic to photography, Rosie thought.

Like a conjuror's magic, streamers of silk flowing from a fist, a live
dove hauled from an empty hat, a woman sawed in half.

Illusions, images, an alchemy of a kind that never failed to as-
tonish her. You pressed a button, a shutter clicked, a lens sucked a
scene into the mysterious recesses of the camera and imprinted it
there. Some of the time it was an accidental process; a second
earlier, a second later, and the scene you wanted or the face you
needed to record had changed in subtle ways, perhaps by the minu-
scule shifting of a shadow or the blink of a subject's eye, something small and unnoticeable save perhaps to the photographer
herself.

Luck, persistence, patience—the alchemist's attributes and qualities.

She even liked the tiny red bulb that hung in her darkened bedroom and the weird glow it cast over everything. She liked the trans-

mutation of a simple roll of film into finished pictures, the smell of chemicals involved.

And even as she watched the first of her photographs emerge from the chemical bath, she felt a terrific sense of peace with herself—an empty house, Martha and the kids gone, only the faint rattling of the surf along the shoreline and the faraway hawking cry of a gull. A sense of real peace, which was something she always relished—her own space in the world, her own refuge and retreat, the only time when she could plausibly think of herself as a loner, not the gregarious Rosie everybody knew but another Rosie, an inner being, someone at whose heart there existed a great quiet, a serenity.

Then the moment of truth. Seeing shimmering images come slowly and inexorably to life beneath the chemical liquid. Seeing her black and white creations assume depth and texture, shape, shadow and light. Watching her private world take form.

Overhead, momentarily, the red light flickered, and she wondered if perhaps the bulb was flawed or some cut in the power source had taken place, but then the flickering stopped and the light glowed constantly once more.

She studied the photograph in the liquid again, waiting. Waiting impatiently but knowing she could do nothing to hurry the process along. Nothing except watch, watch and wait, restraining her eagerness to see the full image form in front of her eyes.

And there it was.

The first one.

The stormy beach. The wild sea and the dull gray sky. And it wasn't a bad shot at all, considering her misgivings at the time and her mood of mild depression during the shooting. It lacked any true sense of composition, but she wasn't ashamed of it.

She removed it from the liquid and hung it up to dry, pegged to a thin string she'd suspended across the room.

Then the second shot. More storm. More wicked weather. It wasn't a good picture, blurry, amateur, something she'd discard later. She hung it alongside the first one.

And the third. It was of the dunes along the beach, one of the shots she'd taken rather carelessly on her first day out. No great shakes. No prizewinner here. Nothing to write home about, for sure. The fourth was also of the dunes from another angle, but it lacked penetration, a sense of texture, the feel of grit and sand she'd wanted to get on film. Just another picture. Another nothing piece of work, which she'd also get around to discarding later.

Then—

Then there was one of the house, one she remembered shooting from a point that directly faced the house.

But there was something wrong with this one, something she couldn't immediately put her finger on, something that was just not right about the image.

The angle?

No, it hadn't anything to do with angle or perspective.

Some strange congregation of shadow then? Was that it?

No, she thought. It hadn't got a thing to do with light, the quality of light. The light was clear, perfect, a photographer's light.

What the hell was it? What the hell was wrong with the picture of the house?

Something strange, like it was another house altogether, but she knew that couldn't be the case; it was definitely this beach house, it was recognizably the house they'd rented for the summer. There was the balcony running around it and a glimpse of the stunted trees at the rear of the place—what the hell was bugging her about this picture?

She hung it up, studied it, stared at the balcony, the windows, the roof, the tiny trees.

The same house.

But not.

Different in some odd fashion. Different in a way she couldn't grasp.

Different.

The trees were smaller, for one thing.

Smaller and younger than they were now. As if they were newly planted, saplings, saplings that weren't as windblown and ugly as they looked now from the house.

Which was absurd.

Absurd, ridiculous, a trick of her angle. A trick of perspective, light, something simple to explain.

Except she couldn't explain the next thing she noticed.

The house did not appear as weather-beaten, as wasted, as it did now. It seemed fresh and new and proud, nothing chipped and flaking, the paint smooth and perfect, the balcony straight and not crooked as it looked from outside.

Tricks of a camera, she thought.

What the hell else could it be?

You don't stand down on the beach to take a picture of an old house and come out with one that looks utterly brand-new; you don't do such things, such things just didn't happen. It was all a trick of light—even the small trees and the apparent newness of the house, these could be illusions created by sunlight, a patina of freshness cast all across the surface of the place by bright summery light.

The small trees, though. They looked newly planted. Less ugly.

How? How did that happen? She remembered what she had seen through her lens and it wasn't a house that looked anything like this one. She remembered distinctly what she'd seen that afternoon when she'd held the camera in her hand. Even the weather in this picture was different from the weather she remembered when she'd snapped the damn thing. Storm and rain. But in the photograph the day was bright and calm and sunny. Puzzled, she set the picture aside, thinking she'd go out later and examine the structure to see how such a picture might have been possible.

But then—

She stared at the next pictures and she knew she'd not taken any one of them. They were photographs that must have been taken by somebody else, perhaps by one of the kids—perhaps by Tommy, but why would he try to take such weird photographs of something as uninteresting as the closet door in his bedroom, for Christ's sake?

And not just one shot, but four, each of which showed the closet door in a different position.

One, it was slightly open. Then two, it was a little wider.

Three, wider still.

And in the last shot, it was open all the way.

Open all the way, and half-visible in the gloom of that space there was a shadow, a shadow vaguely suggestive of a human form but which might have been nothing more than a simple trick of the darkness in that narrow closet.

Four photographs of a goddam closet door!

She felt briefly angry that Tommy (or maybe even Lindy) would use her expensive camera without asking permission, but the anger passed as she realized the sight of the closet door was making her uneasy, unsettling her, especially the shadow in the last shot, which, the more she studied it, the more human it seemed to her. But that was nonsense—unless Tommy and Lindy had been playing some weird game between them, one of them lurking inside the closet while the other held the camera. *Ha-ha-ha*, this is going to freak Rosie out, this is going to blow her mind.

She stared at the pictures she'd hung, and her sense of unease grew. And suddenly the red glow of the dark bedroom seemed to her a claustrophobic thing and all the photographic equipment strange and menacing and unfamiliar. She sat down on the edge of her bed a moment, gazing at the hanging pictures as they dried. Then she rose and stepped out into the hallway, shutting the door quickly behind her and moving to the top of the stairs, looking down in the direction of the kitchen doorway below.

Okay.

You keep a little cool here.

The closet pictures you can explain away as jokes, teenagers' jokes, but how did you rationalize the photograph of this goddam beach house? How did you explain that weird one away?

She started to go down the stairs. She'd go outside, study the house from the same angle as she'd taken the picture, see if she could understand it. At the foot of the stairs she stopped.

And she understood she was not alone in this place.

There was something or somebody else.

She wasn't alone in this godforsaken beach house but in the presence of another entity, something she couldn't quite define, couldn't quite place or understand—but she knew it was close to her, close and pervasive, entering her senses as if it were a vibration. She moved to the kitchen doorway and glanced inside. Those damn kids, she thought. They'd crept back. They were trying to make her nervous.

"Lindy? Tommy?" she called out.

Then inside the kitchen—empty, nobody, nothing.

She clenched her hands together tightly. Rosie, Rosie, you've begun to imagine too many things since you came to this place, you've begun to see and hear too much.

Some form of the bends, she told herself.

Too much fresh air socking it to those city-soiled lungs of yours and the old brain can't quite hack it.

She crossed the living-room floor, paused at the outside door and realized she wanted nothing more than to get to the sands, watch the tide scuttle over the beach, gaze into the sun. She just wanted out.

She reached for the door handle, twisted it, pulled and—

and—

and the goddam door wouldn't open.

Goddam door was stuck, locked stiff.

Jesus, and now there was panic, panic and dread, and again the awareness of a presence close to her, but she wasn't going to turn her head round and look. For Christ's sake, she would just keep hauling on the handle until the door opened, and if that failed, well she'd just smash the window and get outside that way.

Open open open!

The stairs at her back creaked.

Creakcreakcreak.

But she still wouldn't turn her face and look.

Straining, jaws tight, teeth clenched, she tugged on the handle (*creak creak creak*).

And then it yielded, it finally gave way, and she stumbled out on the porch and the sea wind blew against her face and the door slammed shut behind her. She moved down to the sands, and when she was some distance away she turned to stare back at the house.

She was sweating, trembling.

What was it? A form of paranoia or something? A kind of madness that made you hear things that weren't there, made you feel things that didn't quite exist? Made you think you heard the sound of somebody coming down the stairs behind you? Made you take pictures of houses that didn't exist in the way you perceived them?

The camera does not lie, Rosie, unless you deliberately want it to.

And she gazed at the house, seeing the porch, the balcony, the blank windows, the roof, catching a glimpse of the trees beyond.

This is not the house I photographed.

I photographed something else.

The same place in another time. The same house in another age.

Nonsense. Sheer nonsense.

How could any camera take pictures of the past, for Christ's sake?

A travesty of time. All your clocks turned inside out.

What kind of sense did any of that make?

Okay, you're a tough kid from the big city, you've been around, you know a thing or two, Rosie, you've got more spunk than to run like hell out of a house just because you imagined something.

So she started to walk back, but when she was about twenty yards from the porch she stopped, changed her direction, skirted the side of the house and, with her hands on her hips—as if she needed to appear defiant for the sake of some invisible onlooker—stood looking at the grove of ill-formed trees.

And she had the odd impression of just having missed something.

The impression that somebody had, only seconds before, vanished from the range of her vision, disturbing the trees in his passage, making the branches quiver and the leaves rattle.

But that was only the sea wind.

The sea wind. Nothing else.

She turned to gaze up at the house.

And she saw the small girl stare unsmilingly down at her.

14

THE CAR
June 19

What Tommy wished was that he hadn't bothered to pick up that stupid doll in the first place, because it seemed to have affected the moods of both his mother and Lindy and they'd been silent all the way along the beach. Now and then he'd stare in the direction of the blacktop but he never saw any passing traffic. Once, he'd shut his eyes tight and crossed his fingers and wished like hell for the sight of a tow truck, but nothing, nothing ever seemed to travel along this road. He wondered why anybody had bothered to build the goddam thing in the first place. He shuffled his feet in the sand, then when he realized he was fed up with the stuff getting inside his sneakers he moved away from the dunes toward the highway and paused there— looking for a sight of the station wagon and wondering how much farther it could possibly be. It wasn't what you'd call the world's greatest car; in fact, he was frequently ashamed to travel in the thing.

With any luck, it might have been swept out to sea during the night.

Or some thief from Cochrane Crossing would have snuck out and stolen the monster.

He waited for Lindy and his mother to catch him up. And he was filled with a sudden longing for his dad, just to have his dad walking alongside him right now—a sadness he had to push aside because he wouldn't give in to it. But Christ, how he wished for him. He stared along the empty stretch of highway and realized his eyes were moist and there was a small pain in his heart, and he wondered where his father was right this minute and what he was doing. Then he was remembering his dad's tiny office at the University and the stacks of books that lay around everywhere and the rack that held his old pipes and the sweet smell of tobacco that always clung to his dad's clothes and the crumpled cigarette packs scattered on the desk.

Now his mother and Lindy were alongside him. He glanced at Martha and he thought how pale she seemed today, colorless, as if the sea breeze had sucked all the blood from her skin. And Lindy looked different as well, a little older in some way, like she'd added a year to her life overnight.

They moved along the blacktop together.

"It's not much farther," Martha said. "At least I don't think it is."

They walked a little way in silence, reaching a bend in the road, a point where it turned away from the ocean, and the beach rose upward into a bleak headland. You could figure this for the loneliest place in the world, Tommy thought. Then he saw the wagon, a small thing in the distance, sitting at the side of the road as if it had been abandoned for years. Great. The high point of the whole day. Find The Wagon.

Find The Doll. Find The Wagon.

At this rate, you might find something really fascinating, like a clump of goddam seaweed.

Martha was jiggling the car keys in the palm of her hand.

"What if we can't find a mechanic in Cochrane Crossing?" Tommy asked.

"I'm sure there's got to be at least one."

"I wouldn't bet on it," Tommy said.

"Somebody's got to be able fix cars there," Martha said. There was this tiny sharp note in her voice and Tommy realized that his own attitude—his pessimism—was getting on her nerves bad. Cheer up, he said to himself. You've only got five and a bit more weeks of this anyhow and it doesn't hurt to smile once a day. He puffed his cheeks and whistled tunelessly and hoped it would sound happy enough.

When they reached the wagon they stood in a group around it, like archaeologists who've found some really puzzling old relic without any obvious function. They stared at the vehicle as if they were willing the thing to start. It looked totally beat, Tommy thought. Rusted, dusty, little crusts of mud along the panels. It belonged in a car graveyard.

"How far is it to the village?" Lindy asked.

"Another four miles, I guess," Martha answered.

She leaned against the hood and studied the car thoughtfully, looking as if she understood the mysteries of its interior. She was still rattling the keys in her hand. Tommy opened the driver's door and said, "I guess we ought to see if it starts." And he took the keys from his mother's hand, sticking one in the ignition and turning it, hearing the engine rattle and cough, feeling the shabby body vibrate.

It died.

Martha said, "Sounds terminal to me."

Tommy turned the key again, and again the car spluttered and died.

"I guess we've got to walk to the village," Martha said.

Come on, Tommy thought. Kick over. Come to life.

He turned the key a third time.

And this time, when the motor roared, it didn't die on him, it ran with a satisfying hum and he looked through the windshield and smiled at Martha. Then he stepped out of the wagon and gazed at the vehicle proudly; it was the kind of expression that might have been on the face of the man who had just invented the wheel.

"So why couldn't it have behaved like that last night?" Martha asked.

"Cars are temperamental," Tommy said. "You've got to understand them. You've got to understand they've got their own personalities."

"I guess you need a certain touch," Lindy said.

Tommy nodded, glanced at the girl, then folded his arms against his chest. Goddam, he felt good, he felt really pleased with himself.

"Well, it saves us a long walk," Martha said. "If you're sure it's going to get us back to the house."

"I'm sure," Tommy said. "Can I drive?"

Martha shook her head.

"Aw, come on, there's no traffic around."

Martha looked up and down the empty highway. She relented, smiling at Tommy. "Okay. But you don't go more than twenty-five miles an hour. Understand?"

Tommy grinned. "I understand," he answered.

15

LETTERS FROM THE DEAD
June 19–20

It was close to midnight, the sea calm, the children asleep in their rooms upstairs. Martha and Rosie sat out on the porch beneath a pale yellow light that sucked moths and mosquitoes against it. Martha shut her eyes and felt Rosie's hand take the joint from between her fingers; and then, even though her mind was more than a little clouded, she tried to sift through Rosie's narrative. She opened her eyes and glanced at her friend, seeing the drawn look on Rosie's face, a certain hollowness in the cheeks. And what she felt suddenly was that there were certain changes taking place in her friend, changes she didn't entirely understand—she knew only that she was made uneasy by them because they seemed to be happening at a level she couldn't understand. Seeing little girls. Seeing a figure on a porch. Feeling a certain presence. None of these were the kinds of things she would have attributed to Rosie.

Rosie stared at the joint between her fingers.

"She was standing up on the balcony looking down at me. Just staring. She didn't seem to have any kind of expression on her face. So, I decided I'd go indoors again, even though I was more than reluctant. I searched this whole goddam house from top to bottom, Martha. I mean, shit, I looked everywhere. Nobody. Nothing. No little girl."

Martha didn't know what to say. She looked out toward the sea for a time, watching the low silvery moon touch the slow tide. There was a catch in Rosie's voice, an edge of faint hysteria. She put her hand out and laid it across Rosie's knuckles, touching them gently. "Maybe there was a kid in the house and she somehow managed to slip past you . . . Maybe it was the same kid you saw the other day, Rosie. And the presence you felt—well, that was obviously the child's presence."

Rosie shook her head, as if unconvinced. "Who is she? I mean, what the hell is she doing out here? What does she want?"

Martha shrugged. "I don't know."

Then Rosie said, "What kind of person am I, Martha?"

"That's a weird question."

"I mean, how would you categorize me? Would you list me among the completely sane? The rational? Or would you say I was one of the walking wounded?"

Martha smiled. "You're one of the most practical people I know."

"You're sure about that?"

"Absolutely."

Rosie sighed, stood up, looked out across the sands. She gripped the porch rail tightly between her hands. Then she turned and smiled a small, serious smile that gave the impression of some terrible inner uncertainty. "I've never really had much inclination to believe in . . ."

"Believe in what?"

"Hauntings. Spirits. Stuff like that."

"What are you talking about?"

Rosie was shaking her head from side to side. She moved down the porch steps and Martha followed, and they walked together down toward the edge of the ocean. Hauntings. Spirits. Martha turned these things around in her mind, as if she were trying to fix the words with precise definitions. Sometimes words, instead of being her accomplices, seemed slippery and hostile and forever shifting. Maybe that was why she had such trouble when she tried to write.

"Maybe this joint's haunted," Rosie said. "Maybe the child is some kind of . . . ghost." She paused and looked out across the water as if she might find answers inscribed in the ripples of the tide. "Listen, I'm comfortable when it comes to supermarkets and traffic signals and street signs and all the noises of the city. I'm at ease with things I can touch and smell. Soap powders. Perfumes. Showers running across my head. I'm happy with this material world, Martha, and I don't go in for any goddam supernatural nonsense . . ." She hesitated and turned to Martha with a look in her eyes of both fear and slight bewilderment. Martha thought, This isn't Rosie, this is like some other person altogether, whose nerves are beginning to scream.

"I can't believe I'm saying this," Rosie said. "I can't believe these words are coming out of my own mouth, Martha. The pragmatic Rosie is standing here at the edge of a beach and wondering about whether a house could be haunted. Jesus Christ."

"The kid could be anybody, Rosie. Maybe somebody from the

village who comes out here at times to play . . ." Dear God, all this
sounded feeble, straws rattling in the wind. "I don't see how you can
leap to the conclusion—"

"It's not a conclusion, it's a speculation." ,

There was an angry edge to Rosie's voice now, and Martha became silent, hands in the pockets of her jeans, her feet shuffling in
the sand and the soft tide sliding between her toes. She'd never heard
quite that tone in Rosie's voice before. "What about the photographs
you mentioned?"

"I'll show them to you when we go back inside. Maybe you can
make some sense out of them. God, I'm even afraid to take pictures
anymore, I'm afraid to develop the ones I've already taken in case I
see something I can't explain . . ." Rosie turned and looked back in
the direction of the house. The yellow porch light burned bleakly. A
couple of the downstairs windows were lit. "How could some common goddam beach house be haunted? I sometimes get the feeling
here that I'm beginning to lose my grip. But look at that place, Martha. Look at it. It's banal. It isn't Gothic. It doesn't have weird turrets.
It doesn't have mysterious towers. How could a place like this be
haunted?"

Martha was silent. She wanted to say something wonderful, like
You need a good night's sleep, or Things will look different in the
morning—but she couldn't bring herself to mouth these platitudes.
Then she said the only thing that came to mind. "Rosie, there's some
rational explanation for everything. You know there is. We ought to
sit down, see if we can figure it out."

"Like how?"

"I don't know like how—I only know that you can't go around like
somebody about to have a nervous breakdown, Rosie." She was thinking about the strange episode in the tavern now. Where was there a
rational explanation for that business? Armed only with the frail tool
of reason, how far could you possibly dig down to find answers for
events that seemingly had no logical basis? But that incident had
taken place eight miles from this house, eight long miles away—what
possible connection could it have with what Rosie was talking about
now?

She suddenly imagined some membranous strand linking this
beach house with the village of Cochrane Crossing. Some nebulous
pall that existed between here and there. In her mind's eye it took the
absurd shape of a black, filmy umbrella lying across the whole landscape, and she wanted to laugh at her own crazy image.

Rosie nodded, turned away from the house, then looked out across the ocean again. Martha was consumed by a feeling of sudden helplessness, wanting to reach out and in some way console her friend but not knowing exactly how to do that—she had moved into a place that was hard to touch. It was as if she stood behind some shimmering curtain and although she could see her clearly she couldn't reach out toward her. This feeling depressed her.

"Let's go back indoors," she said. "Let's drink some Daniel's and relax."

"In a minute. Just give me a minute," Rosie answered. And she was staring at the house again, her arms folded over her breasts and her expression one of concentration—like she was trying to steel herself for going back across the sands and up onto the porch and through the front door. Then she was bending down, reaching into the tide that slid against her ankles—and when she stood upright again she was holding something in her hand, and Martha, even without looking, knew what it was that had come floating out of the ocean to touch Rosie's legs. Knew, with a strange sensation of something slipping inside her head, a dizziness she thought she couldn't control, that it was the same doll she'd tossed on the tide that afternoon.

Rosie held it in one hand, and in moonlight the small porcelain face looked featureless and the clothing more ruined than ever before. Martha turned her head to the side: I can't bring myself to look at the thing. Why? Why is that? Tide patterns. Think about sea currents and tide patterns and the random heavings of the ocean and lunar forces. A child's doll goes into the sea at one part of the beach and floats back out at another, wasn't that perfectly natural? Wasn't it?

"Look at this," Rosie was saying. "A little girl's doll."

A little girl's doll, Martha thought.

A little girl. A sweet little doll.

Martha shivered even though the night wasn't cold. She turned up the collar of her flannel shirt and clenched her hands together. And she realized that somehow she didn't have the heart to tell Rosie that she'd seen the same damned doll that afternoon. She didn't have the heart to do it because then Rosie would want to see something beyond coincidence, she would want to connect this doll with the girl she'd seen on the balcony—she would want to link everything to her speculation about haunting.

"An old one too, I'd guess," Rosie said.

"Why don't you put it back in the sea?"

Rosie shook her head. "I think I'll keep it."

"Why?"

"Why not?"

There was no reasonable answer to this question. Martha stared in the direction of the house.

Then Rosie said, "You said something about some good old JD, I believe."

And they turned and moved slowly back toward the yellow porch light as if they were drawn there as inexorably as the great moths that fluttered around the scalding glass bulb.

Rosie poured two liberal shots of Jack Daniel's and spread the photographs on the kitchen table, even though she had no great desire to study them again herself. She sat down at one end of the table, swallowed some of the bourbon, glanced at the sodden doll she'd placed on the window ledge and watched as Martha leaned over the pictures. The liquor went through her blood quickly. Good old JD had the most stunning medicinal effect, she thought. You could use it to anesthetize, to tune out all kinds of things you didn't want to hear. She drained the glass and poured herself another.

"This is the closet in Tommy's room," Martha said.

"Right."

"And you're sure he didn't take these pictures himself?"

"I didn't want to mention all this stuff about the pictures in front of the kids, but I did ask Tommy and Lindy—in a kind of roundabout way—if they'd ever used my camera without permission. They said they hadn't. And I believe them."

Martha looked puzzled. "Maybe they weren't telling you the truth, Rosie."

"I believed them. Anyhow, Lindy knows one thing—that my camera equipment is strictly off limits. And I don't think Tommy is capable of any real guile, do you?"

"I wouldn't bet on it." Martha stared at the four pictures of the closet door again. "It's weird. There's some kind of shadow in there that looks like a person . . ."

"Yeah." Back to the Daniel's, Rosie thought—and she turned her face once more to the doll. The blank glass eyes appeared to survey the kitchen with a kind of idle curiosity. Seawater dripped from the doll's lacy clothing and gathered in a puddle on the ledge. Maybe

Martha was right; maybe I should just have tossed the thing back in the sea. "It's the other photo I want you to look at, though. Even if the kids are lying about the first four, there's no way they could have taken that fifth one."

Martha picked it up. She tilted it toward the kitchen light and looked at it for a long time.

"It's this house."

"In a manner of speaking." Good. I'm getting drunk here, Rosie thought. I'm beginning to buzz and then just maybe I can buzz the rest of my way through this supernatural bullshit. Maybe. God bless Kentucky or wherever it was they created the elixir known as Jack Daniel's.

"But it looks different."

"Keep going, kid."

"It looks newer somehow—"

"And the trees are smaller."

"Yeah and the paint's fresh and—"

"And everything is brand-new."

Martha, holding the picture limply in her hand, looked at Rosie. "You're absolutely sure you took this picture?"

Rosie nodded.

"I mean, it couldn't have been lying round somewhere and somehow got mixed up among your own."

"I took it, I developed it," Rosie said. "And here's something else, if you need it—I took my picture during the storm. You see any sign of rain in that shot, huh? That goddam photograph was taken on a clear day, Martha."

Martha sat down and sipped her drink thoughtfully for a while.

"Well?" Rosie asked. "Let's hear it, then."

"Let's hear what?"

"You were talking rational explanations, I seem to remember."

"Yeah. And I don't have one."

Rosie looked down into her drink. She poked the liquid with her index finger and watched the surface ripple. When she raised her face she stared across the table at Martha, at the puzzlement on that pretty, sculptured face, the ridges that ran across the forehead as if Martha were trying to unravel the whole mystery in one shot. Eureka! I have it, Rosie! I have it all worked out! But she was silent instead, frowning, glancing now and again at the picture. Rosie hit the Jack Daniel's a third time because by then a certain mellow feeling was beginning to spread through her—not quite a drunkenness, more a quality of being able to sit in this weird house and relegate the girl she'd seen and the pictures she'd taken to some back burner of her brain where all unexplained phenomena simmered in a kind of cosmic stew she never needed to stir and whose ingredients she never needed to question. Black holes. Flying saucers. All that stuff.

"I just don't have one," Martha said again. "Unless . . ."

"Unless what?"

"Skip it."

"Come on, spit it out, kid."

"Well . . ." Martha scratched a wrist nervously. "Maybe you got caught up in some time-warp deal."

Rosie smiled. "Beam me up, Scottie."

"Christ, Rosie, I can't think of anything better."

They were silent now and the only sound in the kitchen was of water dripping from the ledge where the sea doll sat. *Drip drip drip.* A leak in the fabric of reason, Rosie thought. *Drip.* The thing's full of holes. As trustworthy as a colander. She gazed into the lovely amber color of the Daniel's and marveled at how it could sweep through her veins like some gorgeously legal heroin. She tilted her head back and closed her eyes and felt, for the first time that day, a certain peacefulness. Nothing had really happened. It was after midnight and all was well. And the old town crier was in the streets with his bell and lantern and singing, "Oyez! Oyez!" She opened her eyes. Martha was still checking the crazy photographs. Still looking like she was trying to figure it all out, fit it into some nice neat pattern of reason and logic. Dear Christ, sweet Martha, leave it all alone. Forget it all. Drink more JD. Turn your brain into a jellyfish.

She lifted her glass. She glanced across the rim at Martha. She suddenly longed to hear something from the world with which she was familiar—like music on a radio or something on TV, anything that would be permeated by the ordinary, the mundane. The Fonz even, she thought, because in the Fonz's world there surely weren't any ghosts. It was all laugh tracks and hysteria and hyperactivity.

Martha drummed her fingers on the table because it was clear that this silence was getting to her as well. And she shifted her chair slightly, so that her back was to the doll, and the legs squeaked on the drab linoleum.

"Okay," she said. "So I don't have an explanation. I wish I had. I wish I could ransack this brain of mine and come up with something that would make you happy."

Rosie grinned. "Hey. I just had this thought. We could ask the board, couldn't we?"

"The board?"

"The Wee-ja board, kid."

"Don't be crazy."

"Listen, if we've got some weird spiritual trip going on around here, then we need to go straight to the good old source, don't we?" And she realized she was slurring her words, coming down hard on her *h* sounds and making a mockery of her esses. The board, she thought. Was she being serious? She pushed her chair back from the table and stood up rather unsteadily.

"Where are you going, Rosie?"

"To get the board."

"Come on, sit down, forget it."

"Is it in Tommy's room?"

"Rosie, for God's sake."

"The closet, right?" And Rosie was conscious of herself, as if in a hazy dream, traveling toward the kitchen door, the living room, and looking up the dark stairs. You can't go up there, she thought.

You can't.

Those dark stairs.

Sure. Sure you can. One foot in front of the other. Dead easy. And she moved forward, one hand reaching for the rail, beginning to climb. She could hear Martha call out to her from the kitchen.

"Rosie. Don't."

Rosie don't.

When she reached the landing she opened the door of Tommy's room and, as carefully as she could—which wasn't exactly saying a lot—stepped inside; there was moonlight coming through the balcony door and the window and she could see the closet. Suddenly she wanted to giggle, but then the impulse passed the closer she came to the open closet door—and when she bent down, fumbling inside, she was very cold, as if all the chills of all the years this house had stood had become trapped in one narrow space. She clattered among boxes and books, dragging the Ouija toward her and clutching it against her side as she stood up. When she backed out of Tommy's room she could see Martha watching her from the foot of the stairs.

She was cold still and she didn't begin to feel warm again until she'd made it halfway down the stairs.

"Found it!" She knew now, from the singsong lilt in her voice, that she'd drunk way too much.

Martha followed her inside the kitchen, shaking her head. "I don't want to do this, Rosie."

"Listen, if we got ghosts round here, let's get in touch with them."

"You're drunk and you need to go to bed."

"Bull."

Rosie opened the box, set the board on the table and looked at Martha. "Who knows? They might be fun. They might be stand-up comedians from some Borscht Belt beyond the Great Divide."

"Please."

Martha was staring at the lettered board and the message indicator and she was frowning still, as if she knew no other expression. Rosie grabbed her hand and pulled her toward the table.

"Sit down, Martha. Humor me. Okay? Give me a few minutes of your valuable time."

Martha sat. They placed the tips of their index fingers on the plastic triangle. "Rosie, this is stupid."

"Skepticism is the last refuge of the closed mind."

"I don't even know what that means," Martha said.

Rosie shrugged and looked up from the board at Martha, whose face now appeared to have become half-hidden by mist; and then she blinked and her inebriated vision cleared. "A question. We gotta have a question, kid," she said.

"It's your game. You ask."

"Okay. Okay. Lemme think." Rosie rummaged through the burnt-out passages of her mind a moment. Then: "Who are you?"

Martha sighed, as if this whole thing were a total embarrassment, something she was doing to appease a drunk.

"Tell me who you are." Rosie closed her eyes and waited for a vague feeling of the ridiculous to pass. What the hell was she doing— asking questions of the ether like some deranged biddy in a Victorian parlor, sitting at her fringed table and trying to make a trumpet play sounds of its own accord?

She opened her eyes only when she heard a low whisper of surprise come from Martha's lips. And she looked down at the board, seeing—if not exactly feeling—the movement of the plastic triangle as it slid lightly across the smooth surface. I am not doing this, she thought. I am not pushing this thing. And she could tell from Martha's expression that she wasn't the one pushing it either—then the indicator was going quickly, swinging wildly from one letter to another.

ANNA

Just like that. A N N A. Again and again and again. A N N A A N N A.

Rosie took her finger away from the plastic a moment but it continued to move anyhow.

ANNA ANNNA ANANANANAN

"Anna who?" Rosie asked, putting her hand back in place.

ROSCOE HAS ME

ROSCOE HAS ME

"Who is Roscoe?"

Then there was nothing. No movement. No slight sense of vibration. A stillness. A silence.

Nothing.

For a long time. Nothing.

Then it was moving slowly this time and it felt different, more ponderous, more studied, more careful, as if the letters were being picked at by someone very deliberate.

(Someone, Rosie thought. Some One.)

WHY DO NOT YOU

A pause, a long pause—

WHY DO NOT YOU WANT TO FUCK ME

Rosie could feel a certain tingling along the backs of her arms, the fine hairs stirring. What was all this? What were these weird obscenities coming from this goddam thing? You didn't expect this kind of stuff from Out There, did you? You expected something more meaningful, something of cosmic significance, something to do with the way of things in the afterlife or, at the very least, spiritual guidance. You didn't expect to be propositioned by an errant Entity lingering in an invisible world—and she felt she wanted to laugh suddenly, throw the board aside, scatter the whole goddam thing across the floor. She wanted to mock her own absurd fears of that day.

It moved again. And this time she didn't feel like laughing.

I AM LINDY NIGHTMARE

I AM ALL YOUR NIGHTMARES

Martha pulled her hand away from the board suddenly, getting up from the table, backing toward the kitchen door. Rosie, too, lowered her hands into her lap and realized that maybe she wasn't as drunk as she'd thought.

Untouched, untouched by either woman, possessed by a life of its own, the message indicator continued to move, slowly, certainly, and in a controlled manner.

ROSCOE IS ALL YOUR NIGHTMARES
ALL
AND YOU WILL SEE
YOU WILL SEE

Rosie glanced across the room at Martha, who was standing in the doorway, her hand against her mouth, her eyes held to the board as if she might never turn her head to the side again. "Dear Christ," she kept whispering. "Dear Christ."

And then the board slithered from the table and the plastic indicator went flying alongside it.

And the sea doll on the window ledge blinked its eyes once.

She opened the door of Tommy's room and watched him as he slept in the moonlight. She moved toward him slowly, quietly, the hem of her nightrobe brushing the floor. She stood over him and then, as gently as she could, reached down and touched his forehead with the palm of her hand. When she kissed him she did so as softly as she could. He felt nothing, didn't stir, didn't turn. She watched him a while longer and then she went back along the landing to her own bedroom, closing the door behind her, ignoring the voices of the two women she heard float up from some place very far below.

She lay beneath her blankets, legs spread, a slight smile on her face.

Which was when she realized she was not alone in her room.

There was something else, a presence, and yet not anything she could pin down in physical terms. There was no shadow, no shape, no substance. Instead, the presence permeated the room like a scent, clinging to the very air. She sat upright slowly, feeling the thing weave around her as if it were a web being spun by a spider she couldn't see. It wrapped her in invisible filaments, caressed her flesh, filled her senses. She lay back down again and felt a gentle pressure all across her body. She twisted from side to side slowly, then she could feel her legs being parted and warm air blow upon her inner thighs. What she remembered now was how she'd been touched in the ocean and the experience she'd had in the shower and she understood that everything was connected, everything related in some way, that whatever had touched her then was touching her now—

It stopped.

Just like that, the feeling stopped.

She sat upright and looked around the darkened room, but she saw nothing, she felt nothing.

She heard nothing.

She gazed at the moonlight on the glass door of the balcony and, as she saw the dark shape of some seabird spread itself against the luminous sky, she realized she was disappointed, disappointed and empty that the thing which had started only moments before had gone unfinished.

Like a tease, she thought.

A dangerous tease.

She lay back down and stared at the ceiling.

And she thought: Come back.

Please come back.

I am ready.

16

HOURS OF DARKNESS
June 20

When they had checked the children's rooms and found both kids sleeping peacefully, the two women went inside Martha's bedroom and sat together on the bed in silence. They smoked cigarettes and looked at one another as if they might find answers in the mirrors of their faces. Then Martha rose, stubbed her cigarette, wandered to the balcony door and looked out into the dark. She felt the cold pane against her forehead. And what she thought was that she was looking out into a dreamworld of some kind, that between reality and whatever it was they had experienced in the kitchen there was a stitch undone, an unraveling.

But what kind of vague nonsense was that anyway? You pressed your finger against a material object, something simple, and the whole world went haywire around you and objects moved of their own free will and a child's doll became briefly animated—what were you supposed to say about such a state of things? Let's talk vibrations, Martha. Let's talk of flaws in the earth's structure and underground rumblings and tidal movements. Let's discuss the randomness of the English alphabet and a million monkeys on a million typewriters coming up with a perfect King Lear.

She wanted to weep. She felt a terrible dry tightness in her throat. Roscoe has me, she thought. Roscoe has whom?

Nightmares.

I AM ALL YOUR NIGHTMARES

Or maybe she was remembering that imperfectly.

And who was Roscoe?

Did such a question make sense anyhow? Did it have a grammatical logic to it? Was there any possible answer? (And suddenly she thought of Charlie and of how he'd discuss it—his thin legs crossed and one finger to his beard and his head tipped back, droning about the linguistic significance of unanswerable questions and she felt a tidal loneliness.)

Screw all that.

Rosie was lighting another cigarette and just gazing at the door; white-sober now, all the Daniel's drained out of her system. Then she rose from the bed and went to the balcony door and opened it—stepping outside, the wood slats creaking beneath her. For a moment Martha had no urge to follow her, preferring to remain in what seemed to her the semisecurity of a closed bedroom, but then she too went out on the balcony and watched Rosie's cigarette burn in the moonlight. We should bundle the kids up, get in the car, get the hell out of here, she thought. Drive as fast and as far as possible away from this place. She looked down at the weird trees, made more weird by the silver light. But what kind of reaction was that? Sensible, one might say, albeit in a cowardly manner. Suddenly she was tired and didn't feel like running anywhere.

"Okay," Rosie said, sighing as if she were pulling all the little scattered threads of herself together. "There's this part of me that says bullshit. You know what I mean? There's this section of my mind— the one that controls my responses, the one that makes up grocery lists or reminds me to buy film for my camera—that says, Come on, Rosie, this is just a bunch of good old crap and nothing more. Two tense women fooling around, one of them in a drunken stupor, the other unnerved by some strange stories she's been hearing. Two tense women . . ."

"What about the other part?" Martha asked.

"The other part's more of a problem. It's filled with vague things. Shadows. Creepy-crawlies. Everything's confused and a little ridiculous and also more than just a little frightening—which could be the understatement of the year. It's this other part that's giving me the willies right now." Rosie paused, licked her lips. "It's telling me there's something in this house. Some kind of force. Some kind of thing emerging from a dark place. It's telling me that there are two entities. One called Anna. The other a somewhat rude personality by the name of Roscoe. The problem is—what the hell do I mean by forces? What do I mean by personality? You understand my difficulty, don't you?" Rosie flipped the butt of her cigarette over the edge of the balcony.

Martha nodded. "I have the same trouble."

"And the same fear."

"Exactly."

"So what do we do?"

"You see that wagon down there? And that highway beyond the trees? Something about the combination of those two appeals to me, Rosie."

"You want to get the hell out?"

"To say the least."

Rosie leaned against the rail of the balcony. She was more composed now, more alert, even relaxed; for her part, Martha could feel the house press against her from behind—and even the sound of the ocean, which had seemed peaceful and soporific, made her think of some malignant giant simply slumbering.

"Roscoe and Anna," Rosie said. "I never knew anybody by those names except for a kid called Anna Schlumberger in grade school who had a clear plastic drinking straw in the shape of an elephant. You ever know anybody by those names?"

Martha shook her head; she wandered around the vacant rooms of her memory for a while, but there was nothing.

"Even if I ever had," she said, "what difference would it make?"

"I'm not sure," Rosie answered. "I'm just not sure."

"You're trying to shift this stuff under the convenient label of the subconscious."

"I don't know what I'm trying to do except regain my control, Martha. I lost it for a while—but I can't operate, I can't function without some sense of control. I like little compartments. I like a certain tidiness."

Martha looked down once more at the wagon. "You want to stay here, don't you?"

Rosie nodded slowly. "I've never been a runner. Call it a flaw in the old personality, but I can be one stubborn sonofabitch when I need to be and you know that. Okay, so I'm scared. But I've never been a runner." And Rosie closed her eyes, her mouth drawn into a single tight line, as if she were really trying to convince herself. "And I certainly don't intend to run away from some joker who propositions me by means of a stupid parlor game."

A runner, Martha thought. She admired the way Rosie had abruptly reached out for the controls of her fine tuning, had made adjustments—almost as if nothing had ever happened down there in the kitchen. She could still see the plastic indicator move by itself and the board slide off the table and the doll blink its eyes and she didn't have the capacity to pretend or to obscure everything the way Rosie seemed to—or was it bluff and bravado, simply the old Rosie reasserting herself?

They stared at each other for a moment.

And Martha realized that they were both afraid.

Both scared.

No matter what Rosie said, no matter what bluster, they were both very scared.

17

THE SWING
June 20

It was almost dawn when Lindy rose and stepped out onto the balcony. The atmosphere was lifeless, still, the sea little more than a vague whisper. There were pale rose-colored streaks in the distance. She placed her hands on the rail a moment and then walked the entire length of the balcony, pausing for a while to look out toward the ocean. Sluggish, indifferent, distant. She continued to move, and when she came to the place that overlooked the grove of trees she stopped again. She swept her hair back from her shoulders, conscious of the way her robe hung open and how the early morning air lay cold against her flesh. She leaned forward, studied the trees for a time, then the dark strip of highway beyond. The silences impressed her. How deep they seemed.

And yet there was something concealed by the quietness, an undercurrent of whispered voices, as if just beyond her range of vision people were talking together in low tones. She tilted her head to one side and listened, then she looked along the balcony to the door of Tommy's room and she remembered how she'd gone in there when the kid was sleeping, how she had kissed him—and the memory of that disturbed her.

She strained to catch the whispers again.

Elusive, always just out of reach. Always just beyond her grasp.

She shut her eyes very tight. (Why would she have gone into Tommy's room anyhow? Why would she have done a thing like that? It didn't make sense—but then nothing was making much sense to her these days. Everything around her and inside her was changing, and she could feel these alterations as surely as you might feel vibrations from a stringed instrument held against your body.)

I am different, she thought. *I am not the person I was when I first came to this place.*

And she tried to remember what she had read somewhere about the development of sexuality in young adolescents. Hormone imbalance. Chemical changes. The growth of sexual curiosity, the need for experiment. (Not with Tommy, she thought. Surely not with a kid like Tommy!) It seemed to her that she'd become two different people all at once. Lindy who went to school in Syracuse and lived with her mother in a very ordinary house in the suburbs and who hung out with her friends at a place called Carlini's Pizza Palace and talked about boys and ambitions and movies and rock and roll. And somebody else, another Lindy, whose thoughts and actions and dreams were unfamiliar and alien, a girl who seemed to exist in a twilight condition. Who heard voices. Who just seemed to know things she shouldn't have known and dreamt dreams she shouldn't have dreamed—and felt the touch of somebody when nobody was present.

It was as if the real world had taken one step backward. Had become a shimmering, mysterious place. And she was drawn toward this other world; she was being pulled into it—and such things as school and Carlini's and her friends seemed farther away than mere distance in miles.

She opened her eyes when she heard a very faint creaking sound and she assumed that somebody had stepped out onto the balcony, but when she turned her face to look she realized the noise was coming from the trees below.

She scrutinized the grove for a while but she couldn't see anything down there. No movement. Nothing. Until—

Until she could make out, in the dead center of the grove, the motion of a single branch shaking as if it were being pulled on by an invisible hand. A single branch shaking while all the others were still. Back and forth. Back and forth in an easy rhythm.

She looked away for a moment, and when she turned once again to face the trees she saw the child.

She saw the child sitting on the swing.

And the man who stood directly behind her, pushing the swing.

A man and a young girl, materialized out of nowhere, out of nothing; and she thought, I am not scared. It just seems the most natural thing in the world. A man pushing a young girl on a swing, the creak of a branch, the motion of the child's hair as the draft stirs it, the darkness of the man's arm. The most natural thing.

The man stepped backward, as if tired of the activity, and the swing came slowly to a stop. For a while the girl sat motionless, staring straight ahead, and then she jumped down and turned, holding her arms out toward the man.

They embraced.

They embraced for a long time, the child's head pressed against the man's waist.

And Lindy thought: You are seeing the past here.

What you are seeing is the dead.

The dead.

How could that possibly be?

Then she was conscious of how both faces turned toward her and stared at her without expression, without curiosity, without any sign of interest. She put one hand up to her lips and thought: The dead. They are both dead.

Suddenly the early morning air was filled with the light sound of the child's laughter and in the shadows, in the darkened texture of the light, Lindy saw the girl's face turn back once more to the man's body, then the child was clinging to him, her head pressed into the center of his stomach and her hands clutching him behind the thighs, and then the man's hands locked tightly at the back of the child's neck and he was holding her to him, rocking his body slightly— rocking, rocking, his face turned once again to the balcony, his eyes fixed on Lindy.

Then they moved, passing directly beneath her, and she held her breath and waited to hear footsteps on the porch or the sound of a door slam—but there was nothing, only the dumb silence.

She stepped back from the rail.

Now she was conscious of the chill around her.

The chill, the silences.

She lifted her face, looked up at the sky, the great starless expanse of the growing dawn.

And she wondered what she had seen, what it was she had intruded upon like some hapless trespasser. She placed her arms across her breasts and curled her fingers over her shoulders, thinking about the child locked in the strange embrace with the man.

Roscoe, she thought.

Roscoe and the child who had owned the doll.

The Roscoe she had dreamed.

She leaned against the wall of the house, her robe open against her thighs, and she stared down toward the trees. There was something sad in the emptiness of the grove now, an absence she couldn't quite encompass.

Then the balcony trembled slightly and she turned her face in the direction of the sound.

He was standing very still, his hands held out toward her.

He was smiling.

She looked away, trembling, sensing the presence of something more powerful than she'd ever experienced before. She looked away, waited, didn't move.

And when she next looked, he had gone.

Leaving behind a quietness that seemed to scream inside her head.

A quietness.

A sense of evil.

Exquisite evil.

It was like staring at the closed door of a room she wanted to enter.

More than anything else in the world, she wanted to go inside that room. And she wanted to embrace the man the way she'd seen the child do.

And she would, she thought.

She would.

She would enter Roscoe's room.

When she stared down once more in the direction of the trees the branch was shaking again, and although she couldn't see anybody now, she realized that the creaking of the limb was like the sound of laughter mocking her.

18

DARK SPACES
June 20

When Tommy woke he realized that the closet door was hanging open again. He slid out of bed and stood for a while in front of the dark space. He wanted to step inside, almost as if he were striding forth to meet some grave personal challenge. Last night, he recalled, he had closed the door tightly and wedged it shut with a piece of folded cardboard but the cardboard lay on the floor, crumpled and ineffectual.

Wait, he thought.

Don't do anything.

He let his hands hang at his sides and he wanted to laugh at his own hesitation.

He scratched his curls, gazing at the space.

You want to kick yourself in the dead center of your ass for becoming this obsessed with a goddam closet.

If Norm was here he'd die laughing. And if your dad was here he'd have a reasonable explanation for everything because he was the kind of guy who could sit down and talk sensibly about anything. But you're on your own, kid. This is a solo flight.

And he stepped forward slowly, catching the scent of mustiness, dampness, dark smells that floated out to him.

Then he moved another couple of inches.

He found himself facing the gloom inside, a gloom that was penetrated only slightly by the light from the window.

He looked.

From the upper reaches of the closet, which seemed to extend forever, even beyond the limits of the house, he heard a faint sound. It had the weird regularity of a rat chewing on timber, a gnawing noise; he strained his eyesight, looking up into the dark spaces, and although he couldn't make anything out he had an impression of movement, of something rocking gently back and forth, swinging. A flashlight, he thought. If I'd brought a flashlight.

He thought about the bedside lamp. If he could stretch it across the room he could shine it inside the closet and illuminate those high spaces.

He wondered if the cord was long enough.

He went back toward the bedside table, and as he picked the lamp up, the closet door slammed shut at his back.

He swung round quickly.

Setting the lamp down, he moved back toward the closet.

Only this time, no matter how hard he tried, no matter how hard he yanked and pulled and strained, he couldn't get the damn thing open; it seemed to have sealed itself shut, locked itself in some impossible way. It was like somebody very strong was standing on the other side and holding the handle. Somebody who wanted to both tease and terrify him. He stepped away. He sat on the edge of his bed for a time, wondering.

People ended up in loony bins for far less than being obsessed by a door, Tommy. People were sent to funny farms for this kind of nonsense. Okay, be rational. Be reasonable. Doors don't lock by themselves unless—

Unless what?

He didn't have an answer for this one.

And he gazed at the door once more.

Which swung violently open.

Suddenly, violently open.

There was a shadow inside. Something small and huddled, something that suggested a child, a child standing in the dark spaces—but how could that be, for Christ's sake, why would a kid be standing inside a goddam closet, just standing there and not moving, not moving an inch?

Then the door slammed shut again, filling the room with a wild, deafening echo.

19

THE VISITOR
June 20

When Rosie woke, she did so with a sense of disorientation.

Where, where, where—where was she?

For a while she wasn't sure.

For a while she felt as if she'd been chloroformed and dragged away to some strange place of captivity. Drugged and leaden and alien to herself.

The mysteries of this house.

She swung her legs over the side of the bed and ran her fingers through her hair. There was a dryness at the back of her throat and her tongue felt heavy—slight hangover symptoms, maladies from the bottom of a bottle. She rose, parted the drapes, then stepped out onto the balcony.

She looked down into the grove of trees and then moved the length of the balcony.

When she turned the corner to find herself facing the sea, she discovered Tommy leaning silently against the rail. She paused for a moment, watching the boy's face, seeing the paleness of his skin. There was something so intensely vulnerable in the way he looked that she didn't want to speak.

He turned to her.

"Hi, Tommy," she said.

He smiled in a halfhearted way. And she wondered what this house had done to him, how it might have touched him, whether he had had his own personal encounters with whatever inhabited the place. Whatever, she thought. A spectral tenant.

"You look blue," she said. Quaint. The wrong expression. Kids didn't use blue these days. They talked about being bummed out.

"I'm okay," and he shrugged. "I guess."

She touched him lightly, stroking his shoulder. Beneath her fingertips she could feel him tremble a little.

He was gazing out toward the ocean.

She could tell he was struggling for words, a way to communicate something to her.

I know, she thought.

I know what it is, Tommy.

You feel it just the same as everybody else in this house.

Only you don't want to say anything because you think it's going to sound damned silly, don't you?

She rubbed his shoulder again.

"What's on your mind, Tommy?"

"Nothing."

"Come on. You can tell me."

He rapped his knuckles against the rail for a time. Suddenly she was reminded of Lindy's withdrawals, her little shells into which she retreated—but she had the feeling Tommy's were different somehow, easier to break down, easier to thrust aside. You couldn't ever be sure of anything, though, when it came to the minefields of adolescence. There were explosions when you least expected them.

"It's this house, isn't it?" she said.

He faced her, shuffling his feet on the wooden boards. "I don't like it here."

"Why?"

He stared up at the sky for a time. As she waited for an answer to her question, she thought, He's right, he should go home, we should all go home—what kind of madness was it to stay here anyhow? But it seemed to her that it was another kind of madness to just get up and run. It was an admission of fear, a yielding to a certain kind of spiritual terrorism. Flight, she thought, had never been an answer for anything. Besides, in daylight when the sun illuminated dark corners, and the world was brighter, the weird events seemed less strange—indeed, they were interesting now rather than frightening. It was almost as if she'd taken one step back from all the happenings and was seeing them now in a detached, academic fashion. Dr. Rosie Andersen, parapsychologist. Intrepid explorer of the beyond. If, in fact, there really was a beyond . . .

She repeated her question but Tommy answered only indirectly. He said, "Would you do me a favor? No matter how weird it seems?"

"Sure."

"Okay. Would you come inside my room?"

"If that's what you want."

He was already moving toward the door of his room. He hesitated before pushing it open, and when he finally did he ushered her inside ahead of himself. She stepped inside and paused. "Okay. What do you want me to do now?"

He pointed. "Open the closet."

"The closet?"

"Yeah."

She smiled at him. "You got it."

She laid her hand against the handle, turned it, drawing the door open. "Okay. The closet is open."

"What do you see?"

She gazed into the dark space. "Some books. Some boxes."

"And that's all?"

"Yeah. Except it's cold in there." And it was, cold and damp and musty. "What did you expect me to see, Tommy?"

"I don't know."

"You must have expected something, kid." She watched him for a time; he still hadn't entered the room, lingering on the threshold of the balcony door as if he were deathly afraid to come all the way inside, scared of that kind of commitment.

"Do you . . . hear anything?" he asked.

She listened.

She leaned forward into the dark chill space and she listened.

The imagination.

Just the imagination, she thought.

The faint sound of something whispering from above.

Like paper trapped in a breeze.

Like the steady beat of a moth's wings against glass.

Nothing really.

She turned once more to Tommy. "I don't know if I hear anything, Tommy. I can't really say. What did you expect?"

The boy didn't answer.

Try another approach, she thought. "What did you see in here?"

"I'm not sure . . ."

"You can do better than that, Tommy."

"I can't," he answered. "I can't do any better."

She could hear something stifled in the way he spoke, as if just behind his words there were choked-back tears. She looked inside the closet again, staring upward. That same faint sound drifting down from the dark overhead. That same steady rustling. And she wanted to say, Look, I think we've got a bad case of mice, kid, nothing more than that—but she wouldn't have sounded convincing. Then if it wasn't some rodent infestation, what was making the sound? Something stuck up there in a draft? Always seeking the logical, Rosie, always hunting down the spoor of the rational. And never quite managing to find it.

"What is it, Tommy? What is it that's scared you?"

"I'm *not* scared!"

"You don't exactly seem willing to come into your own room, so I figure something must have upset you."

This time Tommy didn't respond. He just stood in the doorway, arms hanging at his side, his face strangely defiant all at once.

"Look, Tommy, it's no big deal to come right out and tell me what happened to upset you."

"It sounds so stupid," he said.

"Tell me anyway."

"The door. The door keeps opening and closing. Then sometimes it seems to lock itself."

"Lock itself?"

"I told you it would sound stupid!"

"It's not stupid, Tommy." There. The tone of reason, of adult calm. Something she didn't altogether feel. But something she had to go through.

She watched him turn around and go back out on the balcony and then she followed him, calling his name. Outside she saw him move around the corner of the house and she found him staring down into the trees. She put her arms around him, hugged him against her body.

"What else, Tommy? What else happened in that room?"

"Nothing else."

"Come on."

"Nothing," he said again.

"Okay okay okay."

She moved away from him and she thought, He needs a little time, a little space—then maybe he'd come out and tell her what had happened in his bedroom. Maybe he just needed the privacy of his own thoughts for a bit before he raised the subject again. It didn't do any good to be irritated with him or try to force him to say what was on his mind.

She looked out beyond the trees in the direction of the highway.

And she saw something moving out there. A vehicle of some kind, trailing a dark pall of exhaust fumes.

She said, "I don't believe it. Look. There's life on the planet."

She watched as the vehicle came closer: it was a battered pickup truck, an old rusted thing burning oil profusely along the highway. It started to slow down just beyond the grove and then it turned along the pathway to the house. Rosie saw it come to a halt just behind the station wagon.

A man jumped down from the cab. He raised his face and looked up at the balcony, pushing his baseball cap back along his skull. He was short and muscular, dressed in faded coveralls. As he moved toward the house, he raised an arm in the air and called out something that Rosie couldn't quite catch. She walked toward the balcony stairs and started to go down. Tommy following listlessly a little way behind.

The visitor was standing at the foot of the stairs, smiling; he had small yellow teeth and a stubble of beard on his jaw. When he saw Rosie he stuck out a hand, which she accepted and held a moment, conscious of the man's sweat against her own skin.

"Mullery," he said. "Clyde Mullery," and he shifted his feet back and forth as if he were embarrassed by his own name.

"I'm Rosie. And this is Tommy."

"Nice to meet you folks," the man said. He looked at the house in the manner of someone assessing a property for its sale value. Then he glanced quickly at Tommy before he spoke again. "I meant to get out here a few days back. But I come down with this darn cold," and he rapped himself in the chest with his knuckles. "It's only lifting now." He coughed for a moment. Then he reached out and touched the handrail, shaking it a couple of times, watching it shift back and forth. "Beats me how this place still stands. Beats me. Should've been in the sea long ago, you ask me."

Rosie studied the man, wondering about the purpose of his visit. He examined the house as if he were the proprietor, but the place belonged, as she recalled, to somebody named Callahan. So what was Clyde Mullery's role around here? Now she watched as he stepped around her and climbed up onto the porch, where he examined the screen door. She was aware of Lindy beyond the screen, her face in shadow.

"Figure this needs to be replaced," Clyde Mullery said, and he took a small notebook from his coveralls and jotted something down with a pencil.

Rosie followed him. "Are you some kind of caretaker?" she asked.

"Old man Callahan asked me to keep an eye on his property, that's all. I ain't exactly a caretaker." He pulled the screen door back and forward, listening to the hinges. "Four of you here, is that right? Two women, two kids." He looked at Rosie as if he were racking his brain to understand why in hell people would want to rent this godforsaken place.

"Four of us, right," Rosie said. And then Clyde Mullery went inside the house. He stood in the middle of the living room and looked up at the ceiling.

"Got any complaints?" he asked.

Where do you want me to begin, she asked herself. Only some unexplained, apparently psychic phenomena, nothing to trouble yourself over, for sure. "Well," she said, and she hesitated. "Well, we were led to believe the place would be freshly painted and clean before we moved in."

"Who told you that? Callahan's lawyers? Never trust anything any lawyer ever says." And Clyde Mullery smiled. A private joke, Rosie thought.

"We had it in writing," she said.

"Well," Mullery said and let the matter drop. He stepped inside the kitchen. He went to the sink and peered into it. Then he turned and looked at the Ouija board that lay on the floor. He bent down and picked it up and set it on the table.

"So. How do you folks like it out here?"

Rosie shrugged. Tommy and Lindy were standing in the kitchen doorway behind her now.

"It's off the beaten track, that's for sure," Mullery said. "I guess you folks must really enjoy solitude, huh?" And he was smiling again in a way that Rosie was beginning to find a little infuriating. She folded her arms and watched as the man looked once more at the Ouija board. But she couldn't tell from his expression if he understood what it was. Then he turned to stare at the kids for a moment before he said, "Nice-looking pair. Are they yours?"

Rosie shook her head. "Only the girl."

Mullery glanced back at the Ouija. Then he was looking at Lindy this time in much the same way as he had looked at the house when he'd first arrived. Appraising, assessing—something in the expression made Rosie feel vaguely uneasy. "How old are you, kid?"

"Thirteen," Lindy said, her tone of voice flat.

"Thirteen, huh."

Mullery was silent, running the flat of his hand over the board as if he were searching its surface for some secret vibration. No, Rosie thought, I'm imagining this. This is just the hyperactive response of the overstimulated imagination. This house, the way this man looks at the kids, the solid presence of the board on the table—these elements had been casually tossed into the crucible of her imagination, that was all. On edge. Touchy. A little too sensitive. She needed to change the subject. To ventilate her feelings.

"I understand that Mr. Callahan doesn't get around much," she said.

"Yep. Keeps pretty much to himself, you could say."

"I'd like to drive into the village one day and meet him." This was called tossing a balloon in the air—if anybody knew anything about this house and its history it would have to be Callahan.

"He don't see nobody. He don't talk to nobody," Mullery said. "He just sits. He's pretty old. Eighty, maybe. Nobody knows for sure."

He just sits, Rosie thought. She wondered what it would be like to just sit. She had an image of a man rocking back and forth in a darkened room, pale bony knuckles gripping the arms of a chair. She watched Mullery again as he lowered his head to the window, apparently checking the frame.

"Can I ask you a question, Mr. Mullery?"

"I can't promise no answers," he said.

Such hick coyness, she thought. Such backwater reticence. She asked, "Have you ever heard of anyone called Roscoe?"

"Roscoe?" Mullery tilted his head back a moment. "Roscoe, Roscoe, Roscoe, lemme see, lemme see."

Rosie thought she could hear the cogs whirring in his brain.

"Roscoe, Roscoe, Roscoe," he whispered. "I can't say it rings any bells."

Was it paranoia that made her feel Mullery was being slightly evasive here? Good Christ, this place, this spooky place—had it reduced her to paranoia? "Are you sure?" she asked.

"Sure as can be," he answered. "Am I meant to know the name or something?"

"I thought it might be a former tenant." Shooting in the dark, whistling in the wind.

"Nope. Last tenants were called Farmer. Come out of Atlanta, I guess. That would be maybe four years ago. Before that, well, I don't rightly know on account of how I only been working for old man Callahan for four years."

"Why was the house vacant for that length of time?"

Mullery shrugged. "You'd have to ask Callahan that. Guess he didn't want to rent. Who knows?"

"What happened to the Farmers?" she asked.

"Happened? Nothing happened to them, so far as I know. They came out here for a couple weeks, then they went back home." Mullery touched the glass pane lightly and appeared somewhat satisfied with what he saw. "What do you want to know about some previous tenants for anyhow? They leave something behind?"

"Oh. Just some kids' books, I guess. Nothing important."

Mullery crossed the kitchen floor, then stepped back into the living room. Rosie followed, disappointed by his answers. What had she been hoping for anyhow? Something simple, something that would just wrap up the whole puzzle and present her with a solution? Such as what?

"Well," Mullery said when he reached the front door. "I guess you people are just fine. I'll get round to picking up a replacement for the screen door. But it takes time. You got to order these things." He shook his head. And then he was crossing the porch and going down the steps. Rosie watched him; halfway along the path toward his pickup he stopped and turned around. "Roscoe, huh?"

"Roscoe," she said. "That's right."

"Roscoe." He pushed his baseball cap to the back of his head and looked up at the sky. "Nope. I don't get a thing. Sorry, lady."

"Why don't you ask Mr. Callahan about the name?"

Mullery didn't answer.

Rosie saw him get inside his pickup, heard the engine scream to

life, watched the air turn black with fumes. She continued to observe
him as he backed out of the driveway, then he was gone along the
narrow blacktop toward Cochrane Crossing. She went back indoors
and moved across the living-room floor, pausing when she heard the
sound of voices coming from the kitchen. Lindy and Tommy, talking
in low, furtive tones. Some adolescent secret, she thought. Something that belonged in a world to which she did not have access.

She went to the doorway and peered round.

Tommy was sitting at the table, Lindy standing beside him.

They were examining the Ouija board.

And Lindy had her arm against Tommy's shoulder and her hand,
fingers splayed, was rubbing lightly against his back.

Rubbing very lightly.

Rosie stepped back, unnoticed by the kids.

Intimacy, she thought.

A strange, unexpected intimacy. Like the closeness of lovers.

As she moved toward the stairs, she felt as if she had just tres-
passed on a situation in which she had absolutely no rights. None at
all.

Tommy and Lindy. Lindy and Tommy.

She climbed the stairs. Was there something going on between
them?

I am imagining things again.

That's all.

Just imagining them.

They're only kids.

20

CALLAHAN
June 20

It was Rosie who expressed an urge to visit Cochrane Crossing, an
idea that Martha welcomed, because it meant leaving the beach
house for a while. She had begun to see the place as a kind of mirror,

a treacherously flat reflective surface in which you saw the images of
your worst fears, your worst dreams, your most indefinable anxieties.
As glad as she was to get out, just the same she had the worrying
sensation that the car wasn't going to start and that they'd be
stranded. But the wagon started as soon as Rosie turned the key in
the ignition, as if by some whimsical decision of its own the vehicle
had resolved not to repeat its failure of a few nights ago. (A car with a
mind and will of its own: hadn't that been the basis of a recent popular
book? She couldn't remember entirely now. The idea of books and
movies had receded inside her head, artifacts that belonged in the
civilized world.)

She sat up front alongside Rosie, while the kids were silent in the
back. She turned around a couple of times to glance at them as they
traveled the blacktop, but they were each gazing out of their separate
windows, like people doomed to travel together on the same flight—
people with nothing in common save a destination.

She watched the beach house diminish, studied the motions of
the ocean, the sprinkled sunlight pushed back and forward on the
quiet surf. Then, lighting a cigarette, she looked at Rosie. "This Mullery character," she said. "What did you think of him?"

"A little too creepy for my taste," Rosie answered.

"Creepy?"

"It's the first word that comes to mind."

Creepy, Martha thought. So was it all. A whole little universe
rendered spooky, shimmering, evasive. And she glanced back at the
kids again. Earlier, Tommy had mumbled something about wanting
to leave—but he hadn't raised the subject again. And Lindy—Lindy
had slithered inside one of her patented silences even if her expression wasn't sullen and private; there was instead an odd look of peace
on her face, as if she'd become quietly resigned to some fact of life.
(They had to feel the house, they had to feel the presences inside the
house—how could they not?)

When Cochrane Crossing came into view, Rosie slowed the car.

She parked it outside the grocery store.

Through the bleak window, Martha thought she saw a shadow
move. Maybe it was Darlene Richards come to check on prospective
customers.

The four of them got out of the wagon and stood on the sidewalk,
like tourists who have mislaid their map. Rosie looked this way and
that for a time. An empty street, Martha thought—maybe the inhabitants of Cochrane Crossing spent the midday hours pursuing siesta.

Some weird ancient local custom. Or maybe it was a community of, well, vampires—a thought that didn't amuse her as much as it might have done. And as she looked along the vacant street she had an image of the local residents lying in coffins in the crypt of the church, their fangs for the moment having ascended into their gums. You get some weird behavior out of a Ouija board and suddenly you're looking for occult manifestations at every turn. She watched Rosie a moment.

Then she said, "Are we here to get groceries or what?"

Rosie didn't say anything. She had that look on her face that Martha associated with a secret purpose; Rosie was sometimes very good at subterfuge, of using one course of action as a pretext for another. Once, she remembered, Rosie had dragged her to a chamber music recital because she claimed to have a passionate interest in string quartets when in truth she'd only been intrigued by the possibility of a relationship with the cello player; after the concert she'd vanished backstage somewhere and Martha had had to go home alone. It wasn't exactly deceit and it wasn't exactly manipulation. It was just Rosie's way of sometimes doing things, careless and not always well considered. Right now, though, Rosie was lost in her thoughts and her face was filled with a certain sly determination.

The kids had drifted inside the grocery store, Lindy following Tommy. Martha heard the little bell ring above the door, then they were gone.

"Okay," Martha said. "Why are we here? I mean, we're pretty well stocked with groceries. It's not like we need anything."

Rosie leaned against the hood of the wagon, nodding her head. "Boy. Am I so transparent?"

"Like glass."

"Okay. I want to check out this Callahan person. That's what I want to do."

"Callahan?"

"Yeah. I want to know about that goddam house."

The house, Martha thought. The house had become the core of their lives.

Rosie said, "I didn't want to mention anything in front of the kids, Martha. I don't want to spook them any more than I have to."

The process of spooking, Martha thought. How far had it eaten into their young lives in any case? She wouldn't know until she'd had an opportunity to talk with Tommy and Lindy. Even then—what was she going to bring up? Some kind of multiple-choice questionnaire?

Have you ever had strange experiences in the beach house?

YES/NO.

Would you categorize these as supernatural?

YES/NO.

Would you describe your state of mind at the time as one of fear?

YES/NO.

Are you anxious to get in the car and just get the hell out?

YES PLEASE.

"Callahan's a recluse, remember. Have you forgotten that? What makes you think he'll see you anyhow?"

Rosie stared at the store front a moment. "I don't know. I'll take a chance on it. I can be pretty persuasive."

"You can be pretty damned *determined* when you set your mind to it. That's what you mean." Martha gazed along the street again. Nothing and nobody. Absences that hung in the salty air with the tangibility of bedsheets drying in the wind. No people. No adults, no kids. She realized she hadn't once seen a child in Cochrane Crossing. Maybe they were all away at summer camp. Maybe they had a birth-rate problem here.

She shivered slightly. Then she faced Rosie again. "You don't even know where this character lives."

"In a place like this, it isn't exactly going to be a needle in a haystack, Martha," and there was a slight edge of irritation in Rosie's voice. This headlong quality of hers, Martha thought. This strength of will. There were times when Rosie wasn't able to temper her determination with subtlety or patience. There were times when she just charged ahead, bending people and circumstances to her own will. Because Rosie didn't want to leave the beach house, because Rosie didn't want to run away, because Rosie didn't want to think of herself as a quitter, they were all stuck in this place.

"I'll check the phone book. Or else I'll ask inside the store." Now she was gazing across the street toward the tavern, outside of which a couple of rusted trucks and dilapidated cars were parked. (The sea, Martha thought. It eats everything. It eats all the way through metal.)

"I guess they'd have a phone book in the bar," Rosie said. And she stepped off the sidewalk and started to cross the street; after a moment, Martha followed reluctantly. But when she reached the doorway, she paused. I am not going in there. Ever again.

She could hear jukebox music float out toward her as she waited for Rosie to come back. It was Raving Dave Dudley singing "Six Days on the Road"; he sounded like a man suffocating in the exhaust fumes of big rigs.

When Rosie returned, she said, "Callahan lives at number 8 Second Street."

"Second Street? I didn't think they'd have a Second Street in this place," Martha said.

She looked across the street at the grocery store. The kids were presumably still inside. Callahan, she thought. What was the point of trying to see the old man? Even if he met with them, even if he told them anything, what good would that do? She felt a vague resentment at Rosie—here she was once more being sucked into a situation over which she had no control. Here she was along for the unwilling ride.

"You don't have to come if you don't want to, Martha," Rosie said.

Martha shrugged. "I guess the kids will be okay in the store."

"Sure they will." Rosie looked along the street. "We could start in that direction," and she indicated the intersection. She began to walk and Martha followed, glancing back once in the direction of the grocery, seeing nothing but sunlight glistening against the surface of the station wagon.

The church was just ahead of them. Rosie had stopped to look at it. Dirty stained-glass windows, a blunt spire, chipped white walls.

"It doesn't exactly lay out a welcome mat, does it?" Rosie said. "Bleak place."

Martha gazed at the facade of the church a second. What she could not imagine was the sound of worship issuing from such a structure. She couldn't imagine hymns, prayers, sermons behind those cold walls. The stained glass, catching a flare of sunlight, shone in a dull way. Rosie, wandering ahead, had stopped by the steps of the place and was looking up toward the big wooden doors. Martha joined her.

There was the muffled sound of singing coming from inside.

The voices of children.

Pure, harmonious and yet gloomy, devoid of life.

It had to be something to do with the dreary Psalm they were singing:

> *"Now in the hour of deep distress*
> *My God! support thy Son,*
> *When horrors dark my soul oppress,*
> *O leave me not alone!"*

Horrors dark, Martha thought. At least it explained where the children were, although why a choir should be singing in the middle of the week was beyond her understanding. Practice, she thought. Choir practice.

Rosie said, "Nice song, huh?"

"Enchanting," Martha answered, gazing at the stout doors of the church.

"It's what I like about Christianity, the joyfulness of the Psalms. I mean, those lyrics, Martha, they just fill my heart with good cheer."

Martha moved away from the church, and the voices followed.

Out of nowhere, she was filled with a tiny sense of dread.

It stirred inside her a moment, like cold glass around her heart. Then it was gone and she was following Rosie along the sidewalk.

Lindy watched Tommy leaf through the pages of some old comic books in the corner of the store. He did so in a nonchalant way, like he was embarrassed by the idea that comics still interested him. And she remembered how he'd blushed when she'd stroked his shoulder in the kitchen and how he'd sat motionless that whole time, wanting to be touched and yet not wanting it—but she'd felt the way his body had trembled under the tips of her fingers, the quiet arousal of his flesh. She had been impressed by this vague power she had over him, even if it had lasted only moments before he'd risen from the table and gone out of the room. It was like discovering some new potential inside herself, something she was anxious to exercise again—and then she was thinking of the figure on the balcony. He'll come back, she thought.

I want him to come back. I want him to return.

No matter where it is he has to come from. No matter how far that journey has to be.

She remembered the child clutched to the man and the way they had rocked so slowly back and forth—and what impressed her now that she recalled this was a sense she had of a joy that existed between them, an intensity of pleasure, a pleasure she somehow knew was a forbidden thing.

She turned her face to the side a moment, conscious of the store-keeper staring at her with an odd intensity. Lindy pretended to study the jumble of cosmetic items on the shelf in front of her. Ivory Soap and Sure Anti-Perspirant and Nair Hair Remover—and she experienced a moment of passing dizziness, only it wasn't really like that at all. It wasn't any kind of light-headedness she'd ever felt before. She might have been floating someplace above her own body and looking down at herself, as if she were a very tiny moth fluttering against the ceiling. The sounds inside the store—a sluggish ceiling fan whirring listlessly, the whisper of pages being turned—these things seemed inordinately loud to her all at once and she wished she had some kind of switch inside her head that would help her lower the volume.

She shut her eyes and tried to breathe very deeply, tried to relax her muscles—when she felt her whole body change quite abruptly, a sense of yielding, of something just giving way inside her, and then there was slippage and the store seemed to tilt like its foundations had sunk into a cleft in the earth and she realized there was something hot and moist between her legs. She gazed at the woman behind the counter, not really seeing her, then she looked once more at Tommy, whose face was half-hidden behind a Batman comic: everything was going on as normal, nothing in the world around her had changed—but inside her body there was turmoil, spasms of muscles, sudden pulses rapping. And the hot wetness was spreading. Something might have been draining her of her strength.

She leaned against the shelf a moment and all the names of the cosmetics became jumbled before her eyes NAIRVORYURE, just like those first crazy messages from the Ouija, and she understood that if she didn't hold on to something she was going to fall over. She shut her eyes tightly again and tried to concentrate: you knew this was going to happen one day, you knew you were going to begin menstruating, but nobody ever said it would affect you this way— And she clutched the shelf. Maybe it was something more than having your first period, maybe she was really sick and something inside her had ruptured, which was why she felt so goddam weak all of a sudden. She clenched her hands against her stomach and realized that the woman was coming toward her, that Tommy had stopped turning the pages of his comic.

And she heard herself say she'd be fine if only somebody would take her back to her own bedroom in the beach house, where she could lie down in privacy and peace and security. But her voice boomed inside her head and she realized that neither Tommy nor the woman understood a word she was saying, that she might have been speaking in a private language filled with both an impossible longing and an impossible pain.

It was an ordinary frame house in a street of similar houses. The front yard was a jumble of weeds and choked grass and the windows of the place had the blinds drawn. Like a house of death, Rosie thought. A corpse laid out in the front parlor, waxy and white and shrouded.

She stood and stared at the porch, reluctant to go up to the front door but at the same time curious. Then she looked at Martha, who was gazing in the direction of the ocean with an absent expression on her face.

"Well?" Rosie glanced back at the house again.

Martha said, "After you."

They went up the path, past the knotted grass and the tangled shrubbery, toward the front door.

Rosie rang the doorbell, hearing faint chimes inside; she had the impression of a small old-fashioned bell ringing in a large room filled with furniture covered by dust sheets.

An echo, then silence.

She rang the bell a second time, noticing that Martha was already beginning to move away from the door. She doesn't want to be here, Rosie thought. She doesn't want anything to do with this. But what is it that I want? Have I turned into some kind of spook hunter, lusting after spending lonely nights in crypts and haunted houses with a tape recorder and an infrared camera?

"Nobody's going to come," Martha said.

The front door opened just as Martha finished her sentence. The man who stood there was dressed in a stiff black suit, like someone who has just come from a church service. He wore dark glasses and held a cane in one hand, and he had a strange jaundiced complexion, like that of an individual recovering from a complicated illness. For a moment he didn't move. His face expressionless, his body perfectly still, he appeared to survey both women but his eyes were invisible behind the glasses. Rosie took a step backward, an involuntary reflex that irritated her immediately. An old guy in black glasses—why would that spook her?

"Mr. Callahan?" she said.

The man nodded so slightly that the motion was hardly perceptible.

"We're the women who rent your beach house . . ." And she paused because now she wasn't sure what she was going to say, she wasn't sure what words she could come up with that wouldn't sound utterly stupid. She looked at the hallway behind Callahan, a gloomy stretch of space that seemed to lead nowhere.

Callahan shifted his cane from one hand to the other, turning his face away from the women and in the direction of the ocean. He seemed to be listening for something, as if he expected a message from the sounds of the tide. It occurred to Rosie that he carried himself as if he were missing a sense, that perhaps he was either blind or deaf. But when he turned his face back to them she realized he was scrutinizing them closely from behind the glasses.

"The beach house. Of course," he said, and his voice was soft, polite, and his sudden smile friendly. "Why don't you come inside for a while?" and he held the door wide for them, ushering them along the dim hallway toward a sitting room, talking constantly as he moved. "I don't get around so much these days, which is why I haven't been out to welcome you. Arthritis. Curse of the years. Old bones don't have quite the elasticity they used to have. I'm sure you young girls don't know about such problems."

Rosie glanced at Martha. Young girls, she thought. Maybe Callahan didn't see so well after all. And then she was looking around the sitting room, barely able to make out the furnishings because of the blinds drawn on the windows.

"Sit, why don't you? Make yourself at home." Callahan gestured in midair with his cane. "I'd offer you a drink but I don't keep any here. Can't take alcohol these days. Another curse of Father Time."

Rosie and Martha sat together on a narrow sofa. Rosie watched Callahan move toward an armchair and lower himself awkwardly. You didn't expect this, she thought. Whatever you might have expected, it wasn't quite this. She looked beyond Callahan at the walls, making out several framed photographs that hung there—family groups mainly, most of them pretty old. Callahan placed his cane in his lap and was silent awhile, studying the women, his head tilted a little to one side.

Then he smiled. "You both seem a little surprised. I imagine you expected a hermit, did you? Folks around here have the notion that if you don't go to church or stop at the grocery store every other day then you're a recluse or a monster of some kind." He shook his head and laughed. "I'm just old and infirm. No more, no less. Which is why I can't get out to the beach house. Had to hire Clyde Mullery to look after things for me. Bone-lazy, but he's the best I could get. He been out to see you yet?"

Rosie nodded. "Once."

"He's not a bad fellow. Has this peculiar manner you might call nosy. But like I say, there's worse than Clyde around the place."

A silence. Rosie could hear a clock tick somewhere in the room but she couldn't quite locate it. She looked at Callahan. Then back at the pictures. And she was aware suddenly of Martha stiffening a little alongside her, as if she were suddenly very tense, as if she'd seen something in this room to upset her. But what? There were only the pictures and the sound of a clock and the soft drone of the old man as he went on about how he hadn't been able to visit the house in years and how much he missed the place and the number of years it had been in his family: he was talking as if he'd been lusting after conversation for years.

Martha was shifting uncomfortably, crossing and uncrossing her legs, fidgeting with her purse. What the hell's wrong with her now? Rosie wondered. Callahan had stopped speaking and sat in the manner of someone enjoying a pleasant reminiscence, scrutinizing some inner vision. Then he leaned forward a little and asked, "You girls enjoying the old place? It's a good place for your kids, I guess. How old are they? Thirteen?"

Before she could answer, Rosie's attention was drawn back to the pictures on the wall.

Family groups.

Portraits of individuals.

And something else.

Something she knew by heart.

She felt an odd pulse at the side of her head, a swiftness of blood, a knocking.

She rose from the sofa and went toward the photograph and studied it.

It was the same picture of the house she'd developed herself. The same angle of perception. The same, everything the goddam same. From the young trees to the new shingles, everything.

She glanced at Martha, understanding it was this photograph that had made her friend so uneasy.

Callahan was watching her. "That was taken about sixty years ago, I figure. Back when the house was first built."

"Was it in your family then?" Rosie asked.

The old man nodded his head. "It's always been in our family," and his words were drawn out, ponderous.

Rosie turned away from the photograph. "I understand you haven't rented the house in four years, Mr. Callahan."

"That's right." Callahan tapped the rug with his cane. "It must be a good four years by this time . . ."

"It just lay empty all that time?"

"It just lay empty. Right."

"Why was that?"

Callahan shrugged. "I had this foolish notion of living out there myself, I guess. I just never got round to moving . . . It was a stupid idea anyway. What would I do out there all by myself? How would I get into the village for provisions? I don't own a car, and even if I did, I'm in no shape to drive one."

Callahan was turning the cane round and round between the palms of his hands. Rosie looked back at the photograph again. The new house, the young trees, the vacant windows. She wondered if anyone had been inside the place when the picture had been taken, if someone had been working in the kitchen or asleep in an upstairs room—and then she was trying to envisage the photographer, the old-fashioned camera, the tripod.

"Do you know who took this photograph, Mr. Callahan?"

Callahan smiled. "I wouldn't have an answer for that one."

Rosie went back to the sofa and sat down, glancing at Martha, who was looking down at the rug as if in its faded pattern she might find answers that Callahan couldn't provide.

A silence in the room. The distant whisper of the tide. Light lying against the surfaces of the blinds. Subdued light. Ask, she thought. Go ahead and just ask.

"Do you know anybody called Roscoe?"

Callahan sat back in his chair. "Roscoe?" He appeared to turn the name over in his mind for a time, then he shook his head. "I can't say I do."

"Or a child called Anna?"

"I don't know that one either."

Rosie watched him for a bit, wondering if he was lying, concealing something: Roscoe and Anna—the names of some unfathomable mystery. Why would the old man hide information anyhow? Then Callahan was getting out of his armchair, propping himself up on his stick just as the clock in the room began to chime. It was over; this little chat had just come to an end.

Callahan said, "It was downright friendly of you girls to come visit with me. I'd like it if you could stay longer but this is the time of day when my doctor says I have to nap. Nap! That's the trouble with doctors these days. You can't smoke. You can't drink. You have to take naps. You can't do a damn thing but just sit in an armchair and breathe and sometimes I think they'll forbid you to do even that."

He went with them out into the hallway, where he stood, leaning against his stick, as if he had something else to add to the conversation. But he smiled and said nothing. Rosie watched him a moment, conscious of the hallway stretching behind him and a flight of stairs leading upward into gloom.

And something else, something she wasn't remotely sure she saw, whether it was her imagination—

The movement of a person.

Swift. Then gone.

Merely a shadow crossing the top of a stairway and then nothing—

A housekeeper, Rosie thought.

Another person in this place. So what? Why wouldn't an old man have somebody to look after him?

"You'll come again, I hope," he said.

Rosie smiled. "It would be a pleasure."

"You don't mind seeing yourselves out, do you?"

Martha was already at the front door, opening it. Rosie followed, turning once to see Callahan go back inside the sitting room and shut the door behind him—then they were outside where a sudden sea wind was blowing granules of sand along the street. They walked a little way in silence.

"That photograph. That goddam picture," Martha said. She stopped and gripped Rosie by the wrist and her face was pale. "I want to get out of this place, Rosie. I want to go home. I don't care about the rent we've already paid, and I don't care about the rest of this rotten summer—I want to go home."

Rosie listened to the wind rise off the tide. She felt Martha's hand go slack against her skin.

Maybe it was the only step to take, the only move possible. Maybe the mysteries could be left to themselves. And whoever occupied the beach house could play out their little games in silent, dusty rooms with no companionship but the sand and the sea. But something inside her resisted the idea of flight even now, some quality that for want of a better name she called stubbornness. Yet it wasn't exactly that, and it wasn't even the prospect of quitting and running and in some way betraying herself—it was the sense of a mystery left unfathomed, a puzzle unexplored. And behind this another notion was taking shape, something she had just begun to consider when she'd seen the picture on Callahan's wall—the idea of capturing some ghostly occurrence on film, the idea of getting something down on celluloid, of fixing the supernatural in a photograph.

It was ambitious, she thought. And perhaps it was impossible. But suddenly the idea went through her with an arrowlike thrill. "Let's give it another day or so, Martha." This was spoken in a voice she couldn't quite recognize as her own, a tone that was suffused with the steel of aspiration. Photographers were always looking for that most holy of grails—The Shot, The Big Picture, call it what you like. She could see it all at once: a photograph by Rosie Andersen that depicted supernatural phenomena. A picture that would survive all kinds of expert scrutiny, that would pass every test ever invented to uncover photographic fraud. Her excitement was tempered only by the suspicion that perhaps such events would, by their very nature, avoid the permanence of celluloid. But then she was thinking of the photograph that hung in Callahan's home and the one she herself had taken of the house, and her enthusiasm grew. Somehow, in some strange way, she had already photographed a ghostly phenomenon, which implied that she could do it again.

Martha looked incredulous: "Another day? Are you kidding?"

"One more day won't hurt."

"Jesus, Rosie, I can't believe you're saying this."

"Why not? Whatever's going on in that beach house—you really think it can hurt us? Huh? You really think that, Martha? What can it do, for God's sake? Kill us? Could a ghost or whatever it is kill us? Okay, I grant you a few parlor tricks. I grant you some mischief with a Ouija board. I grant you some strange occurrences and some awfully odd apparitions."

Martha was shaking her head in disbelief.

They turned onto the main street and Rosie stopped talking. Something else had just occurred to her. "You know what's funny, Martha? Callahan never once wondered why I was asking all those questions or why I was bringing up those names. It was almost like he expected to hear them . . ."

"Maybe he did," Martha said in a sullen way. "Only I don't care anymore. I just don't give a damn."

They walked to the grocery store.

As they reached it, Tommy stepped out. His face pale, his mouth open, hollow, his expression one of anguish.

He leaned against the window of the store and said only one word. "Lindy."

21

APPEARANCES AND MESSAGES
June 20–21

Tommy thought about it until he couldn't think anymore, until all
the pictures inside his brain became confused and he wanted to take
a leave of absence from his own mind. Maybe hang a GONE FISHING
sign around his skull so that anybody who asked would know he
wasn't at home for a while. A real long while.

But it came back anyway and no matter how hard he tried he
couldn't push it aside altogether, and what he saw was the way Lindy
had clutched her stomach and fallen to the floor and how slicks of
blood had formed around her and then there was the woman in the
store hurrying around with napkins and the way Lindy had talked
about wanting to go back to her room because she'd be okay there
and then he'd helped carry her out to the back seat of the wagon
where she'd lain with a strange look on her face—and suddenly this
wasn't Lindy, this wasn't the girl who'd recently started to flirt with
him and tease him, touch and embarrass him, this was another person altogether and one he didn't know.

Jesus Christ. He'd heard about menstrual periods and he'd always
felt sorry that women had to go through them—but he'd never expected to see anybody so doubled over in pain and babble so much
about nothing in particular. And the blood, he hadn't expected to see
the blood . . . He ran his fingers through his hair and watched the
sea from the kitchen window. From the upstairs part of the house, he
could hear his mother and Rosie talking quietly—it was female stuff
and he was excluded from it because that was in the nature of things,
but just the same he wished he could go upstairs and see if Lindy was
all right.

He pulled open the refrigerator and surveyed the items inside—
bean sprouts and spinach and too many green things (all of which
constituted his own idea of junk food)—and then he realized he
wasn't exactly hungry anyhow. In fact, there was this small knot of
nausea in his stomach which he imagined he might kill if he sneaked

a little of Rosie's Jack Daniel's. When he found the bottle he tipped it to his mouth and felt it singe the surface of his tongue, burn raw against the back of his throat: he stuck it away again. Disgusting stuff and who needed it anyhow except grownups who couldn't handle their own problems without alcoholic help?

He sat down at the table and looked at the Ouija board, then he thought about going upstairs to his own room but that idea had about as much appeal as a trip to a dentist. He studied the board for a bit, then wondered about Lindy—about why she'd started to come on to him recently, stroking him, touching him, almost as if she was doing it for laughs. There was this utter mystery called Female Chemistry. Maybe it had something to do with that. Sometimes it seemed like girls turned into women overnight and they left you stranded in their wake and all you could do was gasp at the way they changed.

He sighed and went outside, watching the sun slip down over the ocean. He leaned against the porch rail and shut his eyes, sniffing the salt air. What he wanted was to take one of his fishing rods and go out on the water and sit there in a small boat and forget about this goddam house with its weirdness and its closet doors and its shadows. But even as he considered this, he realized he still couldn't get Lindy out of his mind. He was trying to picture her lying upstairs in her bed— and his thoughts, sweet Christ, his thoughts were suddenly focused on her body and her long hair and the idea of her hands touching him. And he was thoroughly embarrassed by the whole notion.

He went down the steps to the sand. The tide was slow, distant, the sands flat and glistening. He stuck his hands in the pockets of his jeans and started to walk. He didn't feel like going as far as the sea; he turned and looked back at the house and saw a couple of lights in the upstairs windows and a shadow pass against glass—his mother? Rosie? He wasn't sure.

He shrugged and went around the side of the house.

The sun was almost gone, barely a fragment of dying light in the sky. Tommy squinted in the direction of the blacktop. As usual, it was empty; he wondered if the appearance of Clyde Mullery and his pickup truck had only been a kind of illusion. In fact, he even began to think that Cochrane Crossing itself was like a mirage. If he walked to the village right this moment, would it exist at all?

He moved through the grove of trees.

When he reached the edge of the road he started to think about Lindy again. He turned round, faced the house and looked at the light shining against her balcony door. And he remembered a movie

where some guy had serenaded a girl on a balcony with his guitar.
Somehow the thought made him feel clumsy, like his hands were too
big or his fingers too thick.

He went back toward the trees.

Then he stopped once again.

There was a rustling among the leaves and branches. The sound
of some night bird moving around. He looked this way and that but
in the gathering darkness he couldn't see anything.

Just the same, he had the distinct sensation that something was
near him. Something that moved.

He stood very still. He thought: Lots of things move in the night.
Birds. Rodents. Snakes. A whole bunch of things.

Then he raised his face and stared up at the empty balcony and
the light from Lindy's room.

Martha lit a cigarette and said, "I can't remember my first period at
all. I mean, I was prepared for it and I expected some big deal, but
now I don't even remember it." And she paused, looking across the
kitchen table at Rosie, who was pouring herself a shot of Jack Daniel's.
We're both thinking the same thing, she thought. We're thinking
about the girl lying upstairs in her bedroom and how pale she looks
and how much blood she's lost. Martha twirled the cigarette round in
her fingers. She looked away from Rosie and found herself staring at
the doll on the window ledge and then, moving her eyes a little, at
the Ouija board set out on the table. It was strange how, when one
was faced with a natural upset, like the fact that Lindy was weak and
had lost too much blood, all the supernatural intrigue, all the weird
phenomena, seemed to fade into the background. It was still there—
how could it not be?—but it was like sound-track music, something
you were conscious of only in a limited way.

"She's going to be okay, Rosie," she said. "I mean . . ." Her voice
trailed away.

Rosie threw her drink back and said nothing for a while. Then,
drumming her fingers on the table, she leaned back in her chair.
"Sure, she's going to be okay. I just wish there was a fucking doctor
around here, that's all."

Martha sighed and remembered how the woman at the grocery
store, Darlene Richards, had said that the doctor only visited Cochrane Crossing twice a week—and that even then his visits were unre-
liable. They had tried to call the man, a certain Dr. Mannering, from

the phone in the grocery, only to learn that he was out on an emergency in some godforsaken hamlet called Twynford and wouldn't be back for hours.

"The loss of blood," Rosie said, and her voice was a whisper. "I've never seen so much goddam blood." She filled her shot glass again and downed the liquor quickly. Martha reached across the table and touched the back of her friend's hand a moment.

"Christ, Martha . . ." Rosie pressed her fingertips against her eyelids and then stared into her empty glass. "This was intended to be an idyllic summer. You remember that far back? The four of us. This house. You were going to write and I was going to take pictures. Does any of that ring a bell for you, kid?"

Martha nodded. She needed to say something that might console Rosie, that might assuage her concerns for Lindy—but words, as they had done in the past, came out lacking the necessary quality of compassion. "Look, she's not bleeding anymore. She's sleeping, she's fine . . ." Words. Little empty shells that just rattled together as uselessly as trinkets on a charm bracelet. She stared round the kitchen and she thought: It's this place. This place. We've disturbed something here and whatever it is it's made us unwelcome. It doesn't want us here.

No. No, it isn't like that at all.

Whatever, it needs us here.

It needs us here to torment us.

The house seemed smaller to her all at once, a confining presence, as if all around her it were dwindling. Shrinking. Slithering into the sands and taking all of them with it. She crushed her cigarette and lit another, thinking again of the child in the upstairs room. Thinking of what Lindy had said.

I'll be fine if you don't move me.

I'll be okay just so long as you let me stay where I am.

And the tone of her voice—pleading, begging: she might have been saying, I can only get weaker if you take me away from this place. As if the beach house were the source of her strength. Dear Jesus.

The source of her strength.

She watched as Rosie's hand touched the message indicator on the board. "Maybe this doctor will come soon," Rosie said. She got up from the table and paced the room for a while in a restless way. Then, her shoulders sagging, she sat down once more and gazed at Martha.

"Tomorrow," she said suddenly. "We'll leave here tomorrow. If Lindy's strong enough to travel . . ."

Martha looked at her friend for a while. She felt a conflict of emotions just then, a faint despair that Rosie's spirit, her determination, had broken like this—and an upsurge of optimism at the prospect of getting out of this wretched house.

"Lindy says she doesn't want to leave, Rosie."

"Lindy doesn't know her own mind. How can I agree to staying on here if she's going to get sick? What happens if she starts to bleed again and this goddam doctor still doesn't come? What do we do then?" Rosie raised her face and glanced up at the light bulb; she looked gaunt and weary, her skin stretched tautly over her skull. Martha had an urge just to reach out and hug her, as if the mere act of touching might soothe her concerns away. Then she was thinking again about the girl in the upstairs room and her mind was abruptly crowded with shadows, with all the shadowy movements of the house, the dark corners and the damp closets and the sense she had all at once that the place had a life of its own—a center, a core, a soul, call it what you like; and that this core was inhabited by something that had no right to any kind of life.

"We could get an early start," she said.

"I'd like that." Rosie nodded and took a pack of cigarettes from her breast pocket. Then she smiled weakly at Martha. "It's funny. I think I could stand the idea of sharing this place with invisible tenants, I think I could have put up with apparitions and all the rest of it because deep down inside I still don't believe in that shit, no matter what my senses might tell me—but when it comes right down to it, it's the old maternal thing that makes you reach decisions. Screw the ghosts. Let them have this whole damn place to themselves. Let them have their fun all alone—I just need to know my daughter's going to be okay. I need the confidence of knowing that there's a hospital nearby and physicians that keep regular hours. Goddammit, I need civilization!"

Martha was silent for some time; she'd been too worried about Lindy to think about her own son but now she was conscious of his absence. He'd mentioned something earlier about going for a walk— how long ago had that been? She had no real idea of time now, as if it had become suspended: a whole little world without clocks. She wandered to the window, stared out into the dark, then returned to the table and looked down at the Ouija board. Tommy, she thought: he's out there walking the beach. Maybe he found something intriguing along the sands—a crab, a chunk of driftwood, a stranded sea creature.

Rosie said, "We could drive up to DC and spend a couple of days sightseeing. We could do the whole tourist thing. Check into a nice safe motel. Clean sheets. Bubble baths. We could sit up late and watch TV and gorge ourselves on Kentucky Fried Rat. Doesn't that sound appealing?"

"It sounds wonderful," Martha said. And it did—well-lit streets and illuminated monuments and automobiles and pollution: the idea of poisoning your own lungs on the air you breathed had never quite seemed so attractive to her.

"I've never actually seen the White House," Rosie said, working herself back into a mood that was one of counterfeit cheerfulness. "How can I genuinely call myself an American and say that I've never seen the great beating heart of the Republic, huh?"

Martha smiled. "And I've never seen the Capitol."

Rosie shook her head in mock solemnity. "What are we? Communists or something?"

"Card-carrying members."

"It's a terrible admission."

"Dreadful."

"It's the kind of realization that makes me want to smoke a joint, Martha."

Rosie reached for her purse, opening it, rummaging inside. It was a forced kind of banter, Martha knew, but it was better than nothing, better than the gloom, the weight of this house. Rosie took a plastic bag out and opened it. She spilled some grass and a pack of rolling papers onto the table and began to pick seeds out with her fingertips.

Martha watched: Rosie did this nimbly, swiftly, with all the expertise of long practice.

The discarded seeds rolled across the surface of the Ouija board.

And then Martha knew—

She knew something was about to happen, she could feel it coming in at her from a long way back—a dark sense of presentiment, of premonition. She wanted to rise and get out of the kitchen, but before she could move, the plastic indicator in the center of the board shivered, shifted slightly, rolling toward one corner of the board, then back once again to the dead center.

She stared across the table at Rosie.

And then back down at the indicator, which was moving again, pausing over one letter before sliding on to the next.

PLEASE

And again: PLEASE.

Rosie tried to smile: "What's this? A little politeness tonight?" But her flippancy didn't work—it was a dead thing, a bad effort.

Then the indicator was rolling quickly, moving in zigzag patterns all over the board.

PLEASEDONOTLEAVEMEHERE

Martha clutched the edge of the table. This room had changed, the atmosphere in this kitchen had altered—as if it were suddenly inhabited by an invisible being whose pain and loneliness were palpable things.

DONOTLEAVEMEHEREWITHROSCOE

"Anna?" Rosie asked suddenly. "Is this Anna?"

YES

"Where are you?"

IAMWITHROSCOE

"Why are you with him? Tell us why."

PLEASEDONOTLEAVEMEWITHHIM   HE HURTSME

Martha shut her eyes a second. She had a picture of a small child trapped in a black labyrinth, a lonely voice crying in a locked room. He hurts me.

"Why are you with him, Anna?" Rosie asked again.

Nothing. The plastic gadget had come to a halt in the center of the board.

"Why, Anna?"

Nothing. Rosie leaned back in her chair and looked at Martha.

Silence.

Martha felt an odd sadness, a sense of sorrow that had no particular focus: how the hell were you supposed to feel something about a disembodied voice? Something you couldn't touch and see, couldn't help in any way?

Rosie, her fingers trembling, picked up the pack of rolling papers and removed one. "Well? What do you make of—"

Before she could finish her question, the board had come to life again. And this time it was different, its vibrations altered, the movement of the indicator slower, more deliberate.

MISERABLE

A pause. Martha thought: We don't even need to touch the goddam thing. We don't need to lay our hands on it. It moves and it speaks anyhow. And she tried to imagine spectral fingers hovering over the table.

CUNTS

"Roscoe," Rosie said in a whisper. "Our old friend Roscoe. Charming as ever."

THE CHILDREN

There was a long pause. Martha leaned over the board, tense, expectant, all the nerves in her body burning: The children, what about the children? What was he going to say about the children—
The indicator didn't move.
"Roscoe?" Rosie said. And there was a certain determination in her voice, almost as if she were challenging Roscoe to respond. "Roscoe, we're waiting."
We're waiting, Martha thought.
Like it was a telephone connection to The Beyond.
Nothing more than waiting for some operator—trapped in purgatory—to plug in the right wires. And she wanted suddenly to laugh, wanted to toss this idiot board aside, but she couldn't laugh and she couldn't move because the board and its plastic triangle had become the claustrophobic center of the universe.

THE CHILDREN

"What about the children, Roscoe?" Rosie asked. Her challenge was stronger now, her voice more firm.

THE CHILDREN

Pause.
Then:

STAY

Martha raised her face and looked at Rosie, who was getting up from her chair and moving round the kitchen—

"What do you mean they stay? What the hell do you mean by that?"

But the board was silent and secretive, its alphabet a furtive arrangement of meaningless letters, and Rosie's questions, echoing through the kitchen in a thin muffled way, went unanswered.

The sounds of the women's voices, drifting up to her room from the kitchen, seemed to belong to some other world, some other dimension of experience. She lay flat on her back and stared upward at the ceiling and thought about the strange weakness she felt and the numbness that existed at the backs of her legs: she might have been floating in warm water or drugged by one of those sleeping pills her mother used and which, from time to time, she had pilfered. Turning her head a little to the side so that she faced the balcony door, she realized how glad she was that the women had left her alone—their fussing around and the way they'd been whispering about her made her uneasy; and their presence inside her room had been like trespassing on her privacy.

They'd been talking about leaving. About leaving the beach house and going back to good old Syracuse. Maybe that was the thing that troubled her most. She pushed herself upright and gazed across the room at the oval mirror. Her reflection was pale and her hair looked dry and ragged. She ran one hand through the strands and sighed: Why did they want to leave here anyhow? Didn't they feel the vibrations of this place? Didn't they understand that there was warmth concealed at the heart of this house? Warmth and pleasure? Exquisite pleasure?

She hugged herself, closing her eyes: you feel more secure in this room now than you've ever felt anywhere else. You feel safe. And what you thought of at first as fear has become something quite different.

It has become an invitation to stay.

You misunderstood before.

But not now. Now that you don't feel scared.

She lay back down, her hands beneath the bedsheets. And she stroked her hips and stomach with her fingertips in lazy, circling motions. She imagined the man moving along the balcony toward her room. The sound of his footsteps on the boards. His hand lightly touching the rail. She imagined him turning the handle of her door and stepping inside, the curtain blown back by the breeze and the glass shimmering in moonlight, and then he was crossing the floor toward the bed and just sitting there, gazing at her for a long time without moving, just sitting, just watching—

She sat upright again, listening. Then she rose and, pushing the bedsheets aside, moved toward the balcony door. When she opened it, she leaned for a moment against the frame. Weak, she thought. Still weak. She felt the night breeze stir in her hair and blow against her bare legs.

She reached for the handrail and pressed her body against it as she looked down toward the trees.

Somebody was moving below. Moving slowly through the grove.

Tommy. She recognized him as he approached the house. He paused, looking upward at her. The breeze flapped against her once more, blowing her robe open, but she made no move to cover herself. She stared down at the boy.

Then her attention was drawn elsewhere. She turned her face and looked the length of the balcony.

They were watching her.

The man and the little girl.

The child had one hand held out, palm curled in a gesture of invitation. Lindy stared at the small face, which was impassive and pretty and pale. Then she looked at the man, vaguely afraid but fascinated just the same, unable to prevent herself from gazing at him and knowing, with dead certainty, that if he were to hold out his hand she wouldn't hesitate to go toward him—and suddenly she was trembling, her legs weak, her heartbeat fast.

He was smiling.

Even as he seemed to look straight through her as if she were no more than a sheet of clear glass, he was smiling. She was conscious only of the darkness in his eyes and the way the smile appeared to be little more than an empty expression, something that was chilly and condescending and taunting.

She turned her face away.

Tommy was still standing motionless below. Watching.

She looked back at Roscoe and the child.

The girl had lowered her hand now. With the same impassive look on her face, she reached out and placed her fingers between the man's legs and when she turned to stare back at Lindy she was holding his penis in her hand.

Lindy took a couple of steps forward and realized she'd never seen a man erect in her whole life. She wanted to touch him herself, wanted to wrap her hand around him, stroke him, push him inside her own body. He was large and swollen and she knew he would hurt her but she didn't care. She understood only that she needed the man, she needed him to fill her; and she was conscious all at once of how her own blood was singing inside her head and her pulses dancing and her terrible desire.

She took a few more steps forward until she was only yards away from the man and the child.

When she stopped again.

Because it changed.

It changed completely, as if some demented conjuror, some malicious sleight-of-hand artist, had drawn a cloth of black silk across the whole scene and she was left gazing at an empty balcony, an empty night, a starless dark filled with poignant absences; and Roscoe and the child had slipped through this same silk into a place of invisibility. She gripped the handrail and looked down at Tommy, who hadn't moved, who was still staring upward.

Lindy watched him for a long time, conscious of the breeze playing over the surface of her skin, conscious of the sinking sense of disappointment she felt—before she turned and went back inside her bedroom, closing the balcony door.

22

ILLUSIONS
June 21

Tommy stood in the kitchen doorway and watched Rosie and Martha at the table. He checked the Ouija board a moment, and then, hands slung in his pockets, he went toward the refrigerator, opened it, looked inside. He took out some orange juice, drank it quickly, and leaned against the sink. The two women—who might have held season tickets to wakes—watched him in a guarded way; he knew something had just happened in this room. He knew it had something to do with the goddam board that sat between them.

"Where were you?" Martha asked. "It's after midnight."

"I went for a walk," Tommy answered.

"Along the beach?" Martha asked.

No, he wanted to say. I was hanging out in a pool hall and then I ran into this chick I know . . . He nodded, staring down at the patterned linoleum.

Then he was thinking about Lindy again, thinking about the way he'd seen her on the balcony. He stared at the women for a time. The tension in this kitchen, he thought. You could take a knife and slice it like it was a birthday cake.

Then Martha said, "We're leaving tomorrow, Tommy. We decided it's probably the best thing because Lindy needs to be near a doctor . . ."

And that's not the only reason, the boy thought. He was turning over the idea of going upstairs to his room. But he wasn't ready for that yet—he felt very drained. He pushed himself away from the sink and walked to the table. Rosie was looking at him. "You glad we're leaving, Tommy?" she asked.

"Sure," he said. "Sure I am."

And he was. He truly was. He glanced at the doll a second. There was a sudden sharp pain behind his eyes and he had to rub his eyelids. His mouth was dry: the balcony, he was thinking now. The girl on the balcony. What had he really seen there anyhow?

"When are we going?" he asked.

"First thing in the morning," Rosie said.

"Daylight," Martha added.

Suddenly these two women seemed to him like those ladies who volunteered to take flowers and vitamins to the terminally ill in charity wards. Too careful, too kind. And what was the word . . . solicitous? Something like that. He gazed at the board. That black alphabet. He wanted to come out with a real flip remark like, "You know what? There's something funny about this house." An icebreaker. Something to cause a few smiles. But the tension was getting to him again and he couldn't speak for a bit.

"Is it okay if I go see how Lindy is?" he asked, and his voice was a little raspy.

"She's probably asleep, Tommy," Martha said.

Rosie had a cigarette in her hand; it had burned all the way down to the filter, like she'd forgotten it was there. Tommy studied her: she seemed to be thinking over his question, turning it this way and that in her mind, as if she wasn't sure whether it would be proper for him to go to Lindy's room.

"I'll just look in," he said quickly. And that was all. Nothing more than that. He laid his hands against the edge of the table and he realized he was scared, he was afraid of the prospect of going upstairs. Up up and into the gloom. Passing the closed door of his own bedroom. Jesus Christ.

Rosie finally stubbed her cigarette and said, "I don't see any reason why you can't go up and see her, Tommy. Just don't wake her if she's asleep. Okay?"

"I won't," and he was reluctant to step out of the kitchen, as if what he needed most now was the security of these two women. Then he turned and stepped inside the darkened living room and stared in the direction of the staircase. Up and up and up. He stopped at the bottom step. I can't go up there, he thought—even as he started to climb anyhow. When he reached the landing he hesitated a second outside the door of his own room: What would happen if I just hauled it open right now? Would that closet be shut or what? Or would it suddenly swing open? And what would I see? There was sweat in the palms of his hands and he wanted to turn around and head back downstairs again.

But he went along the landing until he reached the door of Lindy's room; he knocked lightly. When nothing happened, he knocked again.

He waited, squinting now and then back along the landing. Faintly, from below, he could hear the two women talking in low voices. We're leaving, he thought—and he tried to draw some kind of encouragement from this prospect. But there was one more night to get through. There were several hours to pass before daylight. And that felt like entering a tunnel at the end of which, at a far distance, you can see a bright disc coming up slowly. He pressed his forehead briefly against the door. Then he raised his hand and knocked again.

This time, when there was no answer, he turned the handle and stepped quietly into the room.

Rosie, who had been listening to the sound of the boy as he climbed the stairs, got up from the kitchen table and went to the sink where she ran cold water over her hands, then splashed her face. She dried herself with a paper towel. Martha was leaning against the door of the refrigerator with her arms hanging loosely at her sides. Limp, like a rag doll accidentally caught in a washing-machine cycle. Rosie crumpled the towel and tossed it into the trash.

"What makes me angry is how I can't fight back," she said. "I mean, if this Roscoe character was real, I could do something. I could scratch his eyes out. But I feel so goddam useless, Martha. Helpless. I wish the sonofabitch would just show himself, that's all." And even as she spoke she felt her anger fade, her sense of futility deepen. She ran a hand through her hair in a gesture of bewilderment. Ghosts. Spooks. Messages from Nowhere. Telegrams from the Other Side. How were you supposed to deal with stuff like this anyway? She walked to the table and sat down, looking at the motionless board. Now she found herself marveling at the bravado of her earlier decision, that she would stay in this godawful house and take pictures. Big Shot, she thought. You were going to capture some psychic wonders with your trusty Canon, huh? You were going to be Miss Terrific.

Why didn't you just get the hell out of this place earlier?

Your stubbornness and your ridiculous ambitions—

Why didn't you ignore those things? Why didn't you listen to Martha sooner?

She said, "There's not much point in getting pissed off, is there?"

Martha shook her head and said quietly, "I guess."

"I mean, it doesn't go anywhere. The thing we've got to think about is just getting the hell out of here." She studied Martha a moment: there was no color in Martha's face and her eyes seemed bleached, devoid of sight, as if she were just one other item of flotsam the sea had cast up on the shore. But somehow this paleness accentuated her dainty prettiness, underlined it. "I don't care if Lindy's strong enough or not, we've got to get the hell out . . ."

"We ought to start packing now," Martha said.

"Yeah. Give me a couple of minutes to find some energy. I'm beat." Rosie lit a cigarette and watched her smoke go curling up to the light bulb. "I need to get some air—you want to go out on the porch for a bit?"

"Sure." Martha's voice was uneven, unsteady.

Outside, the night air was heavy and the porch infested by relentless moths drawn to the light. The two women sat down on the steps and looked across the dark sands quietly for a while.

"This kid. This Anna," Martha said.

"What about her?"

"I just wonder what she means when she speaks about Roscoe hurting her. She sounds like a prisoner or something. She sounds sad. Forlorn."

Rosie listened for the murmur of the tide. Like a prisoner or something. Here they were again, discussing Roscoe and Anna like they were the next-door neighbors. She sighed and flipped her cigarette out into the darkness. A psychic cage, she thought. The little girl trapped behind spectral bars. She looked at Martha and said, "I can't get a handle on any of it. I keep turning explanations over in my mind. Maybe we're catching echoes of something that happened here a long time ago between this character Roscoe and a child he somehow hurt. Know what I mean? Maybe we're listening to some kind of weird radio station. God, I can't think straight, Martha. Every time I try to rationalize this, it slips away." She paused. She rubbed her hands together. "And then that bullshit about the children. They stay. They stay. What does that mean?"

A breeze cut through the humidity suddenly, then died again. Martha said, "I don't know . . . Unless . . ."

"Unless what?"

"Unless he means to try and keep them here and . . ."

"And what?"

"Harm them . . ."

"Like how?"

But Martha didn't answer.

Rosie thought, Harm them. Harm them. She closed her eyes and wanted to believe still that they were dealing here with two separate worlds and that while one could somehow communicate with the other, could overlap it in some way, just the same it couldn't actually reach out to touch it, to change events or trespass on behavior.

She stood up and leaned against the porch rail. The breeze came back again, fluttering against her hair. Then she thought about the weird photographs and the child she'd seen and the way she'd heard her name whispered from the tide—but her thoughts ran into mazes of their own making, small labyrinths she couldn't find her way through. Turning, she looked at Martha.

"You mean he might perhaps influence them in some way?" she asked. "Make them act in a certain way?"

"I'm not sure what I mean."

That nervous edge in Martha's voice, that awful tension. She might have been biting her words off. Rosie glanced toward the beach, seeing how the sliver of light from the porch fell only a little way across the sand. And for the first time since she'd divorced Herb she felt a sudden desire for his company, for his support, his mere presence—a feeling she shoved aside as a momentary weakness. He wouldn't have been able to deal with this situation any more than she could. Just the same, despite her own better judgment, she experienced a moment of acute loneliness, a thing as sharp as the salt smell in the air. But even if Herb were here, he'd only be bitching about the fact there was no TV and how terrible it was to miss his beloved sports. Who needs him?

She turned round to face Martha again, who was sitting hunched on the steps and looking out blankly at the darkness. There was the faint doomed ticking of moths' wings against the porch light.

Rosie sat down alongside her friend.

For a long time they remained silent, like two people who have run into emotional obstacles that no vocabulary could describe or overcome. A place beyond words; an estuary beyond meaning.

"I'm sorry," Rosie said.

"What for?"

"As I remember, it was my idea to come down here for the summer. It was me and my big mouth. Me and my great ideas. I'm sorry for that, Martha."

"You? I thought I was the one who saw the ad."

Rosie shrugged. In truth, she couldn't remember now; but she knew that even if Martha had been the one to discover this place, then she, Rosie, would have been the one to follow through on the deal. I make an ass of myself with my enthusiasms, she thought. Into the Valley of Death with no regard for the feelings of others. Clumsy, forever rushing forward, never taking the time to sit down and plan things in serenity.

"I just thought it would be so perfect," she said. "The best-laid plans. You know what they say."

Martha smiled a little sadly. She patted Rosie on the knee as she stood up, stretching her arms, yawning. "I think I'll start packing now. Maybe after we leave, this whole place will just fall into the sea."

Rosie looked up at her friend. "Taking Roscoe with it, I trust."

Martha stepped inside the house.

Alone, Rosie listened to the creak of the screen door a moment. Then she rose and followed Martha indoors. As she climbed the stairs, she could hear the sounds of the kids' voices coming faintly from Lindy's room.

And she thought: How could Roscoe possibly harm them?
In a few hours they'd all be gone from this place anyhow.
In a few hours.
The thought filled her with relief.

Lindy looked at Tommy, who was sitting in the chair across the room
from the bed, his hands awkwardly placed in his lap. She tugged the
bedsheets up over her body, so that only her face was visible. She
heard herself say that she was fine, she was feeling stronger now, but
her voice didn't seem to be her own: she might have been a doll sitting
on a ventriloquist's knee, something with no mind of its own. There
was sweat all across the surface of her skin and every now and then
she felt a hot flush run through her body. Then the small room felt
stifling, suffocatingly warm.

Tommy shifted around in the chair; he was obviously uncomfortable. She watched him carefully as he glanced a little furtively around
the place, almost as if he expected to discover something revealing—
like underwear or tampons or a bra, some evidence of her femininity.
He's never been in a girl's room before, she thought. This is his first
time.

She closed her eyes a moment.

He hasn't mentioned anything about what he saw on the balcony.

Embarrassed and probably scared.

She opened her eyes, looked at him, studied the tight little curls
in his hair, the wide shoulders, the firmness of his young body. And
then she was thinking about the balcony again and how the man had
appeared to her and she felt an odd itchiness against her flesh. Something she knew she couldn't just scratch away.

"I guess we're leaving here," he said.

Leaving.

It always came back to that.

Running away.

She clenched her hands together beneath the bedsheets. "Is that
what you want?"

He laughed in an uneasy way. "Sure. Don't you?"

She didn't answer him. She stared in the direction of the balcony.
The black sky beyond. The night is empty, she thought. Bleak and
empty. There is nobody on the balcony now.

Tommy stood up and walked toward the balcony door and peered
out, tapping one foot on the floor as he did so. Why doesn't he talk

about what we saw out there, she wondered. Why doesn't he mention it?

"I'll be glad to split this place," he said. "It's just too weird around here. And I'm bored."

Bored?

Too weird?

Didn't he understand anything?

She raised herself against her pillow and watched him. And once more she felt the peculiar distance from herself, hot flashes rippling and spreading across her body, and her own voice echoing inside her head.

She lifted one hand and saw sweat glisten in the lifelines.

"I'm glad you're better," Tommy said. He smiled and it was a good, warm expression. He moved a little way toward the bed; she realized he was close enough for her to reach out and touch him if she wanted. Better, Lindy wondered. Better than what? She could feel the house reach out to touch her, filling her with a warmth she hadn't known before. And she knew, even if she had no evidence to back up her knowledge, that Roscoe was out there somewhere in the dark and the realization rippled through her in tiny circles of pleasure.

"What do you mean it's too weird here, Tommy?"

"You know. That business with the Ouija board. Other stuff."

"What other stuff?"

He shrugged. Then he sat down rather tentatively on the edge of the mattress. "Other stuff. It doesn't matter."

"Come on, Tommy. What else would you call weird?"

"The closet door in my room, for one thing. The way it opens and closes whenever it wants . . . The creepy shadow inside."

Doors. Jesus, she wasn't interested in hearing about closet doors or shadows.

"Anything else?" she asked.

"Isn't that enough?"

"What about the balcony?"

"What about it?"

Tommy, Tommy. Don't deny what you saw a little while ago.

"The man and the girl on the balcony," she said. "Why haven't you mentioned them?"

He looked puzzled. "I don't follow you."

"Come on, Tommy. You know what I mean. You were watching. You saw them. You couldn't have missed them."

He shook his head from side to side. "I didn't see any man or girl, Lindy."

She pulled herself up into a sitting position. (It's okay. He's too embarrassed still to admit it. He doesn't like to remember what he saw.) "You were walking out among the trees, Tommy. About thirty minutes ago. And you looked up at me on the balcony—"

"Right. I looked up. I saw you," he answered.

"What else did you see?"

"Nothing else. Just you. And you were sorta walking like you were in a trance or something—"

"I understand," she said patiently. "You just don't want to admit the rest of it. I can go along with that."

"Jeez, Lindy, I'm telling you the truth—"

"Tommy—" Exasperation. Why didn't he just come out with it?

He held his hands, palms outward, in the air like a traffic cop at an intersection. "I don't know anything about any man. I don't know anything about any girl. You must have been dreaming."

"I was not dreaming!"

He got up from the edge of the bed and strolled round the room.

"I was not in any trance!" she said.

She subsided against her pillow.

More of those hot rushes. More flashes.

It seemed to her that the pressure of her blood was mounting constantly, raging inside her veins. Deep in her skull there was a tiny pain, something pressing against the brain. Like the sharp touch of a scalpel. And the noise there . . . the buzzing.

"Tommy," she heard herself say. "Are you telling me the truth?"

"I swear," he replied.

She shut her eyes tightly, fiercely.

Okay, he's not lying, maybe he's being up front, maybe he's being truthful—

Then what did I see? What the hell did I see?

Roscoe and the little girl.

The little girl touching Roscoe.

The way I started to move forward toward them. Before they vanished into the mystery of the night.

And Tommy standing below, watching.

Only Tommy wasn't seeing what I saw. He wasn't seeing anything like that. Only me on the balcony. All alone.

What did that mean? That she'd been given some kind of privileged vision or something?

She felt an acute loneliness, a vague sense of despair.

She drew the bedsheets up over herself.

Her whole body was on fire now and she was sticking to the cotton.

Something created by my own fevered brain maybe.

Like a form of madness.

No, no, it hadn't been like that at all.

She'd seen Roscoe and she'd seen the girl.

Then why hadn't Tommy?

Maybe he just didn't have the vision.

Or maybe Roscoe hadn't wanted him to see.

She shut her eyes.

She felt the raging of blood inside her head.

Tommy was saying something about how she should get some sleep, about an early start in the morning, and then he was going toward the door and opening it and her vision had all the surreal, lunatic quality of a broken-down movie—awkward movements, words that were not synchronized with lip motions.

She realized she wanted him to stay.

But he was already gone and the door was shut behind him.

She gazed round the room. She thought: I've gone beyond Lindy. I've stepped into another place where Lindy has just been stripped away, skin after skin. A place in which I no longer know who I am.

A place where personality drifted as casually as starfish on slow tides.

A place where I want to be . . .

Martha folded her clothes and packed them in her suitcase. She worked quickly, as if she were conscious of a clock running down somewhere nearby. Now and then she stopped and looked out through the balcony door at the dark sky. I'm waiting for the first sign of daylight, she thought. Waiting for the darkness to break apart. When she'd finished packing, she shut the suitcase and sat for a while on the bed, smoking a cigarette. Despite the prospect of leaving, she was still tense; she knew there would be no relief until they were miles away from the beach house and Cochrane Crossing. Miles and miles away.

She could hear Tommy and Lindy talking together, a muffled sound that barely penetrated the wall. Every so often there would be a long silence and then Lindy would say something in an upraised voice and Tommy would respond. They're talking about leaving here, she thought. And Lindy still doesn't want to go.

She lay back across the bed, stubbing her cigarette in the ashtray on the bedside table, and she listened as the door of Lindy's room closed quietly; then there was the sound of Tommy coming along the landing.

He knocked very gently on her door and when she called out, "Come in," he stepped inside.

"You better start getting your stuff together, Tommy," she said. She got up from the bed and smiled at him. He was leaning against the wall, looking vaguely dejected.

"How's Lindy?" she asked.

"Okay. I guess."

"You're mumbling, Tommy. And when you mumble like that I know there's something on your mind."

He looked down at the suitcase on the floor. She watched him for a time, knowing that in certain moods it was impossible to get any information out of him until he was ready to communicate.

He raised his face and looked around the bedroom. "This dump," he said. "That's all it is. This crummy dump."

"I know, I know, Tommy."

"I can't wait—"

"Then you better go start packing, kid."

He didn't move. He just stood against the wall, reluctant. He doesn't want to go to his room, she thought. He doesn't want to be alone.

She said, "I'm not looking for anything neat and orderly, kid. Just stuff all your things in your bag. That shouldn't be so hard."

"Yeah. Okay." He pushed himself away from the wall and opened the bedroom door. He peered out at the landing, then turned to her with a pale smile on his face. "I'll go pack . . ."

When he stepped out, he didn't close the door behind him. He left it wide, as if he needed the security of knowing she wasn't shut away from him. She watched him go along the landing to his own room; he didn't close that door either. Then she heard him clumping around noisily and there was something so comforting, so mundane, about his clumsiness that made it difficult to give credence to the things that had happened in this house.

She began to pick up her personal items from the dressing table. A bottle of cologne, hairbrush and comb, hand mirror. She tucked them inside a plastic bag. Then she opened drawers, making sure there wasn't anything she'd overlooked. There were things she could easily just leave behind—Kleenexes, a couple of hairpins, inconsequential things. The detritus of a vacation.

Some vacation, she thought.

Some goddam holiday.

She sighed, returned to the bed, sat down.

Tomorrow—

When she heard the sound, it was almost inaudible.

It was so distant, so quiet, that at first she thought it was coming from a long way off, from a place she couldn't locate.

Then she turned her face toward the balcony door.

The child was standing there, one hand upraised, her fingernails lightly scratching the glass. Standing there, watching, her yellow hair hanging down to her shoulders and her face without expression. She was wearing a dress that might have been fashionable in the early nineteen-twenties, a white taffeta thing.

Martha could not move.

She gazed at the girl's face and she thought, Anna, this is Anna.

The fingernails continued to scratch and then the small mouth began to open and close, forming silent words beyond the glass.

Help. Me. Please. Help. Me.

Martha shut her eyes a second and told herself it was only a dream, a bad dream, an experience related to all the tensions she'd felt recently, it would go away when she opened her eyes, but even without sight she could still hear the repetitive scratching. When she looked again the girl was still watching her. And the tiny mouth was still opening and closing, the eyes unblinking.

She needs you, Martha thought.

She needs your help, she wants you.

Martha stood up.

And then the horror went through her.

It went through her like a long chill finger of ice, burrowing into her bones, her blood, her being.

It was the smile, the sudden smile.

The abrupt flare of light in the eyes.

This wasn't a child she was staring at.

This wasn't an innocent, helpless face.

The light in the eyes was a malevolent thing, like the flicker of flame thrown by a black candle in a sacrosanct place. And the smile —dear Christ, the smile wasn't the expression of any child: it was old and it was corrupt.

It was secretive and used.

There was cunning in it. And mischief.

There was a quality of evil.

This creature.

This creature didn't need anyone's help.

Martha swayed slightly. She felt her stomach turn over and her legs become weak. She had to clutch the edge of the dressing table for support because she could feel the smile press against her like an unbearable light.

Don't look at it. Don't bring yourself to look at it again.

But she did.

This time she saw only the black glass and the starless expanse of night beyond it.

No child.

No little girl.

No—

Body.

23

VOICES
June 21

When Rosie had surveyed the mess in her bedroom and made an attempt to get her stuff together—packing camera equipment, shoving clothes inside her ancient battered suitcase (a relic of her honeymoon, that timeless moment in Florida when Herb had been deceptively romantic—bitter thoughts)—she realized she was fatigued. She wanted nothing more than to stretch out on the bed and yield to sleep, but she had the feeling that sleep wouldn't quite cut it, as if giving up consciousness would be dangerous.

Giving up the drawbridges of awareness.

Letting yourself slip away.

Dreams, she thought. Nightmares.

The sleeping terror.

And no control. None.

She had to check on Lindy anyhow. Earlier, she'd heard Tommy come out of her daughter's room and go inside his own, and now there was the noise of him slinging his belongings around; the boy had all the subtlety of the United States Cavalry.

Rosie stepped out on the landing.

There was an abrupt silence from Tommy's room, the door of which was open. Rosie didn't move for a moment; she glanced at the light flowing from Martha's bedroom.

Another open door.

She gazed in the direction of the stairs. The kitchen light was burning below. She half-expected to see a shadow cross the doorway down there or hear the flimsy squeak of the plastic indicator trek over the Ouija board.

But there was nothing.

Turning, she moved to the door of Lindy's room.

She knocked, received no answer, twisted the handle, went inside.

Her first impression: the balcony door was open and the sea breeze was making the curtain shake, which gave her the odd impression of ectoplasm manufactured at a séance.

Second, Lindy was asleep. Hands clasped together on top of the bedsheets, eyes shut, regular breathing.

Rosie walked across the room, lingered over the child a moment; then she closed the balcony door. The night air had become chill and a little damp. She sat on the bed, looking at Lindy's face. The girl was pale, paler than Rosie liked to see her—but the loss of blood would account for that. She reached out and stroked Lindy's hands. Poor kid, she thought. Welcome to the wonderful world of womanhood. Welcome to that world of inconvenient internal plumbing. But we'll soon be gone from this place and we can take you to a doctor and everything will be fine.

When she rose, she went out to the landing, closing the door quietly behind her. She moved in the direction of her own room. Halfway there, she paused.

It's not the best time to feel thirsty, she told herself.

It's not the best time to have a sudden urge for iced water.

She licked her dry lips and went to the stairs, passing the open door of Tommy's bedroom and glancing at the boy, who had his back turned toward her. She started to descend, staring at the rectangle of light from the kitchen below. Godammit, I'm thirsty, and no ghost is going to scare me out of getting myself a glass of water, for Christ's sake. She went down the rest of the steps quickly and entered the kitchen, which had the appearance of a stage set awaiting the arrival of actors to give it any meaning. The dull light bulb and the table with the Ouija board and the doll on the window ledge and the flat, unreflective surface of the old refrigerator: unreal, lacking a certain quality of depth or texture.

Rosie crossed to the sink and filled a glass with water. From the freezer compartment of the refrigerator, she prised a couple of ice cubes loose. She dropped them in the water and drank hurriedly. I'm waiting for something to happen, she thought. Waiting for the next spectral episode. Expecting it. (Show me your next trick, Roscoe, your next merry jape from the other side.)

But there was nothing. Just the banality of this kitchen.

Even the doll on the ledge seemed featureless, mundane.

It was as if the spirits had vacated the premises, moved on to bring their own special brand of enlightenment to another place.

She put her glass back in the sink.

When she left the kitchen, she headed for the stairs.

She stopped abruptly when she heard the sound of her name being whispered from behind.

Rosie . . . Rosie . . .

Don't look back, she told herself. Don't turn around. Pretend you didn't hear a goddam thing and go back to your room. She continued to climb.

Rosie . . . Rosie . . .

The children stay. The women go . . .

Two voices now, two whispers in unison.

She moved along the landing to her own room, stepped inside, shut the door behind her. The whispers had stopped. She stood in the middle of the room, her hands on her hips, and she thought: Maybe we should leave before daylight.

Maybe we should all get out of here as fast as we can.

She yawned, struggled with her weariness, then went on packing.

Tommy sat on the edge of the bed and stared at the closet door.

He had gathered his belongings together and they lay in a pile in the middle of the room. Clothes, fishing poles (so much for fishing, he thought), assorted shoes. Sooner or later, he'd just stuff everything he could into his bag and haul it down to the car. But right now, as he watched the closed door, he was uneasy. He expected it to open at any moment, the way it usually did, but it was shut tight and that fact bothered him; he had the weird feeling that if he drew the closet open he'd see something he didn't want to.

Maybe he'd spend the rest of the night on the living-room sofa. He stretched out on the bed and gazed at the ceiling, wriggling his toes, cracking his knuckles. Boy, he thought, he'd have a story to tell Norm when they got back to Syracuse, something that would really curl his friend's hair. The prospect amused him; Norm wouldn't believe any of it because he was pretty cynical in his own way but it would be a damn good story anyhow.

He sat upright.

He was conscious of a faint sound coming from the closet.

A rustling of some kind.

Quiet and regular, like a rodent chewing up old papers.

It's no rodent, he thought. Whatever it is, it's no rodent.

You could go open the closet yourself—

Except you don't have that kind of courage, do you?

Then he was thinking about Lindy. What had she been mumbling about before? A man and a girl on the balcony, something like that. Then she'd looked pretty wild, a crazy kind of expression on her face. He turned his thoughts away from her. The sound from the closet had stopped now. Go on, he told himself.

Go open the door. Get the whole thing over with.

He didn't move.

Something else had seized his attention, a different kind of noise. A tapping against the glass of the balcony door.

He turned his face, looked at the drawn curtains.

He stood up very slowly and it seemed to him that he was stuck in a place between the closet and the balcony, like a donkey that can't decide between two carrots.

He shrugged, as if he might somehow cast off his fears with this simple gesture, and then he went toward the balcony door.

Where he paused, his hand stretched out toward the drapes.

She had been dreaming her own death.

Walking the moonlit sands, seeming to drift very gently across the surface of the beach, she had stumbled over her own body. It lay face down, inert, all life gone out of it. When she'd reached down to turn the body over, she'd recoiled at once.

The face was covered with scavenging crabs, tiny sea creatures savaging her eyes, razoring her lips, clawing at her flesh.

And then the whole thing changed quite suddenly and she was standing on the balcony, no longer certain whether this was a continuation of the dream or if she'd just awakened.

Roscoe was standing at the end of the balcony, watching her.

He gave the impression of being extremely tall, powerful, large enough to block the width of the balcony and the night sky beyond.

She stood very still and waited for him to come toward her, but he didn't move.

She could feel the breeze blow though her long hair and move under her robe. Cool, luxurious, it caressed her thighs and pubic hair and rose upward to her breasts.

She took a couple of steps forward.

The breeze died away. When it did, she could hear Roscoe's voice; it wasn't a voice like any other she'd ever heard because it seemed to come from a place deep within her own brain.

A dream voice.

I have been waiting for you, it said.

I have been waiting for you a long time.

She shut her eyes, concentrating until the voice filled her, until it expanded from her brain and ran, as if with her blood, through her entire body. She felt that she was dwindling, diminishing, shrinking away to a point where she would cease to exist.

When she looked again, she realized she must have walked a little farther along the balcony because she was closer to the figure now and she could make out every detail of his face—the fine bones, the dark shadows under the eyes, the high forehead which appeared to have the fragility of an eggshell.

She raised her arms and held her hands forward.

You will stay here with me forever, the voice said.

She trembled. What was there in that word "forever" which made her feel a kind of apprehensive longing?

Forever was both life and death.

She felt as if she might be falling from a great height. Falling into a darkness whose contents she could not even begin to guess. I want to fall, she thought.

I want to fall forever.

She was trembling again.

Trembling and still going closer to the man.

You and the boy, the voice said.

You and Tommy.

And he raised one finger and pointed toward the door of Tommy's room.

The breeze came back off the shore, whipping round her robe and blowing it open. She stared at Roscoe's hand, at the finger indicating Tommy's door.

You know what you need to do, the voice said.

She closed her eyes once more. This feeling—it was like lying underwater, floating in warm liquid. She imagined hypnosis would feel this way.

You've always known.

She looked at Roscoe, whose eyes moved all across her body.

And then he was stepping backward from her.

Gone. Suddenly gone.

As if he'd never been there at all.

But then she heard the creak of a branch from the grove below and she knew, without looking, that Anna and Roscoe were down there in the darkness, watching her, waiting for her to go inside Tommy's room, waiting for her to choose.

No, there wasn't a choice involved.

She knew what she had to do. What she had to do to please Roscoe. As if pleasing Roscoe were the only thing that mattered now in her life.

She stopped outside the door of the boy's room and tapped her fingers on the glass pane. Then she waited.

24

THE CLOSET
June 21

She had this weird expression on her face and for a moment Tommy thought she was probably sick, fevered. He watched her step in from the balcony and he couldn't help but notice the fact that her robe hung open as if she just didn't care how much he got to see. Embarrassed, he looked away. What the hell was that look on her face? Like she wasn't quite at home. A shingle loose on the rooftop. A card missing from the deck. Uneasily, he turned and looked back at her. She was gazing at him in the manner of somebody who isn't really seeing the very thing they're looking at.

"Lindy . . ." and his throat, God, his throat was dry.

She didn't say a word. She moved toward the bed and stood staring down at it. Didn't she even hear the faint sound coming from the closet? If she did, she didn't acknowledge it.

"Lindy," he said again.

She looked at him in a penetrating way. And a bell went off in the back of his head and he realized what she'd come here for and he felt clumsy, silly, impaled on his own ignorance: Jesus, he and Norm had talked about something like this happening and fantasized about what they'd do with a girl who came on to them really strongly, except it had never happened to either of them—until now; and now he didn't know how to behave.

"You're supposed to be in bed." Why doesn't she say something? Why does she just keep looking at me with that secretive expression on her face? And the noise from the closet: doesn't she hear it? She's crazy, he thought. She's fallen out of her tree. He looked at the way her robe hung open and he could see the shadow of her pubic hair and he felt himself start to get excited. But this wasn't something he could experience in isolation, this wasn't centerfold pictures and the privacy of your own bedroom and a box of Kleenex on the bedside table, this was something else altogether. He cleared his throat and looked down at the floor and he said her name again and this time his voice was almost entirely gone. But she still wasn't talking. Still just looking. He wanted suddenly to hide.

Then he remembered his bedroom door was open and he thought about how either Rosie or Martha might go past at any moment, which would be a total embarrassment, so he moved across the floor and shut it very quietly. What am I supposed to do, he wondered, trying to remember the sex books he'd read and the pamphlets that were sometimes passed around in school and the explicit pornography he sometimes sneaked a look at in certain kinds of bookstores. Gone. Everything had slipped his mind. A complete blank, for Christ's sake.

He looked at the girl.

Wet dreams, he thought. This is something you've always pro-duced inside your mind. This particular moment.

She had her hands placed flat against her stomach.

"Tommy," she said. Her voice was weird, melodic, as if she thought the sound of his name musical.

"I . . ." He stopped. He felt strangely awkward, as if he'd somehow become crippled, stunted, unable to coordinate any of his movements or speech. But he couldn't take his eyes away from her. She moved slowly toward the bed and slipped the robe from her shoulders and let it drop to the floor, then she lay down and smiled at him.

"Tommy," she said again, lifting a hand toward him.

He didn't move. A paralysis had seized him. Even the odd noises from the closet didn't bother him now because all his attention was centered on the fact of this girl and the insecurity he felt about adequacy. He looked at the balcony door, then the walls of the room, then down at his mountain of belongings on the floor. I want her to get up and leave.

"Lindy . . . You're not well . . ."

"I'm fine, Tommy. I'm perfectly fine." It's this place, he thought —it's driving us all mad. It's like we stepped inside the boundaries of hell by accident.

"Come and sit with me," she said.

He took a step forward, paused. There was a terrible, tight knot inside him. She had her face turned toward him.

"It's nothing to be afraid of," she said.

"I'm not afraid."

She smiled. "Yes. You are."

He had a sudden, awful thought: This isn't Lindy.

This is somebody else.

A stranger in Lindy's body.

Like a possession. Something like that. And she seemed older to him than ever before, more sophisticated, smarter than anything he could ever aspire to. He found himself looking at the crumpled robe on the floor, scared to look at her, scared in case she'd changed her appearance.

"Tommy," she said.

He didn't look.

"You want me, don't you?" she said. "I can tell."

He raised his face and looked at her long red hair spread on the pillow. This is wrong, he thought, it's all wrong—it's like going inside your geometry class and finding that all the angles in your textbook have become curves. A world out of shape.

"Come over here," she said.

He moved in the fashion of someone controlled by a force beyond him.

When he reached the bed he looked down at her.

Her arms were raised in the air toward him.

He sat down beside her and felt a hand fall against his thigh.

"What if somebody comes in?" he said.

"Nobody will. I promise you, Tommy."

She took his hand and laid it against her breasts.

It was a feeling he'd never quite known before, something he had only ever guessed at; it was a mixture of things—wonder, alarm, a sense of being offered a great gift he wasn't sure how to accept. He moved his fingertips around the nipple and closed his eyes. This isn't really happening, he thought. This isn't really happening to me.

She placed one hand between his legs and as soon as he felt her undoing the zip of his jeans he thought the top of his head was going to explode. He slid down, his eyes still shut, until he was pressed against her. Then he felt the chill air of the room touch the tip of his penis, which she held in her hand now. She was moving her wrist very slowly back and forth. He heard himself say: Please . . .

"Come inside me, Tommy. Inside me."

She shifted herself under him, guiding him.

He had no control, no awareness of himself as a person, as if his senses had quite abruptly departed. With his eyes shut, he realized that nothing existed except for this small area between their thighs, that his brain had dissolved and reassembled itself there. He heard her moan and then he felt her fingernails sliding under his shirt and digging into the flesh around his spine. And when he felt himself come, he thought he was riding the great dip of some giant roller coaster, spinning and revolving, his heart thrown out into space and just left there in orbit—

Silence. Silence then.

He raised his face and opened his eyes and he looked at her.

Gasping, he pulled himself away, struggled to free himself from her hands.

It wasn't Lindy's face.

Or if it was, it had changed.

Changed beyond recognition.

He rolled sideways, unable to breathe.

Unable to breathe, appalled by what he saw, disgusted.

The claws of those tiny creatures were digging into the surface of her skin, their pincers tearing at her flesh, scissoring her face and tugging bloody pieces of her away, eyes and lips and the tip of the nose—

Jesus Christ.

Jesus—

Those crabs. The way they smelled, like stagnant seawater.

The way they slashed the girl's face, time and again, over and over, cutting and digging, peeling flesh back from the bone structure, digging and digging ever deeper into the soft core of the eyes and scavenging the skull beyond and boring deep into the brain and crawling through the red strands of hair that were now soaked with blood. And then he could feel their hard bodies and their pincers touch the backs of his own hands and nip at his flesh, seeking his veins, his life—

He swung round to look at her again.

She was staring at him.

She was staring at him, and the sea creatures had gone. Gone from her face and scalp, gone too from his own hands.

Gone.

Evaporated just like that.

"Tommy?" she said.

He couldn't speak.

What the hell had he just seen? What had he imagined?

He put his hand out and touched her lightly on the cheek, as if to be sure. The surface of her skin was smooth.

But there was something else different. The look of bewilderment on her face. The expression of sheer astonishment.

"Tommy?" she asked again. She sat quickly upright, staring at him with a look of accusation on her face. "What the hell are you doing?" Before he could even think of an answer, she'd become conscious of her own nakedness and reached for the bedsheets, pulling them hastily over her body. "What have you done . . ."

He turned his face away again. She doesn't know. She doesn't remember. She has no idea of what happened. He was suddenly ashamed.

A sick girl, he thought. A sick girl with no memory of anything.

"Did you . . . did we . . ." Her voice faltered. There was the hint of a sob behind her words, a catch in her throat. "We did. I know we did. I can feel it . . ."

"It wasn't my fault," he said.

She was getting out of the bed now, draped in the sheet and

looking on the floor for her robe. Which was when he was conscious of the blood on the bedsheets. A huge spreading stain that he attempted to cover up at once.

"It wasn't my fault," he said once more.

He watched her, but she wasn't looking at him. Instead, her attention had been drawn toward the door of the closet. She was gazing at it in a puzzled way.

Tommy looked, listened. The noise from behind the door was growing louder, more persistent. It's going to spring open. I know it is. I can feel it.

He looked at the flat surface, which suddenly suggested to him the gateway to quite another dimension, a place where solid things were insubstantial and shadows had weight, and strange apparitions might crawl across the face of a girl the way those crabs had done, tearing like that, ripping and clawing.

He glanced at Lindy, but she wasn't paying him any attention. Instead, she was moving toward the closet.

"Don't," Tommy said. "Don't open the door."

She paused in front of it.

It opened, as if it had been blown by a violent wind.

It opened wide.

The child hung there from a rope, her arms limp at her sides, her tongue protruding, her white dress around her like a small shroud and her yellow hair flowing over her shoulders. The child hung there, spinning very slowly, going round and round in a macabre circle of death.

Tommy stared at the darkened lips. The sockets that contained no eyes. Stared and stared, motionless.

And Lindy, covering her face with her hands, screamed.

One sharp, dying sound that filled the bedroom before it faded away.

The closet door closed again.

Slowly this time, like the curtain coming down at the end of a play.

25

POINT OF DEPARTURE
June 21

When Martha pushed the door of Tommy's room open, she could still hear the echo of the scream inside her head.

Then she was aware of several things all at once—Tommy staring at her, Lindy standing in the middle of the room with her hands across her face, Rosie hurrying along the landing, asking, "What's wrong? What's wrong?"

Martha looked at her son.

He glanced at her, turned his face away in a guilty manner.

Some rooms, Martha thought—

Some rooms retain diminishing echoes of the things that have recently happened in them. Violence, sex—fragments that hung in the air, elusive but tangible just the same. She looked a moment at Lindy, at the open robe, the small breasts, and she thought, I know what happened in this room.

It's here all around me. I can feel it.

Rosie had her arm around Lindy's shoulder and was leading her out to the balcony, making small noises of concern.

Tommy raised his face and stared at the closet door.

It isn't just the goddam closet door, is it, Martha? It isn't just that. And she felt empty all at once, as if all the possible reactions she might have had to a situation like this one had simply flown out of her. She went toward the bed and sat down beside her son, and closing her eyes, retreating, she tried to create a picture of Tommy and Lindy—but there were no images, no shapes inside her head. What do you do in a situation like this? How are you supposed to respond? Goddammit. These two kids.

Two kids.

She gazed round the room and thought, It's a haunted place.

Haunted. An innocence lost.

She was filled with a sudden sadness, a sense of emotional dislocation. Tommy. Lindy. Two kids, for God's sake.

She let her eyes rest on the bedsheets, observing the streak of blood already drying on white cotton. Then she reached for Tommy's hand and held it, while she struggled for something to say.

The boy said, "I didn't ask her to come in here. I didn't invite her or anything. She just came inside . . ."

Blood on a bedsheet. A tiny hieroglyphic of betrayal. But who has betrayed whom? She rubbed the back of the kid's hand with her fingertips and wondered how far and how deep this godforsaken house had reached into the souls of these children.

She looked toward the balcony where Rosie was hugging her daughter in silence.

The house, Martha thought. This place. You can blame this terrible sea house for what has happened. The way it touches you, the way it embraces you and tries to frighten you. She shivered: this black place, located somewhere on the far horizons of a terrible night—it's touched us all. And suddenly she resented Rosie, resented her for her earlier reluctance to leave. If they'd gone before now, then this would not have happened.

Tommy said, "Then she screamed when the closet door opened and . . ."

"What happened? What did you see?"

Tommy looked down at the floor. "It doesn't matter . . ."

"Tell me, Tommy."

"We saw this kid . . . A young girl . . ."

A young girl, Martha thought. And she remembered the girl scratching against the glass of her door and the way she'd felt then, as if what she had been looking at was something more corrupt than she could define.

Corruption.

That's what reaches out and clutches your heart in this house. That's what touches these kids. She glanced once more at the blood on the bedsheet, then she pulled a blanket over the stain. She placed the palms of her hands against the sides of Tommy's face and looked into his eyes and she tried to see the uncertain child locked inside his expression, tried to see the child with whom she was familiar, the one she loved—and it seemed to her that, momentarily, her kid was lost and had been replaced by a stranger.

Then Tommy said, "I'm sorry, sorry . . ."

That was Tommy, she thought. All of Tommy contained in a couple of words and an expression of awkwardness. The Tommy she knew. Her son.

Now Rosie was coming back inside the room and Martha felt a curious reluctance to look at her friend directly, as if what had happened in this bedroom had somehow created a fissure in their relationship. Rosie, her face angular and pale, waved an arm in the air and said, "We can discuss . . . We can discuss all this later. Right now, I've got one damn good suggestion to make." She paused: something in her eyes, Martha thought, some little light of hurt. How could your son do this to my daughter? How how how?

"I suggest we get the hell out of here immediately," Rosie went on. "I don't care if we have to leave things behind. Let's get the hell out."

Martha rose from the bed, nodding. "It can't be too soon." An understatement, she thought. A perfect understatement. "I'll go grab what I can."

She moved toward the landing and Rosie came after her. The two women stared at one another for several seconds.

"Our kids," Rosie said. "Our kids, Martha."

Martha felt limp. "I don't know what to say."

"Oh, Christ." And Rosie reached out and put her arms around Martha, drawing her close and holding her tight. "Our own kids . . . I don't blame them, Martha. I can't blame Tommy and I can't blame Lindy." Silence. Then, in a voice close to tears, Rosie went on. "It's this house. I blame this fucking house and whatever lives here!"

Martha was silent for a while. She could feel her friend's heartbeat against her own chest as they hugged.

"I know, I know," she said eventually. And she did: even as she stood on the landing, she could feel the house slither around her, as though it were made, not of wood and glass, but of some viscous substance. She could feel its pressure against her and she thought once more of the child she'd seen . . . Then she stepped back from Rosie, saying, "I better get my stuff together."

Rosie smiled in a pale way. "Quickly."

"Yeah. Quickly."

Rosie turned and went back through Tommy's room toward the balcony, barely glancing at the boy as she passed. She could see her daughter standing outside and something in the way she stood—the ragged manner in which she leaned against the balcony rail—caught at her heart. She wanted to sweep Lindy up and carry her away and make believe that nothing had happened, that everything was as it had been back home. My child, she thought. My baby. She stepped outside and cursed this wretched house, cursed the decision that had ever brought them here in the first place. You can't go back, though, Rosie, you can't turn the pages of the calendar back to a point where a certain innocence might have existed. She placed her arm around Lindy's waist, clutched the girl against her, then led her along the balcony to the door of her own bedroom. I will not let you out of my sight until we leave this house. I will not lose you to whatever powers exist here—

"We're going, Lindy," she said. "We're leaving here. Right now." And she was talking slowly, the way she would have done to a small child. "We're taking a few things with us, essential things, then we're going to get into the car and drive."

Dumbly, the girl nodded.

Rosie thought: She hasn't said a word about anything that happened between her and Tommy. Nothing but silence, withdrawal. Suddenly, Rosie could feel moisture in her eyes. Small, quiet tears. She rubbed her eyelids with the backs of her hands and then she steered Lindy inside the bedroom, making her sit down on the bed.

The girl, her hands idle in her lap, stared at the balcony door.

Rosie kissed her gently on the top of her head, then looked round the room. She was tempted just to leave everything and go, just to forget her possessions and carry the girl down to the car. But she needed the camera and the photographic equipment and at least some of her clothes.

She began to sift her belongings quickly, glancing now and again at Lindy; and she was struck by the sudden realization that the girl was drifting farther and farther away, that her eyes were directed to some inner point, a place deep within her own skull. What is she looking at? What is the kid remembering? Jesus, the absence of light in those eyes and the lack of expression on the face. (Trauma, Rosie thought. And she recalled the streaks of blood on Tommy's bed and the sad, guilty look on the boy's face.)

I'll make you whole again, Lindy.

I'll take you to a place where you'll forget everything that happened in this house.

I'll take you away from the evil.

Sunlight and greenery. No beaches and no ocean.

Then she thought: Move, just move, take what you can and go.

As you should have done long ago. But back then you were impaled on your own goddam bravado. ("I'm not a quitter." That's what you said then. Oh, Christ, you should have quit.) I'll change, she told herself. I'll be a different person.

She stacked camera equipment and dragged it toward the door. She realized as she did so that she'd have to come back inside the house for the rest of what she wanted to keep—but how could she haul this shit down to the wagon and leave Lindy here alone?

No.

It wasn't the safe thing to do.

So she opened her door and called along the landing to Martha, who emerged from her own room.

"Will you stay in here with Lindy while I make a trip to the car?" Rosie asked.

"Sure I will." Martha's voice was flat, expressionless.

Rosie dragged her equipment onto the landing. Flat, expressionless, she thought. What we need here is a sense of life, of vitality, not of death. And she understood the message from the board now. She could see it clearly.

The children stay.

She understood the sense in which the kids would always stay here, trapped in a ghostly memory that no amount of living would ever finally bury.

Ensnared here, in this awful house by the sea.

She watched Martha go inside the room to sit with Lindy, then she gathered up her equipment and moved laboriously toward the stairs. When she made it outside, she staggered toward the wagon, opened the tailgate and stashed the stuff inside. Breathing heavily, she leaned against the vehicle for a moment and looked through the grove of trees. Silent, empty, filled with darkness.

Then she raised her face and looked up toward the balcony.

She realized, as she saw the lights in those upstairs rooms, that she wanted very badly to cry—but knew only too well that she wasn't going to because she wouldn't give Roscoe, whose presence she knew was close, always close, any further satisfaction.

She thought: I have given him his last, his only gift.

And it was the only one I had to give.

Tommy went downstairs slowly, then stepped inside the kitchen. He glanced at the Ouija board as he moved toward the cupboard. His hands were trembling and he couldn't make them stop, like they had lives of their own, dictated to by a brain that wasn't entirely his.

He opened the cupboard and took out the bottle of Jack Daniel's.

He raised it to his lips and sipped quickly. The liquid seared his tongue and burned his throat but he was drinking it only because he had to get his hands to stay still.

He stuck the bottle away again, and as he struggled with the nausea that rose up inside him, he pressed his face flat against the cupboard door.

He felt bad, low, depressed. It didn't matter what had happened between him and the girl, it didn't make a damn bit of difference— even if the possibility of such a thing happening had been something he and Norm had talked about frequently, as if they were making bets about who would get laid first. It just didn't matter to him at all.

He could feel a tightness in his stomach and a strange throbbing sensation in his throat. The girl hadn't been Lindy. It hadn't been Lindy in any sense. It hadn't been the good-looking girl with the long red hair and the slim body. Someone else. Only he wasn't sure who. And he thought about the crabs crawling across her face and the girl hanging in the narrow space of the closet and he wanted to throw up, throw everything up, the sea and the season, the sands and the dune grass, the hauntings.

He clenched his hands together and pounded the cupboard door with his tight fists, then stopped. You're going back home, he thought. We're all going home.

If we ever get out of this place.

Alive.

There was a tense little pain in the center of his chest, as if something small were eating away at him inside.

He turned back to face the table.

The plastic gizmo at the center of the board was beginning to move.

He stared at it, wanting to turn away, not wanting to look and read the words that were spelled out—but unable to avoid the sight of the thing moving of its own accord across the board.

It was a simple message.

A message he wasn't sure he understood.

It read

ANNA

LOVES

ROSCOE

HAHAHAHAHAHAHAHAHA

He raised his hand and brought it down swift and hard on the indicator, which bent beneath his blow and went skittering toward the floor.

Then he stepped quickly out of the kitchen and went up to get his luggage from his room.

Lindy could feel the woman stroking the back of her hand and she had a sensation of being smothered, as if she were locked in some small airless space. She glanced quickly at the woman and although it seemed to her that the other person was familiar, just the same she couldn't attach a name to the face. It began with M, she knew that much, but the rest of it was lost to her. There was a sympathetic smile and a certain concern in the eyes and it was a good face—

Lindy stared straight ahead at the open door of the bedroom.

She thought: This house is altered now. This place is changed.

And she imagined herself drifting through all the rooms of the house, through the history of this place, her face made pale by the tiny flames of kerosene lamps.

Somewhere a piano was being played. A child's fingers hitting the keys with the solemnity of someone practicing. One single melancholic note after another.

She was standing on the landing next, looking down toward the kitchen.

Roscoe sat at the kitchen table, a deck of cards laid out in front of him. He turned them over in an idle way. Once he raised his face and looked toward the stairs, but he didn't seem to see her. Even as she descended, he wasn't aware of her.

When she reached the bottom step, she paused. Across the living room she could see the girl on the piano stool, the yellow hair hanging down her back. The child struck the keys a few more times and then, bringing her fingers down in one crashing chord, she slipped from the stool and moved toward the kitchen. The kerosene lamps flickered across the ceiling as a hard wind blew round the frame of the house. (The furniture, she thought. Why did the furniture look so different, so old? It wasn't the house she knew. But it was. It was all familiar to her.)

Lindy watched the girl step inside the kitchen and stand at the table, where Roscoe was still turning the cards over and over.

Something is going to happen here.

Something sad, unbearable.

Something inevitable.

The child leaned forward and kissed the man on the side of his face. He responded by clutching the small hand and pressing it to his chest, as if in the hope that the touch might somehow soothe away a pain he felt inside. And there was pain, there was something raw and hurt in all of this. Now the man picked up the child and placed her on his lap and they held each other for a long time and what Lindy thought of suddenly was love—she could feel it in the air all around her, a stifling, choking thing that seemed to her more of a prison than a delight.

Doomed love.

A terrible love.

The man set the child down again and looked at her for a long time. From the pocket of his jacket he removed a handkerchief and touched her eyelids with it. Then the handkerchief fluttered to the floor.

Now there were sounds from outside the house. The whinnying of horses and the harsh upraised voices of men and, pressed against the drapes, the thin glare of lantern lights.

Something bad, Lindy thought.

Footsteps along the porch, poundings at the door.

The child stepped slowly out of the kitchen and moved toward the stairs, passing Lindy as she did so. She doesn't see me, doesn't know I'm here.

Lindy turned and watched the girl go upstairs.

She went inside one of the bedrooms, shut the door. And there was a sad finality in the way she did so, an awful resignation.

The voices outside were growing harder, more obscene, and the hammering at the door was heavier now.

Roscoe seemed unaware of it all. He gathered his playing cards together and made a neat pile in the center of the table and then he reached down for the fallen handkerchief and tucked it inside his pocket.

When he had done this, he sighed.

He was motionless for a time.

He reached inside his pocket and removed a pistol, which he turned over in his hands.

Then, just as the windows broke and the room was filled with shards of sharp glass, he opened his mouth and pushed the pistol between his lips.

"Lindy," Martha said. "Lindy, you're trembling. Here. Let me wrap you in something warm," and she pulled a blanket from the bed and draped it round the shivering girl's shoulders.

It didn't seem to help.

Martha looked at the kid's face.

Wherever she was, she wasn't in this bedroom.

She was absent.

The eyes were lifeless.

An absence of light in the pupils.

Dead eyes.

And she realized she had seen something similar to this look before.

The balcony. The terrible child.

"Lindy?"

She might not have asked her question: there was no response.

She raised her hand and, very gently, touched the side of the kid's face and what she wondered, with a feeling of utter despair, was whether the girl, the Lindy she knew, was ever going to come back from the place she had traveled to now.

26

THE LAST TERROR
June 21

Tommy slung his stuff in the back of the wagon and watched as his mother and Rosie helped Lindy down from the porch. She looked like she couldn't stand up without support. Her knees buckled and her head hung backward and after a while he just couldn't look anymore. He went round to the front of the car and leaned against the hood, staring down through the grove of trees. People snap some-times, he thought. They just break inside. He swallowed hard and wondered if he'd contributed to her condition, but then decided he hadn't because she'd been acting weird for days . . . Just the same, he felt miserable.

He looked upward at the sky. Dawn was beginning to appear, little slits of gray through all the darkness, like some huge venetian blind was opening very slowly. He heard the women open the side door of the wagon and then Rosie, whispering to her daughter, was helping Lindy get in. He still couldn't look. He didn't have the courage sud-denly. And a sense of shame burned inside his head.

"Tommy," Martha said. "Did you load your stuff?"

"Yeah," he answered.

He glanced back at the house. It seemed that every window in the dump was lit. It looked like something blazing away on the edges of darkness. A bonfire, he thought. That joint deserves to be torched. He cracked his knuckles. I'll forget it all. The whole summer. I'll let it slip out of my mind and never think about it again and never mention anything about it to anybody. I'll just blow it right out of my memory.

He looked through the trees again.

There was something in the far distance. A sound of some kind, like a slow humming, a quiet vibration. It came and went, came back again. Listening, tilting his head in concentration, he wondered: What now? What else could happen now?

From behind, he heard Rosie say that she had one last thing to pick up from the house, then she was moving toward the porch and he could hear it creak as she stepped up. Don't go back in there, he thought.

It's stupid to go back inside.

Then he turned his face toward the black highway, straining to catch the humming sound he had heard before.

Rosie climbed the stairs to her bedroom.

When she reached the landing, she paused. The emptiness of this house, she realized, was an illusion. Only the human inhabitants had gone. The others remained.

And she could sense them around her.

She could feel their presence as if they were standing in wait just behind closed doors. Waiting to appear, to spring.

Don't think about it now.

You're leaving.

You're leaving and you'll be safe and Lindy is going to be well.

There's only the camera to get.

She stepped into her bedroom.

The camera bag was lying on the bed. She went toward it and picked it up, slinging it quickly across her shoulder.

When she turned round to leave the room, she saw the letters on the wall, written there in bold black crayon by a hand that must have undergone some enormous effort to write such a spidery message. She stared at the words, tried to shut her mind down, tried to tell herself that in a matter of minutes this house would be relegated to some special dungeon of her own private history and locked away forever.

But the words seemed to pulsate even as she looked at them.

ROSCOE

NEEDS

LINDY

Go, she told herself.

Just get the hell out of here.

And do it now!

She moved to the landing.

When she reached the bottom of the stairs, she saw the message again, scrawled across the living-room wall.

ROSCOE

NEEDS

LINDY

No, she thought.

You don't get Lindy.

She rushed across the living room and, expecting the front door to lock in front of her at any second, made it onto the porch and stumbled toward the car.

In time to see a slow-moving procession of lights streaming along the highway.

Moving with all the ponderous grace of a funeral cortege.

Moving inexorably toward this sea house.

White lights, dark highway. A chain of lights coming monotonously through the night.

Martha, turning up the collar of her denim jacket, watched them for a moment. Then Rosie was standing alongside her.

"What is it?" Rosie asked.

"I don't know," Martha said. "But I don't like the idea of visitors from Cochrane Crossing at this particular time."

"And it's too late for a welcoming committee . . ." Rosie's voice trailed away.

Martha studied the lamps of the vehicles.

She felt menace in the sight of those lights.

She turned to look at Rosie. "It doesn't make sense. I can't understand why anybody would be coming out here . . ."

"I don't like the notion of hanging around to find out," Rosie answered.

Tommy was already inside the car, hunched up in the front passenger seat, as if he wanted to keep as much distance between himself and Lindy as possible. He stuck his head out of the window and said, "Are we ready to leave?"

Rosie got in behind the wheel, and Martha sat in back beside Lindy. Martha glanced at the silent, dark-faced girl, then she looked toward the lights. This fear—this fear she felt inside—was a tight, coiled thing. All those vehicles: why were they coming out here? Suddenly, as she watched the lights, she had the sensation of being trapped inside one of those nightmares that open up inside your brain like poisonous plants. The kind of nightmare you can't awaken yourself from. Almost instinctively, she reached out and laid her hand on Lindy's arm, but the kid sat motionless and unresponsive still.

Rosie stuck the keys in the ignition.

The car whined, died, died with the same kind of choking sound that Martha imagined her own heart might be making right then.

"Jesus, Rosie, what's wrong with it?"

"I don't know," and Rosie turned the key again but the car spluttered and fell into a silence that seemed utterly final.

"Oh, God," Martha said. I knew it, I knew this would happen. She listened as Rosie rammed her foot time and again on the gas pedal. Start start start, Martha prayed.

Please start.

Rosie tried a third time.

Mechanical death.

But now the lights had turned off the highway and were coming down the track toward the wagon, filling the windshield with blinding whiteness.

Rosie twisted the key again and again and again.

The vehicles had stopped just in front of them, their lamps illuminating the grove.

Silence. Just cold silence and cold white lamps and the dark silhouettes of motionless vehicles. Martha leaned forward in her seat, every muscle in her body taut. Dear Christ, what did they want? What did the people from Cochrane Crossing want out here?

And this sinister silence now.

This sinister absence of movement.

She thought: *They aren't going to let us leave*
that's what it is
they aren't going to let us leave this place
because because
we have to stay they want us to stay

She put her hand against her mouth, as if this gesture might somehow still her hurrying thoughts.

There was the sound of a car door slamming. Then another. And another. And now the lamps were filled with the shadows of people.

Shadows moving toward the wagon.

They're going to kill us, she thought.

They're going to keep us here until we die.

It isn't possible, it isn't rational, it doesn't add up—

"Rosie . . ." She tried to form a question but her mind was empty.

Through the open windows of the wagon she could hear footsteps crunch on the sandy soil but she didn't want to look at any of the people out there. She glanced at Tommy, who was rubbing his chin nervously as he stared at the lights.

Trapped, she thought. Trapped between the house and the people from Cochrane Crossing.

But they're only ordinary people from some sleepy backwater village—what possible harm could they mean to do us?

"I get the feeling of a mob," Rosie said. "A lynching party." There was no humor in her voice at all.

Now the shadows outside had stopped moving. They had formed dark bunches, dense little knots all around the wagon.

Rosie stuck her head out of the window. "What's going on?" she asked.

Nobody answered, and Martha had the strange impression that the shadows out there were without human faces.

"We're trying to leave," Rosie said. "So if you'd be kind enough to remove yourselves and your vehicles, we'll get going."

Stillness. The faint rustle of the breeze through the grove.

"Jesus," Rosie said to Martha. "They aren't exactly receptive, are they?"

Martha shut her eyes a second.

She hoped Rosie wasn't going to become suddenly flippant and make cutting remarks about these people, stinging little statements they were certain to overhear. It isn't that kind of situation, she thought. Whatever it is, you can't rely on rude asides to get you out of it. She stared at the lights of the vehicles again and she felt hopeless.

"Goddam," Rosie said and she opened her door, stepping out into the dark, where she stood, her thumbs curled in the loops of her jeans, with a defiant expression on her face. "Look, we only want to get on our way. So all I'm asking is that you make a little space there, folks . . ."

Nobody's listening to you, Rosie, Martha thought. There's no point in losing your temper. But Rosie, seemingly encouraged by the fact that at last she had human entities to deal with—rather than spectral—wasn't going to back down.

"What about it?" she asked. "A little space, huh?"

A little space. What good was that going to do when you had a car that was going nowhere?

Somebody emerged from the shadows and Martha recognized the figure as Callahan. He leaned on his cane and stared at Rosie and his face was gaunt in the beam of lights.

"You don't want to be in such a hurry there," he said, and the tone of his voice, in its flat, monotonous way, was something Martha found menacing.

"It happens that we are in a hurry," Rosie answered.

Callahan was shaking his head from side to side. "It's not over yet. He's not satisfied yet."

"Who's not satisfied?" Rosie asked. "Who are you talking about?"

Callahan said nothing. He smiled in a small, sad fashion and poked the earth with his cane. Then he looked round the faces of the others who stood alongside him and he shrugged. Martha recognized the woman from the grocery, Darlene Richards, as she stepped forward into the glare of lights. And then others—Braxton, the faces of the men she'd seen in the tavern.

He's not satisfied yet, she thought.

She rubbed the bridge of her nose, looked briefly at Lindy, who appeared to have no interest in any of this, then she glanced back at the house. Its lit windows somehow emphasized its cruelness, yellowy and harsh and unrelenting. She turned her face once again toward Rosie, who was staring at Callahan.

"He wants the child. Lindy," the old man said. "If he doesn't get her . . . He has to be satisfied, you understand what I'm saying?"

Rosie was silent.

The shadows moved again, as if responding to an invisible signal. They were beginning to crowd round the wagon now.

"If he isn't satisfied, something bad always happens to a child in the village, that's what I'm saying." Callahan poked the soil again with the cane.

Something bad, Martha thought. Like what? Two words that could cover a multitude of happenings—but the way the old man had uttered the trite phrase left her in no doubt that he was scared.

Then it occurred to her that the only real trace of a child population in Cochrane Crossing had come in the form of a church choir singing a depressing Psalm. It was as if the kids had all been hidden away, concealed.

"And we don't have many young ones in the Crossing these days," Callahan went on. "We need to protect the few we do have. Don't you understand that?"

"I don't understand anything you're saying," Rosie answered. "All I know is that we want to leave and you people happen to be blocking our way."

"It's not that simple," Callahan said. He looked in the direction of the house for a time, and a small muscle began to work in his jaw. Then he turned his gaze toward Rosie again. "It's not anything like that simple. I wish it was. You've seen our village. It's a dying place. And it's going to die all that much quicker if our young people leave. Or if they die . . ."

"I'm sorry about your village," Rosie said. "But the fact remains that we're heading out, folks. And thanks for all your hospitality along the way. I'm sure we'll come back and see you some time soon."

No, Rosie, Martha thought.

That's not the way.

Sarcasm and anger aren't going to cut anything here.

"You still don't get it," Callahan said. "We provide for him, don't you see? We're his providers."

"Provide for whom?"

"I don't need to answer that question, do I?" Callahan smiled again, as if with enormous effort. When he spoke again, his voice was filled with weariness in the manner of someone who has uttered the same sentences a hundred times. "Roscoe. John Roscoe, Mrs. Andersen. John Roscoe, who built this house in 1916 because he needed the isolation for his own purpose."

For his own purpose, Martha thought.

His own corrupt purpose. And she thought again about the child on the balcony. The child that had been Roscoe's purpose.

Rosie stepped back, leaning against the hood of the wagon.

Callahan said, "He had a daughter called Anna." The old man paused. "He instructed this child in certain ways . . . I'm sure you have some idea of what I'm saying, don't you? I don't have to try and define evil for you, do I?"

A daughter, Martha thought. A little girl called Anna, whose life John Roscoe had taken and twisted; and she wondered at the perversity of this, at the nature of this kind of destruction.

Rosie didn't speak.

Callahan looked around the darkened faces of his companions. Companions in some macabre conspiracy. Some frightening scheme to provide—

Sacrificial victims to a dead man.

No, for Christ's sake, this was 1984, not some misty place belonging to Greek mythology.

She clenched her hands together and looked at Lindy. The girl was staring straight ahead, her mind locked away in a place you couldn't even begin to guess at.

"Roscoe shot himself on the twenty-first of June 1916 when he learned that the people of Cochrane Crossing knew about his activities with his daughter," Callahan said. "When he knew that action was going to be taken against him for what he'd done to the child . . . On the same day, at the same time, his daughter hanged herself."

Rosie lit a cigarette. Even from where she sat Martha could see that her friend's hand was trembling. (June 21. Today was June 21, wasn't it? But she wasn't sure, because her sense of time had become fragmented, collapsed.)

"This is all fascinating history, Mr. Callahan, but I don't see what it has to do with us," Rosie said.

Bravado. Bluff, Martha thought. It has everything to do with us, Rosie, and you know it. They want Lindy. Roscoe wants Lindy.

This sea house wants her.

Callahan sighed. "Every four years, Mrs. Andersen, every leap year, we rent this house around the anniversary of John Roscoe's death. Every four years we provide him with two children, a boy and a girl. As we provided him with . . ." And the old man inclined his head toward the station wagon. Then, in an uncomfortable voice, he added, "We have a terrible bargain with the dead. Do you understand me now? It's a bargain on behalf of the living. The young people of our village."

Rosie was silent. She puffed on her cigarette and then flipped it away into the dark. After a moment she said, "My daughter is part of this ridiculous bargain, is that what you're trying to tell me?"

Callahan nodded. "She is part of the bargain, yes."

"How? In what way?" Rosie's voice trembled now.

There was a long silence before Callahan stepped forward, a little shakily, toward the wagon. "She knows what she has to do to satisfy John Roscoe."

"What does she have to do? What does she have to do before you and your dog-eared little village can have some goddam peace?"

The shadows moved again, collectively. Martha imagined them swarming the car, seizing Lindy, taking her back to the house. Then what? She thought: A history of death, a cycle of sacrifices. How many times had this destructive cycle come round, how many young people had been swayed by the inhabitants of the sea house and been trapped there? Died there?

Evil, a spreading stain of evil. The essence of the man known as Roscoe, who now wanted Lindy but not Tommy any longer because Tommy had already served a purpose and had been discarded—only the girl was expected to stay.

Permanently.

"I'm sorry," Callahan said. "I'm sorry."

"Sorry?" Rosie asked.

"The child has to . . . She has to do what Anna Roscoe did."

Rosie clapped a hand to her mouth, looking for all the world like someone trying to restrain a laugh. Then she said, "She's expected to hang herself?"

Callahan looked away.

As he did so, Rosie turned toward the wagon and put her hand on the door handle.

But the shadows were moving all around her, hands reaching for her to pull her back from the car. Rosie struggled, kicking her legs, trying to free herself. Martha stretched her arm out of the window and made a grab at her friend, but Rosie was sucked back into the shadows.

They're going to take Lindy, no matter what.

They're going to take her back inside the house and leave her there—and she wondered about the way in which the past intruded on the present, the pact that had been made between a ghost and the people of a small town so that they might survive. A black bargain. A contract in death.

She hung out the window, searching for Rosie, whose voice she could hear. But she couldn't see the woman anywhere because she was hidden among the people who had seized her. Martha looked quickly at Lindy: the girl was slumped back in her seat, silent, adrift, forlorn.

Get out of the car, Martha, she told herself.

Go look for Rosie.

But how could she leave Lindy alone inside? She was suddenly all the protection the girl had, which wasn't saying very much.

They only need to haul the door open, grab the child. I couldn't do much to save her from them.

She stared ahead through the windshield, watching Callahan lean on his cane in a wasted way, as if this darkness had eroded him, as if the task that had brought him out here had weakened him.

She scanned the night for Rosie again.

Shadows and lights and movement, but no Rosie.

Callahan was coming round the side of the car, where he paused by Martha's window and lowered his head. "Let the girl get out," he said.

"No."

"There's nothing you can do," he said.

Martha started to roll the window up, when Callahan raised his cane and smacked it down across the back of her arm, a painful blow that caused sparks in front of her eyes.

"I'm sorry," he was saying. "You can't do anything to save her."

Martha reached for the window once more and this time Callahan didn't strike her; he smiled and stepped back, shaking his head as if to say: It's useless. Can't you see it's useless?

But she shut the window anyhow, glancing once at Lindy and then toward Tommy, who was sliding across the seat up front and positioning himself behind the wheel, where he jiggled the key back and forth in the ignition. Why not, she thought. Why not try? He'd been able to get this goddam thing to start before.

But the shadows were milling all around the vehicle now, as if by the sheer pressure of their numbers they would prevent the wagon from going anywhere. Martha stared through the windows as she listened to Tommy work the key with all the determination he could gather. Back and forth. Back and forth. The scratching of metal against metal.

Come on, come on—

Turn over—

Nothing was happening, the car was dead.

Then the windshield splintered, struck by something heavy, a stone maybe, and Tommy reached out to punch the opaque glass away—which wouldn't make a damn bit of difference since the car wasn't going anywhere.

It wasn't ever going anywhere again and they would be lost in this place for the rest of their lives.

Tommy hammered the gas pedal again and again, thrusting it hard to the floor. Once or twice the engine groaned but it didn't kick over. A faulty connection, he thought. Maybe the battery terminals. Maybe the voltage regulator was shot. A gremlin of some kind. He felt panic rise inside him.

The shadows pressed against the outside of the car. They could smash the rest of the windows or maybe turn the whole wagon over on its side, he thought.

Spin it over like a toy.

Work, dammit. Do something.

Go go go go—

You have to be patient with cars sometimes, even when you don't have the time for that kind of thing. You have to wait until they're ready to respond.

Jesus.

The car was being rocked from outside, pushed this way and that.

He stared out through the shattered windshield and saw the old guy with the cane looking at him.

You're not going anywhere, sonny: that's what the guy was saying. You're stuck here, no matter what. For a second, Tommy was trapped in the man's stare.

Then he floored the pedal once again, hoping the motor would kick into life, hoping he hadn't managed to flood the damn thing, because then he'd never get it working. (And he remembered the few times his dad had let him drive, whenever they were on a quiet street away from traffic—but this was a whole different ball game now. This wasn't some peaceful little Syracuse neighborhood, and his dad wasn't sitting alongside to advise him.)

You're on your own, Tommy.

If you can't get this wagon to come alive, then everybody's up shit creek.

And still the swaying and rocking of the car continued and Tommy could feel the vehicle tilt, the passenger-side wheels rising a few inches from the ground before it fell again with a shudder that went through his entire body. The wheels would drop off before he had the time to get this baby running. He could hear his mother speaking behind him but he couldn't concentrate on what she might be saying because he had only one thought in mind: Start! Start, you ratty old wagon! Run for me!

He twisted the key again. Still there was only the throaty sound of the engine, a quick gasp before it fell silent again.

He banged his hands on the steering wheel. Maybe there was a God of cars, a God out of Detroit you could pray to and if you asked nicely enough He'd intervene and with one mighty touch resurrect your faded engine.

The key.

Turn the key.

Press the pedal.

Hope.

Now the side windows were being systematically smashed, and through the broken glass he could make out faces—desperate, determined, looking like white skulls in the harsh headlights of the surrounding vehicles.

No more time, Tommy.

No more time. The clocks have run out.

Someone reached inside and tried to grab Lindy, but Martha made a claw out of her hand and scratched the guy's fingers and the intruder withdrew, moaning with pain.

Tommy twisted the key again.

Dear Christ—

The engine muttered, threatened to fade into silence, and then stuttered to life.

Don't die. Keep turning over. There's a nice wagon. Let me stroke you.

He slipped the gear lever into Drive and the wagon lurched forward, and suddenly the shadows were scattering all over the place, shouting aloud as they dispersed.

Go, sweetheart.

Go.

The cumbersome wagon bounced on the rutted track and Tommy had difficulty steering because the wheel responded crazily to every crack and bump in the earth below. He clutched the wheel tightly and realized he was heading straight for the parked cars and pickups in front of him, that he couldn't avoid a collision no matter how he managed to steer.

The lights blinded him, the night air rushed in at him.

He swung the wheel quickly to the left, and the wagon, vibrating and shaking, grazed the bumper of a pickup truck. Then Tommy could feel the wagon go into a spin, tires roaring on the soft soil. He struggled to get it back under control, but then it was sliding down a slight incline toward the trees.

"We have to get Rosie, we have to find her," Martha was saying.

Tommy braked and prayed the car wouldn't stall. He came to a stop a few feet from the grove and slammed the gears into reverse and backed the vehicle up the incline, colliding this time with a Jeep—a tinkling of broken glass, a busted taillight, the sounds of people shouting through the dark. Sweating, the palms of his hands slick and wet, he thought: Rosie, how do we find Rosie in all of this?

People were running toward the wagon as Tommy swung it back onto the track. He headed for a gap between the parked vehicles and almost made it but the space was too narrow and he struck another car and he could hear the metallic clatter of his bumper falling off. Jesus. Jesus Christ. We'll never get out of here. Never. He swung in a circle around the cluster of cars and trucks, so that he was facing the house again. The nightmare house. He braked again as the shadows formed in front of him: something was thrown through the broken windshield, a stone maybe, and it caught him on the side of his head. Dizzy. Blood running from the wound. But you don't have time for dizziness or pain. You have to find Rosie and get to the highway.

He moaned, turned the wagon away from the sight of the house and pressed the floor button that would put the lights on full beam.

He drove forward again, weaving among the vehicles, no longer caring if he hit anything, living or inanimate. It didn't matter a damn to him. His pulses were buzzing and his heart was going wild and his head throbbed badly and there was blood running into one eye so that he couldn't see very well.

"Tommy! Tommy!"

Rosie's voice. He blinked through the broken windshield and could see her running out in front of his headlights, waving her arms and shouting his name.

He aimed the wagon toward her even as he saw her surrounded by a couple of people who tried to grab her by the arms and hold her.

Okay okay okay, Tommy.

What you do is aim straight at that little cluster and hope they disperse, hope they leave Rosie alone and scatter: then you better keep your fingers crossed that the brakes work real good or else you'll run right into Rosie.

He gathered speed.

The cold air stung his wound.

He could see Rosie's face in stark white detail, the astonished look as she realized the wagon was hurtling straight toward her. The shadows fell abruptly away from her, scampering for safety—and Tommy stabbed the brake, hearing the car skid to a halt a few feet in front of the woman. Then Rosie was climbing in, slipping behind the wheel, her breathing labored and her knuckles bone-white on the wheel.

She turned the wagon in the direction of the highway.

The night was filled with the sound of cars and trucks being started behind them.

"They're coming after us," Martha said.

Rosie was out of breath. "I'll give them a damn good run for their money," she said. "As good as Tommy gave them." She put her foot hard on the gas and then the highway came up and she swung the wagon right.

"Why don't you go the other way?" Martha asked. "Why are you heading toward the village?"

"Because I don't know where the other way leads, do I? At least I know if we get beyond the village we're going in the right direction for the freeway."

Tommy twisted his head. The lights were burning behind them. The freeway, he thought. The blessed freeway, where they'd be safe, lost in the anonymity of the Interstate system. He shut his eyes and sighed. Which was when he started to tremble uncontrollably, exhausted from the effort of driving.

When he opened his eyes he looked up at the sky. The harsh blackness had yielded to a subtle gray dawn. He glanced at Rosie, whose expression was one of grim determination, then he looked back at their pursuers. She couldn't outrun them all. It just wasn't possible.

She was taking the curves insanely but still she couldn't conceivably stay ahead of the pack behind.

One twist, one curve after another, the dawn air streaming through the windshield. Tommy's eyes watered.

"They're getting closer," Martha said.

Rosie didn't speak.

The sign came up ahead. COCHRANE CROSSING.

30 MPH.

She ignored it, roaring through the empty street of the village as fast as the wagon could travel. It went past in a soft gray blur, houses, the grocery, the tavern.

Then the church.

There were lights on in the church.

Tommy gazed at the doorway.

A bunch of kids stood there on the steps. A dozen, maybe more.

They just stood there motionless, staring at the wagon as it flew past.

The children of Cochrane Crossing, he thought.

The haunted kids of this dump. Like vacant zombies on the church steps.

And then the wagon was moving out of the village, rattling over the railroad tracks and heading for the open countryside beyond.

"They're still coming," Martha said.

"I can't go any faster without this whole damn car just falling apart," Rosie answered.

The lights were immediately behind them, filling the wagon, shining on their faces and glinting in the rearview mirror. Faster, Tommy thought. Fly fly fly.

Just fly.

He stared at the woods going past, the occasional meadow, the infrequent sight of the ocean. And he thought: They can't chase you forever. They have to quite some time.

Crack. Something hit their back bumper. He turned to see a pickup right behind them, nudging them. Rosie swore and floored the pedal, as if she might get this decrepit wagon to find reserves of speed it couldn't possibly have. Crack again. The pickup strayed to the left, then righted itself and knocked once more against the wagon.

Again and again and again, bumper against bumper.

He wants to knock us off the road, Tommy thought—and his head was filled with visions of the wagon crashing through the fence and plunging to some terrible destiny below. Flame and explosions and the scent of charred flesh. (At least they wouldn't get Lindy if that happened.)

The narrow highway stretched ahead.

A sign flashed past and Tommy barely had time to read it.

Barstow County, it said.

The county line.

And that was when he realized the lights of their pursuers were receding.

He looked back. The lights were dwindling, diminishing against the growth of dawn.

"They've stopped," he said. "They aren't coming anymore."

Rosie looked in the rearview mirror. "You're right, Tommy," and she sighed.

In the back Martha laughed nervously. "They've given up," she said. "I can't believe they've given up."

"Maybe they don't cross county lines," Tommy remarked. "Maybe they don't like to travel very far from Cochrane Crossing."

Rosie nodded. "I'd bet on it." And she slowed the wagon.

Late afternoon. The day had turned hot and clammy. They parked the wagon at a deserted rest area and stepped out to stretch their legs. Except for Lindy, who remained in the back seat, impassive, her hands in her lap, her face pale. Martha and Rosie sat at a table and smoked cigarettes in silence. Tommy wandered between the trees.

"I'd like to drive straight through," Rosie said and she looked toward the wagon at her daughter. "I think I want to get home as soon as possible . . . Lindy . . ." She left her sentence unfinished but Martha understood. "Would you mind?"

Martha shook her head. "We can take turns driving."

"Yeah." Rosie flipped her cigarette away, watched it smolder. "She's got to snap out of it sooner or later. She has to."

"Sure she will." Martha looked at the shadow of the girl in the car. You come to the end of a nightmare, she thought. For Lindy, though, it had been something more than that. Something darker and deeper than a nightmare. She raised her face and looked at the trees. Birds, the sounds of birds, the rustle of leaves, life. Life and not death.

Sunlight and not darkness.

She studied the palms of her hands a moment. Then: "She needs some kind of treatment. Counseling, maybe. Christ, maybe we all need that, if only to convince ourselves that it all really happened."

"I don't think I need that kind of convincing, Martha." Rosie attempted a smile, a frail offering.

Martha was silent. She watched her son. The Hero, she thought. The Savior of the Day. And then she was thinking about the beach house again and she shivered, despite the clammy heat that made her clothes stick to her flesh.

She gazed back at the car, at the motionless form of Lindy.

"She'll be fine, Rosie. She'll be just fine.

Lindy heard the birds and could feel the sunlight hot against the side of her face. But these things—these sense impressions—came to her from a distance away, perhaps even from a world with which she was not familiar, a strange place whose shapes and forms and sounds formed an alien collaboration: somewhere she knew she did not belong.

She stared straight ahead through the broken windshield.

And then she was opening and closing her mouth slowly, her dry lips parting and shutting.

Words, quiet whispers.

Roscoe, she said.

John Roscoe.

Wait.

Wait for me.

Because one day I'll come back.

About the Author

Campbell Black was born in Scotland in 1944. His first novel won the
Scottish Arts Council Award in 1972. His play, *And They Used to Star
in the Movies*, has been performed in London, Dublin and Edinburgh.
His other novels include *Brainfire* and, under the pseudonym Thomas
Altman, the best-selling *Kiss Daddy Goodbye*. Mr. Black lives in Ari-
zona.